THE STONE AND THE SECRETS

SECRETS ~ BOOK 3

JAN DAVIS WARREN

ISBN-13: 978-1-942265-52-8

To my sweet great grandchildren, Judah, Jordyn, and JP, you may be wee babes right now but God's plans for you are huge. Jeremiah 29:11 As you grow into a beautiful young woman and handsome young men, may you hear the Lord clearly and heed His calling and direction for your lives.

Your great grandmother would love it if, someday, at least one of you continued our family legacy of storytelling, for the world is in desperate need of happy endings.

May we always remember the greatest stories ever told, with the happiest of endings, are found only in God's Word.

CHAPTER 1

*L*ady Elise Stanton scooped a handful of soft earth. She stood and released it a little at a time watching the direction the dust drifted. The breeze blew it south and a little east.

Perfect.

She wiped her hand down the front of the borrowed tunic. She would wash it and the pants before returning them to the stable boy who'd lent them to her. The pants were a bit baggy but a piece of rope worked well as a belt and also held her dagger.

She lifted her creation and tingled with excitement, as she ran her fingers down the ten-foot length of the wing's edge to check the seams for tears or gaps that could affect the experiment. According to her calculations, the frame needed to remain flexible, but the surface of the wing had to remain smooth and taut, if it was to carry her weight in flight.

If her calculations of updrafts and wind currents were correct, she should be able to sail safely over the deep ravine and remain airborne long enough to glide down to a grassy knoll not far from the castle moat. The area was large enough to give her room to stop...she hoped. The moat was a vile open cesspool, not a place she would want to land.

Finding an updraft while in flight to take her high enough to land in the courtyard would have been ideal, but perhaps a bit too ambitious for a first attempt. She smiled at the thought of the tower guards' wide-eyed alarm as she sailed by them.

The wing itself was beautiful in its simplicity. Elise's heartbeat sped up with pride and the excitement of fulfilling months of studying large birds of prey in this area. There was no logical reason why man, or in her case, woman, could not also learn to fly...with the proper equipment, of course.

She paced off sixty-three steps down the slope to the cliff's edge. If she were not in flight before she reached the last ten-steps, she would have to abort.

The locals didn't call that spot *dead man's leap* for naught. The ravine was lined with large, jagged boulders, and falling into it would not turn out well for her or her apparatus. As an added precaution, she anchored her favorite yellow silk scarf under a rock to mark the spot. The loose end flopped and waved in the breeze.

Elise climbed back up the steep incline to where she'd left the large wing lying on the ground. She bent and grasped the center of the wing, lifting it until she was able to stand with it extended over her head. It wasn't terribly heavy, only awkward to keep level. The breeze was already pushing and tugging against the broad surface.

Long leather straps dangled from under the wing to her left and right. After walking her fingers out to grasp the strap on the left, she wrapped the loop around her wrist until it was tight then repeated the process on her right. The straps would keep her secured to the wing while in flight. It could be catastrophic if she lost her grip once she became airborne.

Pride goeth before destruction and a haughty spirit before a fall... Scripture memorized as a child sprung to her mind, but she ignored it and the sudden chill of negative possibilities that pricked her conscience. Science wasn't advanced by doubled-minded cowards.

Besides, she had prepared. She'd practiced hanging by straps around her wrists from the largest oak tree in the garden several times over the last three weeks until she'd built up her strength and could do it longer than the fifteen minutes, she projected her maiden flight would take. Those practices had revealed the need for padding around her wrist, which she wore today. Hopefully, the lamb's wool covered by leather bands would reduce the swelling and irritation the suspension caused.

Fear tightened around her chest, as she braced herself against the push of the wind. What if... She drew a calming breath and closed her eyes.

Her heartbeat sounded as loud as thundering hoofbeats in her ears.

A sudden gust tugged at the wing, forcing her to plant her feet to keep from being pushed down the slope before she was ready. Something was off. She adjusted the wing until it was balanced and centered.

"Maybe I should do another trial flight with the present size dimensions and substitute my weight with a sack of potatoes." She huffed. Talking to herself was almost as good as writing down a thought. Visualizing the sketches on her workbench helped to justify this trial. "The smaller models of the wing flew fine after a few modifications to the width and design. Besides, I've already made all of the adjustments from the previous tests to the current design." Her thoughts turned to Cook, who would certainly complain and might even tell Elise's mother, if she asked for any more vegetables for her experiments.

If Elise was going to do it, now was the time. Her parents were occupied with visitors, as was the castle's staff. If she was gone much longer, she'd be missed and her father would send her brother, or even worse, might come to find her himself. She couldn't bear the thought of what he might do if he saw her creation before she completed her flight. She must hurry, for there would be no words to soothe his wrath, if he felt her experiment would endanger her life.

She stepped forward, gaining momentum on the slope. The yellow scarf grew larger in her sight.

"No!" A rider raced toward her. She heard him but couldn't see him.

"Wait!" His voice grew loud and demanding.

Her vision was blocked by the length of the wing, but the voice didn't sound like her father or her brother.

Too late to heed the horseman, the wind caught the wing and lifted her feet off the ground.

She was flying!

A million butterflies in a drunken frenzy stirred within her midsection and stole her breath as the ground beneath her rushed by. She struggled to keep her wits. The air current tore against her forcing her to tighten her grip. The invisible force beneath her, be it friend or foe, gathered the wing within its power, taking charge and gaining speed.

The wing shuttered then smoothed out again when she shifted her weight to compensate for the increased angle. The ground grew farther away. Fear shrouded the thrill of it, but she was determined not to abort the experiment.

A stronger gust tugged at the wing and dragged it ever higher. She sped toward the cliff's edge. The scarf was almost beneath her, waving frantically, as if to warn her off.

Indecision tormented her mind. But what kind of scientist would she be if fear directed her path?

Strong hands clasped her legs and pulled her relentlessly downward. The wing resisted, whipping hard from the right to the left like a dog shaking a rat.

The man's horse squealed with fear, fighting the rider, as the wing fought against Elise's efforts to control it.

Caught firmly from below by the unyielding would-be rescuer, made it impossible to balance the wing or wiggle free.

"Unhand me!" She kicked with all her might to no avail.

"Stop fighting me, you daft woman!" The man tugged her down until he grasped her waist. In swift succession, he cut the leather straps, freeing her wrists.

Freed from her weight, the wing shot up like a giant winged beast until it blotted out the sun. The rider got the frightened horse under control by the time he reached the cliff's edge.

"Let me go!" Elise struggled against her assailant, then stilled. She watched in anguish, as her beautiful creation sailed on without her.

Suddenly, the wing stalled in midair, as if caught between two opposing currents.

She held her breath.

The same force that held it captive suddenly released it, and the wing sailed straight up. The hope that quickened within her allowed her to take another breath and release it with a soft plea. "Please fly." The wing dipped then sailed higher. Just as quickly as hope bloomed, the wing stalled and plunged toward the earth.

"No..." Elise wanted to look away, but she had to know its fate.

The air current that bore the wing aloft was overridden by a stronger down flow that slammed it onto the rocky ravine below. The horror of it left her speechless and limp.

A sob caught in her throat.

"That could have been you." Her brother's best friend, William Degraf's, voice was gruff with anger. His heart thumped fast and hard against her side. "What were you thinking?"

She glanced at the man who held her so tightly she could

barely draw a breath. "I would've been fine." Her voice was a hoarse whisper. Another glance into the ravine was evidence of the truth. That could have been her crumpled on the rocks. "Let me down. You're crushing me." Her demand was louder this time, and she pushed against his hard, muscled chest and strong arms, which held her prisoner.

He muttered something under his breath, bent over and set her on her feet, before dismounting. His jaw muscle ticked with pent-up anger.

"You ruined my experiment. My flying wing is destroyed. It will take weeks to fix, if it's even repairable." Her body trembled, as she glanced down again at the wreckage scattered out over the sharp rocks below. She refused to accept the defeat as her cause, but his.

"By the saints." William ground out a curse and scrubbed his hand over his well-trimmed beard. She'd known him all of her seventeen years. His reaction was a familiar one whenever he was vexed beyond words, but she'd rarely seen him this angry.

"Why are you here?" She demanded.

He paced away, stop, turned her way, opened his mouth, then shut it again and paced some more. He was tall, strong, brave, and handsome. She had loved him for as long as she could remember, but once she had reached a marriageable age, he had refused to encourage her interest.

He drew a deep breath and let it out before he faced her.

"I needed to see you--." He halted as if he hadn't planned to say whatever had been on his heart. She could see the surprise in his eyes briefly before he dropped his gaze. He cleared his voice. "Your mother sent me to find you and bring you home." Without asking permission, he reached out and cut the protective cuffs that covered her wrists then frowned when he saw the welts that had formed.

"Why didn't she send John or father?" Elise glanced at the bruises that also lined her wrists. It was evident she would have to create a better way to protect her skin the next time. She refused to rub the burning sensation, as the shock wore off and the feeling returned. To resist the temptation, she hid her hands behind her back.

"I'm here because you failed to tell anyone where you were going. I'm a better tracker than your brother, and your parents have guests who've come to celebrate his commission in the king's army." His voice was deceptively calm, but his hands were fisted at his side. "John and I are leaving day after tomorrow." He glanced at the sun's position in the sky. "My family is expecting me for the same reason, and I don't want to be late."

"You needn't wait for me. I arrived here on my own, and I can get back the same way." She pointed to a wagon and a team of horses tied beneath a large shade tree. "I need to retrieve my wing before I go." It would be a difficult climb down and a harder climb up with the extra weight and awkwardness of the wing. It might even take multiple trips to gather all of the pieces.

He stepped toward her and stopped, his gaze flicked from her head to her feet and back. "What are you wearing? Does your mother know you dress like a peasant when you're traipsing around dangerous places without escort or guards?"

"No, and you mustn't tell her." She met his gaze and tilted her head giving him her most beseeching smile. "Please, William." She motioned toward the wagon. "My dress is there. I'll change back into it before I go home."

"But what were you going to do once you *flew* away? Your clothes are here?"

She hadn't thought of that. Rather than give him the satisfaction of knowing she'd forgotten that minor detail, she remained silent. It would have to be put on her list.

His eyes lit with amusement, but he refused to smile. "Go and change, and I'll retrieve that mangled mess if you promise me you won't try to *fly* it ever again." His tone remained serious, as if he had a right to give her orders.

"Nay. I'll get it myself, for I have every intention of recreating that wing, and it *will* carry me safely into the sky, as long as I don't have any further interference." She raised her chin with stubborn defiance, then turned toward the cliff, scanning the rocky edge to find a safe way down.

With a grim expression, William stepped in front of her, his fists on his hips. She recognized the intent in his eyes a split second before he reached out and hauled her over his shoulder. He stalked toward the wagon, leading his horse behind him.

"Let me go this instant." She squirmed against his unyielding hold knowing she could get free by using the more aggressive measures she'd been taught since childhood. Her parents were diligent to teach their children to defend themselves in case of kidnapping—or worse. Hands unbound; she could reach the dagger at her waist. She didn't want to harm him—though she was sorely tempted to poke him with the tip of her dagger just to show him she was able to get free if she so desired. The idea was forgotten as fast as it had come. She didn't feel like being dumped on the ground, for she had bruises enough from her adventure.

William heaved her into the back of the wagon without speaking then tied his horse to the tailgate. The expression of pinched lips and deep scowl he gave her when she got to her knees was a warning that left no measure for misunderstanding. He would not stand for further interference in his plan to take her home.

In silence, he untied the team, climbed up to the driver's seat, and set the horses in motion with a snap of the reins.

"William, please. I can't leave my creation out there. I spent too much time on it to let it be destroyed by the weather or animals."

Her plea was ignored.

She heard something that sounded suspiciously like, *good riddance*, but he kept the horses headed toward Castle Brighton.

She had no intention of being the subject of a lecture on proper attire for a lady or to embarrass her parents in front of their guests. There wasn't much time if she wanted to change back into her houppelande before she reached home. The long shapeless gown boasted of overly long sleeves that would hide the bruises already forming dark purple bands on her wrists. She unfolded the dress and tried to smooth out the wrinkles.

If William told her parents… The potential consequences of her actions stirred up memories of past punishments. Setting a farm wagon on fire, by making repairs with a forge-heated axle before it cooled properly, resulted in her being restricted to her room for several days. She also had to write a report for her father, of her mistake in vivid detail, with a promise to consider the consequences of her actions. Today's disaster proved it had been a promise easier said than done.

Dread settled in the pit of her stomach, as she fumbled with the dress.

Perhaps, if she promised William she'd try and be more careful in the future, she might persuade him not to mention where he found her, or of the flying wing or its disastrous fate.

If he told her parents everything, then her only hope to earn their forgiveness would to be on her best behavior and help her mother with the guests. With her noble upbringing, she knew how to act the dutifully gracious daughter to visitors, when the need arose. Thankfully, living in a remote area that bordered Scotland and England, there wasn't often the need to play hostess, though her mother insisted she would need such practice when she married.

She glanced at William's broad back and smiled. Such lofty rules of etiquette wouldn't be necessary as a soldier's wife.

With him facing forward, she gathered the dress and pulled it over her head. Once hidden within its layers of fabric, she tugged off the soiled tunic then raised her arms and pushed her hands up into the sleeves of the dress.

The fabric caught and wouldn't budge. No matter how hard she twisted or pulled, she couldn't tug it down or push it up to escape.

She was stuck.

The oversize hair comb she'd worn to keep her long hair out of her face had caught on the delicate lace trim, or possibly on the intricate embroidery on the bodice. Her arms ached, being hopelessly caught in the lengthy ornate sleeves. Her back muscles burned, and a cramp had formed in her neck at the awkward position of her limbs.

She swallowed hard. There was only one way to resolve the issue, and she hated it.

"William." She waited but he didn't respond. "Please, I need your help." There she'd said it. Tears of humiliation clogged her throat.

"What?" His weight shifted on the seat and she heard the springs give as he turned around. "What the…?" He laughed.

"It's not funny." She couldn't keep the growing panic out of her voice. "My hair comb is caught, and I can't move to free it."

"I should deliver you to your mother like that and let her help you as you explain why you're stuck in a dress and wearing peasant's garb."

"But then my parents will wonder what part you played in my situation." That small measure of satisfaction wasn't worth the fear that scenario produced in her thoughts.

He cursed and stopped the team. His weight rocked the wagon as he climbed into the back with her.

For a man who rarely cursed, she seemed to have provoked him to do so several times in the short time he'd been with her.

He knelt beside her. "How can I help?" His voice was solemn, though a hint of humor edged it. She could feel his gaze on her.

"Reach inside the open neck and see if you can find and pull my hair comb free." She held still. "I think it's stuck on some threads or maybe lace." The ache in her shoulders and arms grew ever more painful until she wanted to shout for him to hurry. "Don't look. I already took off the tunic."

"How am I going to find the comb without looking?"

"William."

"Fine." His grumble made her smile. He was a good and honorable man and had protected her in worse situations as they grew up.

His hand groped her head, mussing her hair as he explored the fabric. "I found it, but it's not coming free." He blew his breath out in frustration. "I have to look, Elise or risk tearing your dress, and then what do you think your parents would say?"

"They'd probably demand you marry me to protect my honor." She chuckled but felt him stiffen.

"They'd more likely have me hung than have you marry a lowborn innkeeper's son who's just joined the king's army." His tone carried disappointment. At least he hadn't laughed.

"William Degraf, you know well that my parents count yours as their equals." She knew the separation between noble and lowborn was considered by both classes, as an impossible chasm to cross and too dangerous a challenge to the status quo except in private and special circumstances. Her mother and his had been best friends since childhood, which defied such social laws, at least at Brighton.

"There." He dropped the ornate, gold comb in front of her and climbed back to the driver's seat. The wagon pulled away, nearly toppling her off her knees and onto her face. She hurriedly tugged the dress fully on and shed the pants.

Once she had her hair and dress in order, she moved to the front. She nudged him over and climbed onto the seat beside him.

They rode in silence until she could no longer stand it.

"I'm sorry you had to take time away from your family to come and fetch me." She was repentant now that she'd calmed down and could appreciate how valiant he was in rescuing her. Even if she hadn't needed his help, he hadn't known that.

"Good thing I did." What was that in his tone?

"Are you still angry with me?" She couldn't stand it if the last time they were together, he was at odds with her.

"You scared ten years off my life with that reckless stunt." He turned and gave her the half-smile he allowed when something amused him but he wanted to keep to himself. "I must say, that wing was one of your more interesting inventions. It nearly pulled me out of the saddle when I grabbed you. I'm glad we both survived." With a flick of his hand on the reins, the team sped up. "Time to get you home before your father sends out the guards to hunt for the both of us."

"How long will you and John be gone?" She missed him already.

"We've signed for two years with an open-end contract to stay longer if we're needed, but we'll get leave to come home for short visits periodically."

"I know the king's edict makes it compulsory to serve, but my mother was disappointed that John didn't allow them to hire a substitute to take his place. Instead, he chose to serve in the army himself. I know she would have rather he stayed home and found a bride." She leaned closer to William to block the wind. It was late Spring and the trees had already leafed out, but there was a nip in the air. The wind seemed to have increased, as they drew closer to the castle. That would need to be added to her notes for the next time she tried the wing. A chill ran down her spine, at the thought. Did she dare try again?

"I think your mum blames me, because John decided to join after I did." He shifted closer when she shivered. "But my father had joined the army when he was nineteen and now tis my time to serve."

Growing up, she'd heard the servants tell the tragic story of a handsome young castle guard who joined the king's army, because his true love married another. The beautiful young maiden sacrificed her love for him and married the old innkeeper, because he'd promised to buy her mother's papers and set her free to live with them, but the maiden's mother was poisoned soon after the marriage. Fortunately, the sad story had a happy ending. The wicked old innkeeper died and the handsome young knight returned home to marry his true love. William's parents still ran the Black Swan Inn and had raised a happy family.

Elise always felt the familiar flutter of longing when she thought of a man loving a woman so much that he joined the army to deal with his broken heart.

Though the names were changed, the sad tale of the evil innkeeper and the young maiden was told often as a warning to all young women that came to work in the castle lest they too be tricked into trading their current life of honest servitude for empty promises.

Elise placed her hand on William's arm as a gesture of understanding, and the muscles flexed beneath her touch.

Was he also leaving because of the love of a woman he thought unattainable? There was a twinge of jealousy when she tried to imagine which of the village maidens who mooned over him would stir him with such passion. None came to mind.

Once back at the castle he accepted her parent's thanks without mentioning where he found her or about the wing. He left without another word to her, though he glanced her way and winked before departing. As always, her secrets were safe with him.

She wished she had more experience with matters of the heart. He was her perfect match, if only he'd admit it.

CHAPTER 2

The going-away party for Elise's brother, John was festive, with plenty of good food and music, as minstrels had been hired for the evening. Trying not to dwell on her creation being at the bottom of the ravine, she caught the sadness in her mother's glances when she looked at John. She'd had that same look when Elise's older sister, Sarah, moved to London to live with the Duchess of Yorkshire last year. The duchess was a distant cousin of her father, who'd needed a companion after a fall left her with a broken leg. From Sarah's letter, the duchess' recovery had been slow, but she insisted she still needed Sarah's companionship now that she was well. In the recent weeks, she had even resumed her social calendar, insisting Sarah go with her to the many gala events her royal status required she attend.

John had promised to stop in and check on Sarah when he had time away from his training.

Elise was never interested in such social matters, for her passion for science and inventing was not shared by most, which didn't leave anything substantial with which to hold a conversation.

She guessed it was hard on parents to have their children grow up and move away. Hers would probably feel the same when she left home, which would not be anytime soon, unless the new School of Scientifica in London started accepting women.

The fifteen guests all left the next day, releasing Elise from the need to help her mother with the job of hostess. By the frown on her mother's face when Elise arrived home with William the previous day, she was still in store for a lecture or two about wandering off alone, once her mother had rested. Not something she looked forward to, but she was used to being the recipient of numerous lectures over the years.

Elise escaped to her workshop, an ancient stone building with high ceilings. Her father had restored the old tool shed for her use when she was about ten-years old. It was far enough away from the main castle and stables for safety, in case any of her more volatile experiments went awry. The one-room workshop had space for a small forge and the walls were lined with her tools. A large oak workbench gave her space to spread out blueprints and notes. The place gave her privacy, which she needed to come up with a plan on how to slip away alone, from the castle long enough to retrieve her wing and return without being seen.

When she opened the door, she gasped in delight. The mangled wing lay in a pile in the corner. A note rested on top.

"This is my parting gift. Please don't make me worry about you taking flight again while I am gone. I'm keeping the scarf as my reward." He'd signed it, *Sir William Degraf Knight of the King's army.*

A rush of delight warmed her all over. His dream had always been to become a knight like his father. As children, he'd often signed missives as such, SWD for short.

She glanced at the heap of torn fabric and broken frame. It must have taken him hours to gather it all and bring it here.

When he'd found the time was a mystery, since after he left her at the castle, he had his own family celebration, and he and John had left at first light this morning.

William's thoughtfulness sent a rush of affection for him through her. He knew her too well. She'd barely slept for worrying about the wing being destroyed. Her mother also knew her well and made Elise promise not to wander off again without proper escort. Elise was honor-bound to keep her word to take a guard with her, but she'd dreaded the thought of dealing with the dozens of questions about her invention and how it had ended up in the ravine. She had no desire to discuss the details of her failed experiment to a guard pledged to report to her father. Although, ending up in William's arms might have been worth it.

She smiled and ran her fingers over William's letter. He did care about her. Turning over the page, she noticed a mysterious jumble of lines and symbols at the bottom. Was it a secret code that held a deeper meaning? He knew she loved mysteries and if she couldn't decipher it, she'd have to concede her failure and seek him out for the answer. Perhaps that was his intent.

Determined not to fail, she studied each symbol then took quill and ink to connect the lines drawn from one spot to another. The first image revealed a bird or a dragon with large wings.

Below that was a second group of marks. Once connected, they resembled a stick man on a stick horse taking a journey represented by arrows that led to another picture of the man and horse, but in this image the rider held a person with long hair in his arms—a woman. He had drawn a frown on the man's face. Obviously, the crude pictures were his interpretation of their encounter at the cliff.

At least he'd regained his sense of humor over the incident that nearly plucked him from his saddle, represented by the large bird with long talons hovering over the man and woman on the horse.

There were squiggles scripted below the picture in a language she didn't recognize. William had a gift for languages and had learned several from travelers who visited his parents' inn. Hopefully, she could find the answer within one of the many volumes that lined the castle's library walls. Elise's heart fluttered with the possibilities of a deeper, more personal meaning in his message.

She ran her finger across the crude images, stirring up a buried childhood memory.

It had been years since she'd thought of the ancient, cryptic symbols she had seen on the stone walls in the cave John and William had discovered while exploring.

The boys were eleven and she was nine at the time. They had occasionally allowed her to tag along, but their invitation usually meant they needed someone small and agile enough to accomplish a task they couldn't. This time they were convinced that the mysterious cave they found was filled with treasure and they needed her to squeeze through a partially collapsed opening to see what was inside.

A chill pierced between her shoulder blades.

There had been no treasure. Only evil dwelled in there.

With a promise they would share their wealth with her, she'd been eager to do her part--until she'd squeezed through the narrow opening. The smoke, from the burning torch they'd given her to light the dark space, made from moss and dried grass wrapped around a stick for a handle, burned her eyes and throat.

The cavern had collapsed long ago leaving only a small portion of the once large stone room intact. What was left of the tall ceiling was covered with soot, as if scorched from many fires. She noticed some crude drawings on the only wall still intact. Fascinated, she moved closer and held the torch higher.

The horrifying pictures depicted sacrifices to several monster-like demons. She stepped back. Something crushed beneath her foot and she glanced down. There were blackened bones scattered on the cave floor. She saw skulls from animals…and then noticed several human skulls in a heap, with blackened, empty eye-sockets.

Her terrified screams caused the boys to yell and demand she come out. She dropped the torch and backed toward the entrance. Someone grabbed her dress and pulled her out. Before John could reach for her, William clutched her tight and carried her away, with a promise to protect her always.

The trio had arrived back at the castle out of breath and barely able to tell their story. She was crying and so distraught that her mother had to take her to bed. Her mother was pregnant with her sister, Hanna at the time and not feeling well. As her mother's handmaiden helped Elise and her mother to bed, Elise heard her father shouting at the boys for their irresponsible actions, by putting Elise in danger and upsetting her mother. Their usually calm and unshakable father could be heard throughout the castle. It was a display of anger she had rarely seen from him except when provoked beyond reason.

Elise learned later that her father made the boys lead him and three castle guards back to the cave. He returned the next day with workmen who broke open the entrance until it was large enough for her father to see inside. He recognized the symbols as belonging to an especially blood thirsty druid cult that had been banished from England long ago. He had the workmen destroy the entrance so no one else would wander into it ever again.

Even after her father's assurance that she was safe, she'd suffered with nightmares for several weeks until her mother and the local priest prayed over her and commanded the evil to depart in Jesus' Mighty Name. Only then was she able to sleep without visions of the monster-demons trying to steal her away in the night and burn her in the fire.

Her mother helped her memorize scriptures from the Bible. One of her favorites is still *Isaiah 26:3 Thou wilt keep him in perfect peace, whose mind is stayed on thee: because he trusteth in thee.* The Word of God still produces a feeling of calm, peace, and safety.

Bowing her head, she thanked God for William, for he had rescued her today like he did back then. She prayed that God's hand of protection would be upon him and her brother, and God's Word remained steadfast in their hearts and in the face of any enemy.

~

Seven months later.

During the time William and her brother were off serving in the army, Elise turned eighteen and, according to some, should have already been married with a couple of babes on which to focus her attention, not on science and creating inventions out in her workshop.

A third potential suitor arrived one morning with the intention to court her. He left the castle in haste before noon with minor burns, which he suffered when he got too close to her forge as she tried to explain the process of heating and shaping iron. With that last disappointing encounter, her parents ceased trying to match her with titled, but brainless young men who didn't know an axle bolt from a seat spring.

She'd eagerly pondered the possibility of leaving home to study at the School of Scientifica in London. For she had recently heard from her father, that a childhood friend of his, Lord Isaac Canterbury, was now a professor teaching there. Professor Canterbury petitioned the school's board to allow a few select women admittance. Since the school was in need of funds, they were considering the addition of a few females, but their entrance would be conditional. They would have to pass the same tests of efficacy as the male students. In addition, the female students would be required to sign a contract of commitment for one year of study, because they wanted to discourage all but the most determined, lest their goals were only to find a husband.

As she waited to hear the board's decision, John returned home on his first leave. William had returned with him, having earned a recent promotion to John's second in command, but it had been three days, and William had yet to come to the castle.

She had failed to uncover the meaning of the final symbols from his letter and dreaded his smug look of triumph as he revealed the answer. But she would quickly forgive him, for she was eager to tell him about the school and to show him her latest invention. She'd sent him a thank-you note for retrieving her wing, but never received a reply.

Elise was in her workshop when her little sister Hanna came to tell her lunch was near ready. The ten-year-old talked of nothing but the newborn foal down at the barn, until she was distracted by one of the servant's children who came to play.

Elise had ignored most of Hanna's chatter, as she studied her latest modification. The new design for a seat spring failed to give enough support to the driver and his assistant. They said the seat hit bottom so often they were both stiff and sore and not the least shy about telling her so. The springs finally broke causing the men to drive the wagon back to the stables standing up. The design was sound, but she had failed to take into account having to support two large men over rough ground. She had spent the morning repairing the old springs she had removed and helping the blacksmith's assistant replace them. The defective springs waited on her workbench, mocking her failure.

The broken remains of her wing remained hidden in a

trunk. Maybe one day she'd work on it again. The knowledge she hoped to get from the school might give her the confidence to try again.

Elise washed and put on a fresh dress before going down to the family meal. She managed polite conversation with her family, but between her recent failure with the springs, William's lack of appearance, and not knowing if she would be accepted in the school, she wasn't in a good mood. After the meal, and hoping to lift her spirit, she went to the stables to see the new foal. She watched with delight as the little filly frolicked on long wobbly legs about the large box stall, while the mare ate hay and patiently ignored her offspring.

The rattle of the hinges on the barn door announced a visitor, and Elise glanced to see who entered.

William hesitated when he spotted her, but when their gazes met, he strolled toward her.

Her knees grew weak with the sight of him. No suitor ever produced such feelings. When he grinned, her midsection quickened from a flutter to a tempest as if a thousand butterflies had taken flight inside.

"Lady Elise, it's a pleasure to see you're looking well." The intensity of his smile gave her the impression he meant his words.

She had always thought him handsome, but he had grown taller, and broader shouldered in the service of the king.

"Sir Knight." She grinned when he gave her a slight bow. He had muscled out into a valiant warrior. Before, the top of her head had come to his cheek and now she would have to stretch to reach his chin. She put her hand to her stomach, waiting for the flutters to abate, while he examined the foal.

"This filly is sound and healthy. She'll make a fine addition your father's stable." He stepped out of the stall and secured the half-door. "Have you remained safely on the ground while I've been gone?" He studied her as if the question were more than idle words.

"As a matter of fact, I have set aside the wing for now to focus my attention on creating a plow with a double blade to break fallow ground more thoroughly. It should make getting the ground ready for planting much faster. I'll be ready to test it in a few days."

His gaze hadn't wavered from hers, as if he were memorizing her features. Heat warmed her face. "William, about your letter—."

"Oh good, you're still here." John stepped into the barn and motioned to William to follow him before he turned and left.

William smiled. "Lady Elise, I beg your leave."

Before she could speak, he turned away and exited the barn. William's eagerness to escape her company was a mystery. It was as if he had been avoiding her, though she couldn't imagine why. Men could be so vexing.

That night a rider came with a missive for her father. The board of the School of Scientifica had agreed to accept a few women and she had been sent an invitation to take the admittance tests scheduled in two weeks. Her parents had left the decision up to her.

According to some, eighteen meant a young maiden would soon pass the prime age for seeking a suitable husband.

To Elise, having reached eighteen years of age unwed, meant it was time to stop mooning over William and devote her life to science. A year or more away at school would be good for her.

John and William returned to their regiment within the week. Eight days later, her father escorted her and her handmaiden to London to get them settled with his cousin, before Elise had to take the entrance exams for the School of Scientifica. If accepted, she would be assigned rooms for her and her servant, at the school

CHAPTER 3

"Help! Please save us." The dense fog distorted the origins of the plea. The king's troops remained helpless to intervene. It would have been foolhardy to try and attack in these conditions, for they would be unable to tell friend from foe. Waiting for the morning sun to burn off the fog took an enormous amount of restraint from the warriors, who were ready to help.

The woman's continued frantic pleas pierced William's heart. With three younger sisters, all he could think of how he would feel if it had been them—or Elise, as prisoners in the clutches of those murderous marauders.

Yesterday afternoon, on a routine assignment to escort an annual shipment of sacramental wine from the vineyard in Summerset to the Cathedral in London, they'd discovered the whole of Summerset ravaged and burning—none had survived, human nor animal. The destruction of the monastery, vineyard and nearby village was a senseless act of savage brutality against the peaceful monks, who grew grapes and made sacramental wine for the Church.

William swallowed the bile that rose in his throat at the

gruesome memory of the carnage. Fury burned within him to see those responsible pay for what they'd done.

A scout was sent ahead to track the enemy, as the rest of the king's troops buried the dead. The task took hours digging the mass grave and putting out the fires.

As soon as their tasks were complete, they sought the savages behind the massacre. Their scout met them on the road and had informed their commander the enemy was camped two hours away, in an empty field of at least thirty acres, which was surrounded by a dense forest protecting the enemy from attack on three sides.

By the time their troops had arrived at the encampment, an impenetrable curtain of vapor obscured the moon and their enemy's exact position and numbers.

The thick fog forced William and his fellow soldiers to make camp on the opposite side of the glen from the marauders.

By the muffled sounds of the enemy's laughter and merry-making, they were either unconcerned or unaware of the presence of the king's troops camped nearby. The two wagon loads of stolen sacramental wine were a prize they obviously couldn't resist. As much as he despised the wine being defiled by those murderers, the more they drank the easier it would be to subdue them tomorrow in battle.

Once darkness fell, William's commander and friend, Lord John Stanton, sent their scout to spy on their enemy and count their numbers. He was to locate the captives so their troops could focus on their freedom first, tomorrow. After three hours, he still hadn't returned. With the vile treatment the enemy had brought against the innocent inhabitants of Summerset, William didn't want to think about what they would do to a king's soldier, if they caught him spying on them.

William and several volunteers offered to search for the missing scout, but the commander refused them all. They would have to wait until morning to find out the fate of their comrade.

Until then, additional sentries were assigned to make sure the troops were not surprised by the enemy.

Tension was high as they waited for first light. Every three hours fresh sentries took the place of those patrolling their perimeter until almost dawn, when all the soldiers and their mounts readied for battle.

A sudden quiet settled around their camp.

William rubbed his hand down his mount's neck to ease the tension within him and soothe his restless horse. The fog muffled the sounds of the impatient soldiers and their mounts.

He found the unnatural quiet more disturbing than the shouts of war. It was as if all nature held its breath in anticipation of the carnage about to be spilled out on this once peaceful meadow.

As the dawn edged away the darkness, men of faith prayed softly for divine protection and help to fight valiantly.

To ward off the fear of impending doom, William had prayed all through the night until he'd found peace in their righteous cause. He rubbed the corner of Elise's yellow scarf tucked beneath his chainmail. The silk was soft upon his neck. He imagined her smile and believed, though it was unlikely after all of this time, that he could still smell the faint scent of lavender and wild flowers.

"Help us!" From the direction of the enemy's camp, two maidens screamed in unison, shattering the silence, their cries distorted and eerie through the fog.

William fisted the reins of his mount to keep from charging forth, for they were under orders to wait, but the vision of the murdered monks and villagers remained seared into his mind.

The screams of female hostages had taunted the king's troops well into the night, then stopped leaving the impression that something terrible had happened to them. But now, the pleas had resumed, giving hope that at least two were still alive, but for how long?

Yesterday, after they had found the village ravaged, the commander sent their fastest rider to the next shire to contact the king's earl constable for reinforcements. Being in charge of the king's army, the constable had gone to the training camp to inspect the newly trained troops.

The commander had received orders an hour ago to wait for the reinforcement's arrival before engaging the enemy, but the hostages' pleas tortured each soldier's heart. Their grumbles grew more vocal with their impatience. They wanted to free the hostages and wreak revenge on the enemy.

As much as William agreed with them, the orders they received were clear. He hadn't risen in the ranks to second in command by ignoring orders, especially from the king's earl constable. Hopefully, their reinforcements would arrive sooner than later.

William's warhorse pranced in place, also ready for action. The sun would soon burn off the dense fog, giving them their first glimpse of the enemy.

The sun etched the sky with gold streaks until the dense, gray cloud imprisoning them began to dissipate. Figures moving across the other side of the glen appeared first as dark apparitions then what had been hidden behind the fog was revealed.

Armed with swords, axes and lances, both mounted and on foot, the enemy was an unkempt lot. They wore a mish-mash of ill-fitting clothing, most likely stolen along the way.

William glanced down the line at his fellow soldiers. They had proved themselves brave and honorable over the last year, an elite group of fighters who had honed their skills under John, as their commander, until they could sweep through any opposition as a unified and deadly force. Good lads, every-one.

"Have faith, men. Pray for the hostages. Reinforcements will be here soon." John rode among the troops on his magnificent black warhorse to encourage the soldiers. Their numbers were small, less than forty, and they had no idea how many they'd face, knowing many could be hidden by the trees. By the carnage the invaders had left behind, it could be as many as a hundred.

John waited only as long as it took for the sun to burn off the fog completely to clear the battlefield, then he rode out to the front of the English line, faced their enemy, and raised his sword.

"Surrender in the name of God and the King or die!" John's demand carried across the battlefield with unmistakable authority.

The enemy yelled obscenities and paced back and forth until silenced by the raised sword of a man who was large in both height and girth. He stepped to the front of their line. Their leader, by his boldness and the attentiveness of his men, had a bushy, black beard and long matted hair that hid his features. He turned and yelled an order in French.

"Amener le prisonnier."

Bring the prisoner. William understood the heavily accented French.

Two marauders dragged the English scout into the open. Naked, he was covered by dark bruising, dried blood, and deep lacerations, evidence of the enemy's brutality, and by his drooping head, barely conscience. His captors drug him to the front of their line.

The scout rallied when saw his comrades, straightened, and pulled free of the hands that held him. He saluted his fellow English soldiers, but his defiant shout was muffled with a punch to the mouth by one of his captors.

With an order from the bearded leader, his captors jerked the man's arms out and held him fast. Black-beard walked up to face the English soldier. Whatever he said to him could not be heard across the glen, but the marauder pointed his sword toward the English troops then turned and struck the prisoner a deadly blow.

William gasped in disbelief, as their comrade was thrown to the ground in a bloodied heap before his comrade's stunned silence.

Outrage roared within the English ranks, barely held in check by their commander's raised sword.

The Frenchman issued another order, and a different pair of marauders hauled out a woman. A cloak covered her head to toe, making it impossible to see her face. The hostage's pleas echoed across the meadow. Her captors jerked her to a stop near the dead Englishman, each gripping an arm of the female prisoner. The woman continued to scream, but did not struggle against her captors.

"Oh, please 'elp me. Dinna let 'em kill me!" The woman's high-pitched, low-born speech convinced William, that she was not from this region. She sank to her knees; her arms stretched above her head by her unrelenting captors. Her anguish sounded real enough, but…

William's anger turned into suspicion when Black-beard didn't move toward her.

Something wasn't right.

William scanned the enemy lined up ready to fight. Not one was focused on the woman, only on the English soldiers.

A trap!

He kicked his mount into action. Before William could reach John…

"Charge!" John shouted, with sword in hand, he spurred his horse into action. His mighty stallion leapt forward closing the distance to the enemy in powerful strides, with William and his mount close behind.

His fellow soldier's shouts filled the glen with promises of revenge. The surrounding forest echoed back their voices, until it sounded as if hundreds were about to descend on the marauders, causing their enemy to pause to scan the English's numbers.

With a shouted curse from their bearded leader, they charged.

More of the enemy horde poured out of the forest like a plague of locust, too many to count. They spread out and encircled the English troops, tightening the circle, intent on killing everyone in their path.

Demonic laughter drew William's attention, as he raced forward. The kneeling hostage cackled her delight, as she was helped to stand then released by her captors. As an actress bows before her audience, she curtsied before the English. The hood of her cloak slipped back as she straightened revealing an older woman who cursed at them in French. The hostage ploy had worked, but her act would cost her and her fellow marauders their lives. There would be no prisoners, trial, nor time to repent.

Their enemy badly outnumbered them, but slaughtering ill-equipped villagers was far different than fighting well-trained English soldiers.

Pride rose in William's heart, as his comrades faced the enemy in a tight formation.

Swords clanged against sword. The stench of blood and anguished cries of the wounded and dying enemy filled the battleground.

A fellow soldier raced toward the enemy, having slain three in his path. He raised his arm, and another enemy came up beside him and struck him, knocking him to the ground.

Without hesitation, John rode up and protected the soldier while a fellow soldier slayed the enemy before the marauder could kill their downed comrade.

William saw Black-beard close in on John. The evil marauder's lance hit John in the side, knocking him from his horse. Black-beard rode in with his battleax raised to finish him off.

William spurred his horse. The gelding leapt over prone bodies, and its momentum knocked over Black-beard's mount, sending the big man to the ground. From six different directions English arrows, and lances struck Black-beard before he could get up, ending his life.

A marauder on foot rushed forward with raised sword intent on finishing off the injured John. William turned his mount and rode between the enemy and his friend, taking the blow to his leg in his stead. The marauder died at the hand of one of his own when he tripped and fell into a fellow marauder's blade, having been knocked off balance by William's intervention.

William's mount, also injured by the enemy's attack, stumbled and fell, trapping William's injured leg beneath it. Unable to pull free, he watched helplessly as John struggled to rise, to fight on, but his strength fled with his life's blood. William heard John called out for God's help then stilled and fell silent.

The shouts of a large troop of English soldiers filled the glen. Their reinforcements had arrived.

"Praise the Lord!" William watched many of the cowardly marauders scatter into the woods, but they would not be allowed to escape their punishment, as English troops pursued them.

Relieved of leadership by the commanders of the reinforcements, William could turn his attention to getting freed from under his injured horse. He pulled his dagger and cut the saddle's girth making sure his trapped leg would not get caught in the stirrup if the animal got to its feet. He ran a hand down the panting animal's neck and spoke encouraging words, until the horse rallied and stood. The wound in its side still bled, but as long as the animal remained on its feet it should recover.

William hurt all over, but his right leg felt strangely numb. One glance confirmed the worse. His pant leg was torn and bloody. He feared his leg was broken, for he couldn't stand. He pulled the yellow scarf from his neck and tied it tightly above the wound to stem the bleeding.

An anguished groan drew his attention to John who lay a few feet away. Relief rushed through William knowing his friend lived. The enemy's lance must have slipped under his chainmail. The strike had been a fluke.

The black stallion stood over his downed master, pawing the ground in warning to protect him. Not even English soldiers could approach without the risk of being injured by the great horse. Having helped raise and train the stallion, Shadow knew William, and allowed him to drag himself close to John.

John's wound still bled. William fought against the increasing weakness and pain in his body. With a desperate prayer to save his friend, he pressed his fist into his friend's wound to stop the bleeding.

William struggled to stay conscious but a dark abyss swallowed him up.

CHAPTER 4

The loud battle cries of many warriors shook the earth. Elise put her hands over her ears, but she couldn't shut them out. She could see John and William mounted and readied for battle. She focused on William as he turned toward John. "It's a trap!"

"Lady Elise. Wake up."

Hands on her shoulders were unrelenting in their effort to shake her awake.

She opened her eyes to find her handmaiden, Isabella, leaning over her.

"What?" Elise rubbed the sleep from her eyes. Her heart pounded with the fear of what she'd dreamed. For over two weeks, she'd had reoccurring dreams of John and William being in danger. Her hand shook, as she grasped the neck of her nightgown to loosen it. It was as if boney fingers had closed around her throat, cutting off her breath.

Isabella's brow furrowed, as she touched Elise's forehead. "You have no fever." She put a hand on Elise's elbow to help her sit up. "By your distress, I reasoned it was another worrisome dream. Was it about your brother and the innkeeper's son, again?"

"Yes, but this one was different—the danger more intense." She rubbed her arms. The worry over what she had seen in the dream chilled her to the bone.

"Try not to fret. God will protect His own." Isabella patted Elise's shoulder. "I'll go down to the kitchen and make you a pot of tea. That should help warm you." Isabella was six years her senior and had been a blessing to her in spite of Elise's insistence that she didn't need a handmaiden to accompany her to London. Her objections had fallen on deaf ears for her parents had sent Isabella anyway. Over the last ten months, since Elise had come to the school, Isabella had been more than a hired servant, she'd been a much-needed friend. Not all of the male students and teachers were happy to have a female scientist and inventor in their midst.

"Thank you, Isabella. A cup of strong tea sounds good." After Isabella left the room, Elise slipped out of bed onto her knees. There remained a feeling of impending doom she couldn't shake. "Please, God, protect John and William." The ninety-first Psalms flowed from her memory.

Was her dream a warning of what is to come or merely the result of the restlessness Elise had been feeling of late?

Her father told her, on his last visit to London, that John had been out of the country several times. His soldiers were used mainly for the protection of high-ranking diplomats as they dealt with treaties and negotiated trade deals.

Elise received a letter yesterday from her mother. According to her, John and William had recently been reassigned to protect the borders. After the recent peace treaties, the assignment was considered far less dangerous than most. John would not have been happy if he suspected their father's influence had assured him the safer post.

She stood, took a deep breath and released it slowly, hoping to dispel the dark thoughts. There was nothing she could do but trust God in this matter.

If she were ever to give place to her fears, then those who believed she didn't belong at the school would use her worry as a sign she was too highly strung and emotional to be taken seriously as a level-headed, clear-thinking scientist.

Being here was a rare opportunity to study science, for few women were allowed such a privilege. Fortunately, Professor Lord Isaac Canterbury was a good friend of the family, and he believed no one with a quick mind and a passion to learn should be exempt from a pursuit of science, no matter their gender, social standing, or economic situation.

Elise stretched and yawned. Awaking before dawn had become a habit of late and not always caused by worrisome dreams.

As she dressed for the day, her thoughts turned to William. Not all of her dreams of him were filled with danger, sometimes she'd dreamed of being in his arms.

At nineteen, she'd hoped she and William would have been married by now. Her sister Sarah had waited to marry until last year. She was twenty-four when she married her husband, Trevor Barrington, the Duke of Denham. They were very happy and the reason Sarah made it her mission to find a good match for Elise, in spite of her protests.

If William didn't declare for Elise soon, then she hoped one day to find a man of like interests, who would appreciate her as an equal and encourage her as a scientist.

She raised her chin with fresh determination. Life was for living, not grieving over things she could not change.

The door to her room swung open.

"I prepared this for you to take with you to the workshop. I know you want to get an early start on your class project." Isabella carried a small silver tray, which held a plate with a thick slice of buttered bread. She'd also included a cup, saucer, and a teapot, which had been covered with a padded cozy to keep it warm. Her handmaiden set the tray on the side table.

"Thank you, Isabella. This is just what I needed." Elise snatched a pinch of thickly buttered bread and chewed it as she put on her leather, protective apron that was easier to wear than carry. She put her work gloves and the tools she'd need for her assignment into a tote bag to take with her.

"Though, I am grateful to fulfill my dream of seeing London and experience the city life." Isabella frowned. "Its stench and crowded streets have cured me from the notion of ever wanting to live here. London is a bigger and a more disturbing place than I could have ever imagined." She straightened Elise's bed covers and tidied the room. "I'm glad Lord and Lady Stanton insisted you not come here without me. London is certainly no place for a respectable young woman alone."

"Sounds like you miss our little village in Brighton." Elise gathered her class notes and tucked them into the bag. "I thought you enjoyed the parties Sarah insisted we attend." Elise couldn't help but cringe at the thought of being paraded around as if she were a prized filly of good breeding looking for a buyer. "Finding a husband certainly wasn't my reason for coming to London, but my dear sister keeps trying."

Due to no fault of her own, Elise had angered the hostess, at the last party Sarah had insisted she attend. By the woman's cutting remarks, Elise had drawn too much attention from the men chosen as possible suitors for her rather shy daughter.

"I know Sarah means well, but going to those parties was a huge waste of time." Elise stuffed another crust of bread into her mouth. She'd missed dinner the evening before so she could complete a drawing of a new design to improve a fireplace flue, allowing the flow of smoke to escape more efficiently through the stovepipe.

"The men attending those parties wouldn't say your presence had been a *waste of time*." Isabella handed Elise a napkin to wipe the butter off of her hands. "They still come to call and when not admitted to the school grounds, leave their cards.

They all seem eager to get to know you better." She waved a hand toward the bowl on the table overflowing with gentlemen's calling cards. Isabella pursed her lips as if she had tasted something vile. "Lord Blackstone's been unduly intense in his pursuit of you. At least half of those calling cards in that stack are from him. I'm glad you know how to deal with his kind, for I fear he will not heed your rejection."

"According to Sarah, his kind usually has a short attention span where women are concerned. Hopefully, she's right and he will turn his energy to maidens who would gladly accept his less-than-honorable intentions."

It had been maddening not to have a single intelligent conversation with any of those titled popinjays she'd met at those parties. Not one knew what it took to temper iron into a fine sword or how to make a primitive forge to repair a broken hitch. They laughed at her when she asked them what they would do if their carriage broke down and they were stranded away from all civilization with no blacksmith available to help them. Instead of answering her question, they tried to change the subject to the latest court gossip, their wealth, or flattery, which they believed to be more acceptable conversation between the rich and titled.

Elise rarely stayed a minute longer than etiquette demanded, then gave her regrets to the host and hostess. She'd returned to the school determined never to go to another such event for the rest of her life, only to succumb to her sister's pleading again and again.

Elise put the strap of her bag over her shoulder and picked up the tray. "I will be at the old blacksmith shop at the back of the compound if you need me."

"You should wait for Mr. Harrison to escort you." Isabella smoothed a crease from the bedding.

"If I see him, I'll asked him. Maybe he'll get the door for me or offer to carry the tray."

When Elise stepped outside, she paused to gaze at the pinkish glow that lit the horizon with the first blush of dawn. The promise of a new day was like a signal for the birds to start their songs. There was no sign of the school's nightguard but she wasn't afraid. She'd often gone alone.

The ankle-deep fog that covered the ground would linger until the sun made its full appearance.

Like Isabella, Elise found the stench of London's over-crowded humanity a far cry from the clean country air where she was raised. Thankfully, the acrid smell of a heated forge was the same wherever she went.

She smiled at the thought of creating something useful out of blobs of iron or other alloys she had access to in the work-shop. She'd already learned a great deal from her experienced teachers in crafting with wood and iron. It was also very exciting to explore the scientific uses for the different elements and chemical formulas that could equally heal or destroy. The possibilities for designing new and improved tools and machines stirred her imagination and often invaded her dreams, where the impossible was made possible.

She had kept secret her design for a flying wing, but one day she was sure her design would work, though the exact use of such an invention was still a bit vague in her thoughts. When she used the wing's design in miniature to make a child's size toy, she'd worked out the flaws and found a tail helped stabilize it. She had made several for the children around the school and called them kites, after a small bird of prey that swooped in the sky.

Her personal notes were cluttered with new designs and concepts never before attempted. She guarded those notes and kept them with her for fear of losing them or having more of her ideas stolen.

One of her more detailed designs for a self-closing hinge was stolen by a fellow student, Chester Fields, who claimed she had not designed it but merely copied it as her own. There was no one who believed her, for his duplicate of her work was in his handwriting and appeared original. One of his friends perjured himself on Chester's behalf by swearing he'd helped him work out the design. Elise had been threatened with expulsion if she pursued the matter. Since then, she'd cleverly hidden her initials within each design, which would only be seen if she pointed it out.

The morning fog swirled around her skirt and hid the stepping stones that led to the blacksmith's building. Thankfully, after so many months, she could walk the path without misstep.

The sound of activity on the street as tradesmen started their deliveries was muffled by the large stone wall that surrounded the thirty acres of the School of Scientifica. The ancient walled structure reminded her of the high fortress surrounding Castle Brighton.

The school's compound was guarded by two men, one man for the day and one for the night, which also helped to protect the students' inventions from being stolen, as well as protect the public from any failed experiments that might result in harm.

There was no sign of the nightguard, Mr. Harrison. Around dawn, he usually took a break and was probably in his cottage warming his feet next to the fireplace as his wife fixed him a hot cup of tea and a bite to eat. He would appear in a while to complete his morning rounds and admit the tradesman, so they could deliver their goods to the school.

She loved this time of the morning, before Professor Canterbury and her fellow students arose. No one was around to interrupt her with their endless questions and prattle while she worked a problem through. For security and safety, the blacksmith's building was the most isolated from the main structure, which housed the class rooms, sleeping quarters, and dining hall. The forge burned hot, inviting trouble when surrounded by distracted students.

Juggling the tea tray in one hand, she managed to unlock the heavy door and push it open with the other. She could have used Mr. Harrison's help, but he was still not in sight.

After setting the tray on a nearby table, she closed the door. She moved the tray closer to the warmth of the old stone forge and stirred up the fire, which had been banked by the last person who'd used it. Probably by the person who'd used it to forge the beginnings of the iron staff, which leaned against the wall nearby. The heat from the forge also helped to displace the ever-present chill that seemed to permeate the thick stone walls of the old building.

She added more wood to the fire, dropping one of the logs on the floor.

A large wharf rat scurried out from the woodpile, barely missing her foot.

"Eeww. You'd better run away, you nasty thing." She hated vermin. They got into the students' supplies and experiments, destroying hours of hard work by gnawing holes in wooden containers or contaminating elements. The gardener had set multiple traps, but the rats were everywhere in the city.

Elise returned her attention to the experiment the professor had assigned her. Professor Canterbury fully believed meteorites held secrets yet undiscovered by mankind, because he'd found several unusual metallic compounds within them. One of the stones in particular seemed to draw his interest of late.

She focused on her notes, which she spread out on the work table to confirm her calculations. The instructions were clear. She needed to adjust the elementary Chinese's formula for black powder to test its reaction and then test it again after adding small amount of crushed meteorite from the professor's collection. He'd hoped the heat and chain reaction would leave a residue which would allow them to identify any hidden minerals in the meteorite's composition. Such an experiment could be dangerous unless she was extremely cautious, but if it could help identify the stone's origin then it would be worth it.

She wished William was here to discuss her plans. He was as smart as he was handsome and being able to talk to him had helped her solve several problems with the experiments she'd wrestled with over the years.

Blowing out a breath of frustration, she realized that it was futile to try to wipe William completely from her thoughts.

She threw another piece of wood into the fire.

Why, when other men seemed eager to court her, was William being so resistant to declaring for her hand? She was not the same naive young woman he had last seen. She'd learned far more than just science since she'd been in London. Going to those parties and listening to men talk when they thought no woman was around to hear them was certainly enlightening. It was unsettling how much more attention men gave to the physical attributes of a woman than to her intellect.

She blushed at the memory of their words as they expounded about her looks and heritage. No one should be measured merely by those attributes, male or female.

Watching the men and women flirt, she'd realized the odd expressions William often wore when she was around were similar to those of the men she'd observed at the parties when they were physically attracted to a woman. Enlarged pupils, tugging on their shirt collars or tunics, sweating palms, silly grins, and soft speech were a few of the signs she'd made note of.

She shook off her disappointment in the whole matchmaking system. How daft. Though the scientist in her wanted to create better solutions to the problem, as the daughter of nobles, she understood the matchmaking process was primarily to enhance bloodlines, lands, and bank accounts. It was sad how many of the men were expected to fulfill their family's expectation of making a good match. At least they had more choices in the matter than the women, who had two choices—marry who their family chose or join a nunnery. Thankfully, her parents had given her grace to fulfill her thirst for knowledge...for now.

She drained the last sip of the strong tea and placed the empty cup and teapot on the tray out of her way.

It was time she concentrated on the matters at hand. No more time for idle thoughts that stirred up old problems, but led to no clear solutions.

The glint of dawn pierced the upper windows of the old building. A narrow band of color created by refraction from a large chip in the lead glass, which acted as a prism, painted a rainbow of color across her notes. It was like getting a word of encouragement from God. The rainbow was His visible promise that He would never flood the earth again, but it was also a reminder of His love for all who believed on Him and received His Son Jesus as savior.

Elise drew a deep breath and released her worries to the Lord...again. Fortunately, there was no limit to how many times per day she could do so. If she could only learn to leave those worries in God's hands and not pick them up again.

Studying the compounds before her, she confirmed the instructions. It took three basic elements mixed together to make black powder that would combust once the combination was introduced to fire. After that initial reaction of the gun powder was noted in her papers, she would proceed to next step.

Adding a small amount of powdered meteorite to the compound would fulfill her assignment. She must conclude by identifying if the powdered meteorite was from a stony meteorite or from a far rarer stony-iron meteorite. The reaction of the combusting black powder would superheat the elements in the meteorite dust. Hopefully, the reaction would separate the different elements in the process, making them easier to identify. Nickel was often found in the stony-iron, but the possibility of finding even more rare minerals was the basis of these experiments. At least, that was one of the professor's theories.

Fully focused on the work before her, she took a deep breath and let it out with a whispered a prayer for wisdom, then mixed the gunpowder according to the formula. Equal parts sulfur, saltpeter, and ground charcoal made two cups worth of the combination, enough to fill a medium-sized clay pot used for such purposes. That should be more than enough to use for several experiments.

She had her black powder. Unsure of the exact ratio of the ground meteorite needed for the best reaction, she would start with a small amount. Once these elements were combined, she feared they could become unstable and dangerous.

She wiped her brow and put an eighth of a cup of the black powder into another shallow, uncoated clay pot especially made for these experiments. The compound reminded her of coarsely ground black pepper, but not the smell, which was that of charcoal and sulfur.

She found the glass container with the ground meteorite dust prepared by the professor for her to use. It was well marked and left where the professor said it would be. She carefully measured and mixed in exactly half of the ground meteorite dust into the black powder mixture.

The larger chunk of the meteorite, bigger than a man's fist, from which the pre-ground chip was taken, remained on the workbench awaiting further study, along with several other various sized samples collected by the professor in his extensive travels.

After she'd exclaimed her excitement over the experiment, the professor confided that the meteorites' value was beyond monetary. The rarity of their find alone made them worth a great deal. A few collectors had offered him thousands for his collections. He'd refused the offers, because those wanting his meteorites would put them on a shelf, and their true worth to mankind would never be realized.

Elise wondered if the professor's wife, Caroline might disagree. Her love of shopping was the unkind brunt of many jokes around the school, but Elise had heard Lady Canterbury make some surprisingly intelligent observations after one of his lectures on meteorites. Which was the woman's true character and why hide it? Was she the frivolous shopper she pretended to be, or the earnest academic she'd revealed that day? A mystery for another day.

Elise pulled on her heavy leather gloves. Using a rusty set of long steel pinchers, she grasped the pot and readied to set it carefully inside the fire. Her heart raced in anticipation. Stretching as far as the tongs would allow, she held the thin clay pot containing her experiment over the heated coals.

Something furry pushed beneath her shift and leather apron and rubbed against her bare leg.

"By the saints!" She jumped and dropped the pot.

The pot shattered.

Bang!

The fire in the forge brightened and spit flames upward into the chimney as well as scattering sparks onto the stone floor in front of the forge. Before Elise could grab a bucket of water, kept for such an emergency, the sparks died leaving only a few black smudges, but no damage.

She staggered back, heart pounding at her close call.

"E-e-yowl!" The angry response of a cat having its tail stepped on had Elise jumping back again.

"Tabitha, you naughty cat!" Elise scooped up the uninjured feline. The multicolored tabby that roamed the school grounds was unrepentant by the sound of her loud purr, as she rubbed her face against Elise's arm. She seemed unfazed by the explosion, which would have sent most creatures running away. Not Tabitha. She'd been the author of too many similar incidents in the past, though most explosions were more the verbal kind from the students whose experiments were ruined.

With a firm hold on the errant cat, Elise would have to deal with her first before proceeding. She surveyed the items set aside for the next step in the project.

The small amount of meteorite dust had fed the reaction creating more than mere sparks, as was expected. If such a small amount could increase the normal reaction of the black powder, with that kind of explosive reaction, she'd need to warn the professor of the danger of using more. It would be safer to conduct any further tests outdoors. Perhaps she could convince the professor to put the experiment into a reinforced steel box to contain the explosion. The remaining residue would also be easier to locate to test later.

Once she put the cat outside, she'd move the containers of black powder and meteorite dust into separate storage cabinets. They needed to be put somewhere safe and far away from the stone edge of the hot forge.

If she had accidentally knocked the entire contents of both into the fire, it could have been a disaster.

Tabitha batted the dangling strap on Elise's apron. The familiar stench of sulfur clung to the cat's fur. "You stink. Your mistress will certainly insist you get a bath." The cat tensed as if ready to escape and growled. She obviously understood the word *bath*, so Elise tightened her hold. There were too many dark places in the building for the feline to hide, and Elise had no more time to waste if she was to get those elements put away before other students appeared. "A thorough scrubbing would serve you right for scaring me half to death." Turning her attention to the overweight tabby, she stroked her fur as she continued toward the exit.

"How did you get in here? I know I closed the door." The cat continued to purr ignoring Elise's scolding.

The nosey tabby was disliked by many of the students

because of her antics. She often caused accidents when she showed up underfoot and tripped self-absorbed individuals or by jumping up on tables, disrupting entire experiments. Instead of chasing rats and making herself of some use, her biggest delight seemed to be in knocking the hard-to-get and costly glass beakers off the table to shatter onto the stone floor. The furry little troublemaker belonged to the professor's cat-loving wife, Caroline, or the pest would have been banished from the school long ago.

"I have no treats for you today. Go back to your mistress if you want to be pampered." Elise carried her captive to the door and found it opened. She put the cat out and closed the door again, making sure this time that the latch was secured.

The hair on the nape of her neck rose.

"Got you!" Strong arms clasped around her waist, pulling her roughly against a man's chest. His ale-saturated breath blew hot and rapid with excitement against her neck. "And no one will hear your screams."

"No!" Elise slammed her elbows into her assailant's ribs and stomped hard on his instep. He released her with a string of curse words that would make any maiden blush. Unfortunately, she'd heard worse since she'd come to London.

"You little minx!" Lord Richard Blackstone laughed and paused. He rubbed his bruised sides before staggering toward her again. Usually dressed to perfection, his clothes were wrinkled and smelled of stale smoke, ale, and cheap perfume. "You've ignored my requests to call on you, so I've come anyway."

She'd heard rumors that he frequently gambled and drank to excess until the wee hours of the morning, which his present condition confirmed. He must have seen her leave the building on his way home.

"I am not interested in getting to know you, Richard, so please leave." Elise stepped back and glanced around for a weapon. In his drunken state, there was no telling how far he'd be willing to go to get his way. Backed into a corner, she spotted the iron rod leaning against the wall. She grasped it, took a warrior's stance with slightly bent knees, one leg in front of the other, as she'd been taught, and readied for battle. Growing up in a family that insisted they all learned to use all manner of weapons, she had sparred many times for fun, never expecting to have to use that knowledge at the school.

By the scowl on his face, he was not going to back down and leave peacefully. Perhaps a fierce rebuke would cool his drunken desire. She pointed the flattened end of the rod at her opponent, hoping fervently she wouldn't need to use it.

"I told you to leave or suffer the consequences. I do know how to use this." She stood her ground.

Her attacker stepped into the early morning light streaming through a small window near the tall ceiling, temporarily blinding him. He raised his hands in surrender when he spotted her weapon.

"Lady Elise, I've not come to harm you but to offer you my hand in marriage." He paused when she didn't lower the steel rod. "I've chosen you to be my bride." Richard grinned and edged closer as if those words would solve the problem before him. "I decided that if I must marry to fulfill my grandfather's will, I'd rather have a wench with spirit who excites me than be stuck with someone dull and boring. You have beauty, breeding, and noble lineage almost equal to mine." A smug expression curled his lips. "I've already spoken to my grandfather, and since he approves of my choice, he will speak with your father to make the necessary arrangements."

"It is not a matter of what *you* want. I'm not the least bit interested in you or your grandfather's will!" Elise steadied her weapon. She dreaded what she might be forced to do to protect herself against the drunkard. "My father will never agree to a marriage I do not want, so you can find a bride elsewhere." Elise loathed the ingenuousness of the upper-class and privileged who were looking for a mate solely to enhance their noble bloodlines and assets. "Might I suggest Justine Ebert as a better choice for your bride? I have it by good authority that she would be more than happy to marry you."

"I am not interested in that plain-faced cow with her over-bearing mother." His blood-shot eyes narrowed with intent. "Your elusiveness has driven me mad with desire. I want you."

"You don't know me, Richard. I was not being elusive but adamant in my rejection of you." She had met the egomaniac only twice, the last time at Justine Ebert's family estate, where Elise had rejected him by ignoring his efforts to converse or dance. She had slipped out while he was distracted by Justine's mother, hoping her disappearance would be enough to turn his interest elsewhere. Apparently, it hadn't worked.

She edged away from the hot flames of the forge. The containers of volatile black powder and ground meteorite dust rested on the edge of the worktable nearby.

If he should knock the two containers into the fire…

"Leave now or you could get hurt." If she could reach the door, Elise stopped when Richard blocked her only way of escape. His intent was plain by the lust in his eyes. She thought she heard the door open but dared not take her focus off him.

"After we're married, the first thing I'm going to teach you, my dear, is you will do as I say. I'm Lord Richard Blackstone the third, Duke Archibald Blackstone's only grandson and heir. When I inherit his fortune and his title, I'll be so rich that no one will dare to tell me what to do, not even the king." He smirked and staggered around the bench that separated them as if pursuing her was a game he was intent on winning. "Once I have my way with you, you'll have to marry me, for no other man would want sullied goods."

"What goes on here?" The nightguard, Mr. Harrison yelled out.

Distracted, Richard stumbled and fell against the table. Cursing and spewing out his fury, he swept the entire contents into the fire.

"Run!" Elise dropped the rod, leapt toward the outer wall, which was lined with heavy work benches, and ducked down behind the nearest one.

BOOM!

The entire amount of black powder and meteorite dust hit the fire together. The explosion rocked the building. Elise watched in horror from her place under the workbench. Mr. Harrison was thrown out of the doorway, and Richard was knocked down, landing under the worktable where her tea tray once sat. That table had probably saved his life.

Elise's heart pounded from the concussive power of the blast. Her clothes and hair were covered in dust. The sparks from the forge spread in a wide perimeter from the blast. Her ears rang making it hard to hear.

The explosion scattered hot coals, setting the arrogant young man's hair and the front of his clothing on fire.

"Aarrgghhh!" He jumped up and danced around rubbing at his burnt beard and eyebrows. Screaming obscenities, he turned in circles, disoriented, while flames ignited more of his alcohol-stained garments.

She staggered to her feet, grabbed the bucket of water nearest her and doused him, putting out the blaze.

"You'll pay for this, witch!" Dirty, ash-filled water dripped from what remained of his beard and ran down his burnt tunic and pants. Blisters appeared on his once handsome face and arms. Sputtering curses, he limped out of the building where the door hung off its top hinge. She saw the guard being helped away by two men.

Still shaken by the intensity of the blast, Elise was grateful to be alive. She needed to get out too. Her notes lay scattered on the floor and she gathered them and stuffed them in her tool bag. Sunlight pierced through holes in the walls and roof of the normally dark room. Transfixed, Elise gazed at the destruction of the workshop. The back of the forge had been blown out, along with the glass in every window.

There had been less than two cups of the elements, but thrown into the fire together had produced a significant explosion. If she had prepared more... She shuttered to think of the consequences.

Save the stones.

The voice in her mind quickened her to move. She should save the professor's precious meteorites, if any survived. She staggered toward the forge, avoiding the scattered firewood still ablaze. Bending over, she used a broken table leg to sift through the area where the meteorites had been. The burning debris had set them aglow, but they were all there. She found the tongs and picked up the meteorites, and dropped the hot stones inside her thick work gloves, then doused them with water to cool them before they burned a hole through the leather. At least she could give these back to him.

"Thank God, Lady Elise, you're safe." Isabella rushed into the building carrying a travel tote, which had clothing sticking out from the top, quite unusual for the very tidy handmaiden. "I was having my tea, by the open window of my room, when I heard the explosion." Tears clouded her voice. "As I cried out to God for your safety, I saw Mr. Harrison thrown through the open door onto the ground outside. Before I could move, a man limped from the building screaming foul things about you." Isabella's expression of horror, as she glanced around at the damage, stirred Elise into action. Her ears still rang from the explosion, though she'd heard some words but had to read Isabella's lips to fill in the rest.

"Why did you bring a bag?" Elise shoved the meteorites into her tool bag and then allowed Isabella to usher her outside through a large hole in the wall. Where are we going?"

"It was as if the Good Lord spoke into my ear. I was to pack for travel and get you away immediately to a safe place. You're to hide until the truth is known." Isabella grabbed Elise's arm. "That daft young Blackstone is demanding you be punished… for being a witch. He told any who would listen, that you tried to kill him." She led Elise to a small gate used by the gardeners, which was the only way through the wall at the back of the estate.

"It was he who almost got us both killed." Elise was in big trouble if he made accusations of witchcraft to the wrong people. Science was suspect to the uneducated. A simple chemical reaction could appear magical and frightening to the uninformed.

"Did you see if Mr. Harrison was badly injured? He was there when everything exploded." Elise body ached all over as the shock wore off and fear took its place. She should have sought the guard out and not gone alone. He would have sent Richard away and this would never have happened.

"I saw two strangers bending over him. He was well enough to talk with them." Isabella tightened her grip on Elise's arm and hurried her forward. "The explosion has drawn many spectators. We must hurry."

Daring not to slow their pace, they hurried away from the school toward the docks, threading their way down alleyways to keep from being seen.

Ash and dirt from the explosion fell in Elise's eyes from her hair, causing her to stumble. Her dress caught on a crate, and she ripped it free in her haste to escape.

Sounds of raised voices seemed to be coming from all around them because of the tall stacks of trade goods lined up on the docks to be shipped.

Several large fishing boats were moored nearby. As the voices got louder and closer, Isabella picked one and led the way up the gangplank. They hid behind some crates stacked on the deck. It wasn't until they glanced up that they noticed two men watching them from the railing where they stood. The tallest one smiled and gestured with a finger to his lips for them to remain silent.

"I'll give a reward to the first one who spots the witch." Richard's voice echoed with authority. His words incited the gathering crowd, like someone throwing bloody fish guts in the ocean to attract hungry sharks.

The tone of the angry mob grew louder and more frenzied.

"Find the witch!"

"Hang her!"

CHAPTER 5

The voices drew closer. Elise and Isabella stayed hidden behind the crates stacked on the boat's deck. The two fishermen gazed down at the crowd but remained silent.

"You, up there. Have you seen two women trying to escape through here?" Richard demanded, sending a ripple of fear through Elise. "I'm offering a large reward for their capture."

Elise held her breath. What poor fisherman could turn down a large sum of money?

"Nay, no witches came around 'ere. Ye might look down by the fish market. I hear one can find all manner of evil down there if ye know where to look." The man turned away, ending further conversation. He barked an order for two crewmen to bring in the gangplank and for others to get the boat underway.

"I'll check your boat first." Richard yelled.

"No one boards me boat without me permission. Move along or ye'll be covered in the sweal I've been saving for just such an occasion."

Elise smiled as her imagination stirred up an image of her

pompous enemy covered in smelly garbage usually dumped in the sea, once the boat had cleared the harbor.

The fisherman stalked toward the two crewmen, who'd hesitated after Richard's threat to board. "What are ye waitin' for? A fancy invitation? I gave ye an order. Get that gang plank on board or suffer the consequences."

The crewmen hurried to do as they were told.

It took an hour before the boat was readied and cleared the port. Elise's ears still rang and her head pounded. The smell of sulfur from the explosion clung to her skin and clothing. Every move she made left a powdering of fine dust around her.

Once the fishing boat was out in open water, Elise and Isabella left their hiding place. Isabella wrapped a comforting arm around Elise as they waited near the crates for the captain to complete his duties and address them. A new fear grew within Elise when Isabella trembled and her hold on Elise tightened as the captain approached. Would they be any safer on this boat than at the hands of the mob?

"My name is Captain Keet, and this be me first mate and brother, Frank. Now that we're away from the screaming lunatics and prying eyes, would ye like to tell me yur names and the real reason for boarding me boat?" The man who had saved them had the stance of a soldier, the same as William and her brother. It was then that she noticed he was missing a hand. Fortunately, his attention was on Isabella and didn't see Elise's surprise.

"My name is Isabella Canellas. I am the handmaiden for Lady Elise Stanton of Brighton." Her voice was strong and authoritative. She released Elise and stepped forward.

Captain Keet turned his attention to Elise. He ignored the filthy state of her appearance. "I take it ye are Lady Elise Stanton. Any kin to Commander John Stanton?"

"Indeed. My brother's a commander in the king's army." She couldn't stop the tears that suddenly sprang to her eyes at the mention of John. What would he and her parents think about this mess she had gotten into this time?

"He used to tell us stories of his home in Brighton and of a younger sister who had a knack for getting herself and others into trouble." Captain Keet reached forward and clasped Elise's hand with his left one. "Me and me brother served under the commander for over a year. He be a good man. I'm glad to give aid to his sister…and her handmaiden." He turned his attention back to Isabella and smiled, causing the usually stoic hand-maiden to blush. He raised his stump and rubbed the forearm. "The commander saved me life, but I lost me hand in a surprise attack while protecting some whining coward of a diplomat." A flash of anger crossed his gaze but he blinked it away. "We heard the commander and his second in command had been injured. 'Ave you heard how they're doing?"

"John and William are hurt?" Elise's heart pounded with fear, which was heightened by the sympathy she saw in the captain's eyes. "How did you hear?"

He hesitated, as if unsure how much he should relay.

"Please, you must tell us all that you've heard about them." Elise swiped her tears with a finely embroidered handkerchief Isabella had pulled from the bag containing their belongings and pressed into her hands.

"We gave passage to six of the soldiers who were there when it 'appened. They were recovering from their injuries and on their way back to London to be reassigned." He hesitated again.

"Please." Elise drew a sobering breath and stiffened her spine. "We're strong enough to know the truth."

"They said the commander and 'is second were injured in a fierce battle against a horde of bloodthirsty marauders. According to them, the commander had two of the bas…" His gaze found Isabella's and he paused, as if searching for a better word.

"Blackhearts," Frank supplied.

"Aye, blackhearts. The commander had two of 'em on the run when a third one came up and thrust a lance into 'is side, knocking 'im from 'is horse." Captain Keet cradled his injured arm close to his body as if reliving his own painful ordeal.

Frank put a hand on his brother's shoulder. "His second in command, Sir William Degraf appeared as out of nowhere. He protected the commander from a killin' blow, but was struck full force in the leg."

Captain Keet glanced down at the ship's deck before his gaze rose and met Elise's. "I'm sorry to deliver such bad news."

"I knew they needed help." Elise couldn't hold back the grief that stole her strength. She collapsed to her knees onto the deck. Isabella knelt beside her.

"Enough of this. For weeks you've been troubled with dreams which stirred you to fervently pray for your brother and William. Yes?" Isabella tone was stern.

"Yes, but..." Overwhelmed with a sense of hopelessness, Elise could hardly speak.

"No buts. The Lord stirs folks to pray for intervention for those who can and will be saved." She took Elise's arm and helped her stand. "Wipe away those tears and go to the bow and pray for their recovery. Know God hears our prayers even if He doesn't always answer in the way we expect." She gave Elise a pat on the shoulder and turned her toward the bow of the ship where none of the crew was working. "When you're done, we'll get you cleaned up so we can face tomorrow with a renewed hope in God's promises." Isabella turned to the captain. "Where are you bound for, Captain Keet? Would it be possible to drop us off somewhere we can get transportation to Brighton?"

"Nothing good will come of allowing these women to stay on board."

Elise heard several crewmen grumble, as she walked toward the bow. Fishermen were a superstitious lot.

"Ye ladies are welcome on this boat, but the delivery of me

cargo is me first priority. We'll drop ye off in Scarborough afterward." The captain's tone conveyed his responsibility to the cargo, women, and his crew.

Elise prayed until she felt God's peace. She met with Isabella, who led her to the captain's cabin to clean up. After a light meal of bread and cheese it was time to find out how they might help on this trip. If they could do something useful, they might change the minds of the crew who believed women on a boat were bad luck.

Though normally a fishing boat, the fishing had been so poor for weeks, that Keet and Frank were forced to take on transporting cargo. But storing a lot of cargo on deck was dangerous for it and the crew, if they ran into bad weather. The deck was presently crowded with crates causing the crew to move with caution around a narrow edge by the railing. If the cargo should shift, it could pin a crewman beneath it, or cause the man to jump overboard to keep from being crushed. A day and a half into their trip, a crewmember slipped while edging around the narrow space along the railing and fell into the water. Fortunately, the sea was calm, and the man was rescued immediately, with only a sprained wrist, but the grumbles grew about this being only the beginning of bad luck.

Eager to find a solution to transporting the cargo safely, Elise explored the hold of the ship, and came up with a plan. Enlarging the opening of the ship's hold would allow even the large crates to be stored inside. The use of a heavy-duty block and tackle system would allow the cargo to be moved below where it would be more secure, leaving the deck free, for the safety of the crew.

Once she had it sketched out on paper, she presented her idea to Captain Keet and his brother. They were skeptical at first, but after she explained the potential benefits and simplicity of the concept, they agreed it was worth trying. The captain, his brother, and the crew worked in shifts to make the improvements. In three days, they had the cargo safely stored. The added boom fashioned out of a spare mast, would extend the reach and make it possible to move the cargo onto the dock with minimal need to handle the heavy crates, which turned the crew's grumbling skepticism to hopefulness as they practiced assembling and disassembling the mechanism in readiness for their arrival.

After a week the ship arrived at their destination ready to deliver the cargo they had been hired to transport from London. Every crate of farming equipment and supplies arrived without damage or loss, which, as the women watched from the ship, seemed to surprise and please owner of the shipment.

The new system for moving the cargo from the hold to the dock worked better than Elise, or the crew, could have hoped. She could see the men were happy not to have to haul each crate down the gangplank by hand. The pulley system handled two heavy crates at a time and placed them on the dock without a mishap.

Three other captains wanted to come aboard to get a closer look, so they might duplicate it, but Captain Keet refused.

"No sense givin' the competition any good ideas." The captain sounded pleased. "Our boat has something no one else has, at least, for now."

As they sailed to Scarborough, Elise had more leisure time. She noticed Isabella spent her days on the deck, as if everything about the boat interested her. In her zeal to learn more about fishing, sailing and process of navigating, Elise noticed Captain Keet was always nearby eager to answer her questions. According to her evening chats with Isabella, Captain Keet had earned her respect—not an easy task, for Elise knew the woman well, and she had no tolerance for any who lied to appear more knowledgeable than they were.

In turn, her handmaiden used her knowledge of healing to doctor the captain's bruised stub, which he'd caught in some rigging. His missing a hand hindered the captain doing simple chores, but it didn't keep him from doing his part.

Keet and Isabella had become close, as if they had been drawn to each other from first sight. Isabella lit up when she was around him. Her laughter surprised Elise the most, since her serious handmaiden rarely found things worthy of more than a slight tolerant smile. The captain brought the best out in her. She blossomed with his kind attentiveness, and her stern features softened, making her pretty.

Elise was truly glad for Isabella and wished her the best. She would make a ship's captain a fine wife with her attention to detail, education, and honesty.

The sea voyage and prayer for John and William's safety helped Elise find the peace to quiet her soul, and she'd pledged to give them into God's hands.

According to the captain, they would dock at Scarborough tomorrow, if the wind continued to be favorable. It would take another two to three days for the women to reach Brighton and home, depending on what transportation they could find.

Tears clouded Elise's vision and she swiped them away. She'd been too busy to realize how much she'd missed her family.

She leaned against the railing and watched the water pass the hull in short choppy waves, each undistinguished from the water replacing it, very much like her days away from Brighton and William. Regret pooled in her gut leaving her nauseated with a helplessness to fix her mistakes. God would have to take care of the mess at the school. If she had focused on escaping when Richard first appeared or somehow persuaded Richard into letting her go…

Thunder clapped overhead, making her jump. It was then she noticed the hurried activity of the crew.

"You need to get below m'lady." Frank ushered her to the hatch that led down to the captain's small cabin she and Isabella shared. "Stay below." He glanced up at the darkening clouds. "It looks like a bad one."

"Is there anything I can do to help?" Elise saw the concern in his eyes as the waves slammed hard against the hull, making it hard to stand.

"Aye. Pray hard." Frank pushed her through the hatch and closed the door with a firm snap.

"Oh, good you're here." Isabella pulled out a cloak from the belongings she'd stashed in the bag.

"The storm came up so fast." Elise allowed Isabella to wrap the cloak across her shoulders. "Thank you. I got chilled just walking across the deck to get inside." She rubbed her arms to generate more heat.

"We were supposed to dock at Scarborough tomorrow, but with this storm…" Isabella chose one of the two chairs bolted to the floor next to a table, which was also secured to keep them from being thrown around the room in rough waters. She motioned for Elise to join her. "We should ask for God's protection for us, the brave crew, the boat, and the honorable men who own it."

Elise sat and bowed her head. She had hoped, by providing the new cargo system, the men would forget about women being bad luck. This storm would justify their superstitions, although of late she felt as if she brought bad luck wherever she went.

The storm raged on for two days making it impossible to find a safe harbor. It ceased with the same suddenness it appeared. The sun came out long enough for them to make port and dock at Scarborough.

Elise and Isabella were glad to be safe from the storm and out of the small cabin. They stood on the deck enjoying the fresh air.

The captain anchored in the only slip undamaged by the hurricane-like winds that had also hit the town. The broken hulls of two boats bobbed against the waves, held fast by their anchors. Their slips ripped apart by the violent winds slamming the boats into them. The tip of the tall mast of a third boat was all that could be seen above the water.

"If we'd been docked here as we planned, our boat could have been destroyed like theirs." Captain Keet turned to Isabella and smiled. "No matter what others may think, you've brought me good luck with your presence. The boat is all me and Frank have to make a living. Our widowed mum depends on us."

Isabella smiled up at Keet with such adoration that Elise dropped her gaze. She cleared her throat. "Thank you, Captain, for getting us here unscathed. I will make sure my father sends you payment for our passage."

"No payment is necessary." He brushed his hand across Isabella's causing her to blush.

"I hate to further impose, but could you secure our transportation back to Brighton? I know some stablemen dislike dealing with women directly and tend to be unreasonable in the price. Isabella and I can both drive a team, or if necessary, we can ride horses. Whatever is available is fine with us. We just want to get home."

Isabella nodded in agreement.

"I'm not about to let two beautiful young women travel without an escort. Me mum would never forgive me." He turned to Frank. "Ye and the crew can take the time I'm gone to go over the boat and fix whatever needs fixin'. What say ye?"

Frank grinned, his gaze taking in both Keet and Isabella. "Take yur time, brother. If we get the repairs done afore ye return, we'll take the boat out and catch some fish to help pay the crew's wages. Either way, I'll meet ye back here when I'm done."

While Keet had secured their transportation, Isabella and Elise had purchased only enough food and supplies they'd need for their trip, saving the remaining amount to secure lodging along the way.

Keet surprised them with a carriage for the journey to Brighton. How he did it was somewhat a mystery, for he never revealed how much it cost, only that the bloke who owned it owed him a big favor. Whatever the cost, it made for a pleasant journey. Isabella spent much of her time sitting on the driver's bench next to Keet as he took charge of the team with the same firm control that he took charge of his crew.

Elise watched as he struggled one-handed with the reins, using his injured arm, as much as possible. He had done the same with the ropes on the boats. If she could design a cuff with something to aid him, like a second hand, it might be a way to thank him.

An image of the design came together in her mind, but without pen or ink it would be impossible to work out the details. Hopefully she could find some when they stopped for the night.

Fortunately, in her haste to pack, Isabella had remembered the gold coins Elise's father had left for her the last time he visited.

During their three-day journey to Brighton Castle, as Isabella and Keet deepened their growing relationship, Elise, having acquired both ink and paper at the first inn they stayed, was kept busy sketching something that would, hopefully, make Keet's day-to-day activities easier to manage. Keeping her mind occupied kept her worry at bay. There was nothing she could do for John or William or change what had happened at school.

Her design for the cuff was completed by the time they neared Brighton Castle. She could hardly wait to get to work on it.

When they arrived at the castle's courtyard, the servants met them. The stable hands took charge of the horses to feed and care for them while Keet was introduced to the staff.

"Elise!" Hanna ran out and nearly knocked Elise down as she launched herself at her. "I've missed you."

"M'lady, I'm so glad you're home." Hanna's nanny stood behind her. Miss Violet had been Elise's nanny, too. "I'm sorry to tell you that your brother has been injured in a terrible battle." Miss Violet's lips trembled with emotion, but her words were clear and calm. "Your mum has gone to see to his injuries and then fetch him home. Mrs. Degraf has gone with her, for William was also injured in the same battle."

"Captain Keet told us what happened. We've been praying fervently for God's protective and healing touch to be on the both of them." She hugged her old nanny. "Where Father?"

"He's been gone on a business trip to Spain. He returned only yesterday and left immediately when he heard the news. He hopes to catch up with your mum. There are three of the castle guards traveling with the women, so they'll be well protected." She glanced at Keet, who had turned his attention to Isabella. They were in deep conversation, so the elderly nanny lowered her voice and leaned closer to Elise. "You know your mum. She could take on half the king's army and win. Besides a sword or two, she took plenty of healing herbs and oils to doctor whatever ails the boys." Miss Violet glanced up and met Keet's gaze. "We welcome you, sir. Come, and we'll get you a room where you can clean up. Dinner is in one hour." With that, she nudged Hanna back toward the castle. "We have lessons to return to."

"But Elise is here," Hanna whined, which turned into an expressive pout.

"I'll see you at dinner, Sunshine." Elise hugged her and sent her on her way.

"I shouldn't stay more than an hour or so, long enough to rest the horses. I need to return to the boat." Keet glanced at Isabella with regret.

"I've something that might change your mind." Elise

unfolded the papers with her design. "I would like to make this for you, but it will take a couple of days to fashion. It won't be as good as having your hand, but it could help you with your work." She watched as he studied the drawings.

"You think this is possible?" Keet's expression held hope. When Elise nodded, he said, "Perhaps Frank won't mind if I'm a day or so late." He smiled. "I'm glad for a reason to stay a little longer."

During the time that it took for Elise to fashion the cuff, the traveling priest arrived. He always stayed at the castle when he was in the area and had his own room next to the castle's private chapel.

With a few trials and errors, Keet got the hang of putting on the harness that held the cuff in place. Strong leather straps secured the harness across his back and his shoulders so he could use the hook that she attached to the cuff to pull heavy objects without the cuff coming off. The polished hook with its pointed end was a bit intimidating to gaze upon, but it was the simple curved design that made it functional for many tasks.

"How does that feel?" Isabella tugged the straps snug across Keet's shoulders.

"Fine." Keet stretched his arm out, and with the hook, carefully drew Isabella within his embrace.

"I think what he's not saying is that the harness and hook are a marvel of scientific genius. And thank you." Isabella gazed into Keet's eyes. He grinned and nodded his approval.

They turned toward Elise.

"We have something else to tell you." Isabella blushed, and Keet stood tall and proud.

"I asked her to marry me, and she said aye." Keet's wide grin broadened until the happiness within the ex-soldier-turned-fisherman exploded into hearty laughter. "I shall be going home with a bride and a new hand. I can't tell which I'm most proud of."

Isabella poked him with her elbow, and he gave an exaggerated wince of pain.

"All right woman. It's you I'm most grateful for." He hugged her tight and laughed.

"You better believe it, Captain Keet." Isabella allowed him to pull her into another hug. Once he released her, she turned to Elise. "We would love for you to attend our wedding. Father Amos will marry us tonight in the castle's chapel, with your permission."

"Of course." Elise squealed with glee and hugged her friend. "I begged the good father to delay his journey with the hope this would be the outcome."

"What?" Wide-eyed with surprise, Keet turned to Elise. "You conspired to keep me here until I woke up to the idea of getting married?" When his frown turned into a grin, Elise was able to release the breath she held.

"I simply wanted to gift you with that cuff. You were the one who decided you'd found the one you loved and didn't want to leave without her." Elise was filled joy for her friends, but she would miss Isabella. She would never be able to thank her enough, for she had saved her life by her quick thinking and getting them away from the school when she did.

"Oh, my goodness." Isabella's happy smiled turned to panic. "The wedding is tonight. I have so much to do. I need to pack my things and then get ready for the ceremony."

The ceremony was simple but beautiful. It was the kind of wedding Elise had always dreamed about. All who attended were moved by the priest's reverent admonition of the holy vows. There was none of the haughty display of materialism that often accompanied a noble's wedding.

The newlywed's departure, early the next morning was a joyous occasion. The well-wishers ran alongside for a short distance and tossed flower petals into the carriage.

Elise envied Isabella for having found true love with a

husband who would be loyal and protect her all the days of their lives.

William was her one true love. He was never far from her thoughts or prayers.

A weary messenger arrived that afternoon with a missive from her mother.

To Miss Violet,

Thank you, and all of those who have faithfully prayed for us. John and William are alive, but they've been gravely wounded. As soon as they are able to travel, we will return home.

I'll need you to make the two first floor guest rooms ready, each with a spare cot, for John and William will need constant care until they are better.

I've sent a missive to Sarah with strict instruction not to come to Brighton, for there are rumors of unrest in the land. I also sent a messenger to Elise informing her of what has happened. Knowing her, she will disregard my request to remain safely in London, and return home to help. Ask her to remain at Brighton.

Please have everyone continue to pray for John and William's healing. We expect to return with our brave young sons within the month.

In Christ we trust,

Lady Evangeline Stanton

CHAPTER 6

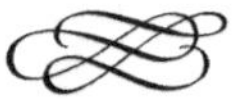

er parents had arrived home with John and William a week earlier, a good thing for the leaves had begun to turn crimson and gold. The fall harvests were complete and the early morning air was crisp with the first hint of winter. God's merciful hand had been on their mission to get the wounded men safely home. Late October and early November's weather had remained mild and the roads passable allowing them to make the journey before cold rains soaked the earth and made traveling miserable.

Elise drew her covers higher to ward off the morning's chill. She rubbed the sleep from her eyes, yawned and stretched. Her body was stiff and weary, as if she had not slept at all. Between her worry for William, who refused to see her, tormenting dreams of being chased by Richard, and John's nightmares, which echoed through the halls of the castle day and night, she hadn't been able to rest long enough to alleviate her exhaustion.

William had insisted he be taken to the inn so his mother could watch over him, though it had been their plan to bring both of the men to the castle. Elise feared his decision to go to the inn was to keep her from seeing him without his leg, though she couldn't reason why. If he would only let her see him, she would tell him that his sacrifice was not in vain. She would use her skills to fashion him a new leg—a better one.

Her emotions concerning him swung, from love and desperation to see him, to anger at his stubborn refusal to see her or any outside visitors.

Both men had been so badly injured that the army surgeons insisted that they be discharged never to return to active service. They told her mother they didn't expect John to live, but if he did, he'd be less than a man and not fit for battle.

That was the wrong thing to tell their mother. According to the two servants that had also accompanied them, their dire predictions made her furious. She yelled at the doctors, declaring them daft in three different languages, before proclaiming that John and William would be healed and good as ever.

In spite of her mother's determination to see John healed, Elise's once strong, and invincible big brother seemed to grow worse. He was pale and in so much pain, he remained captive in his bed without the strength to sit up.

Elise had waited a couple of days, until her parents had gotten John settled and they were somewhat rested from their journey, before her guilt drove her to explain the real reason she'd come home.

She'd tried to keep the details of accident to a minimum, explaining Richard had showed up uninvited with an unwelcomed marriage proposal, but she left out the part about Richard's intent to take her against her will to make her marry him. Perhaps it was Elise's expression of revulsion whenever she used Richard's name, but her mother pressed her for more. She tried to divert her mother's attention and lighten the mood by telling them about Isabella and Keet's marriage, but her parents knew her too well.

When questioned about the cause of Elise's desperate cries for help during the night, she was too exhausted to make light of the terror she and Isabella had faced when they were forced to flee for their lives. All because Richard Blackstone stirred normally peaceful people into a frenzy of hate and greed by his lies and offer of a large reward for their capture. Her parents had been furious at Richard for what he did. As much as she would have liked to forget the whole event, she knew her parents would not allow the matter to go unchallenged. This incident was another of life's hard-earned lessons. What is done can't be undone no matter how hard she prayed.

Her father would want to investigate, so she was not surprised at his sudden need to make a trip to London on business, a week later. He had encouraged her to write a detailed account of the incident for him to give to the authorities. In it, she had explained, in detail, the reason for her professor's assignment and the elements she'd prepared to complete the experiment. Combined, those elements became the catalyst for the explosion, but she made it clear that it was Richard who swept them into the fire, which caused the damage and almost killed them all.

As embarrassing as it was to admit her part in the incident, she was glad to tell her side. It was also liberating to rid herself of the responsibility of keeping Professor Canterbury's meteorites safe. Her father promised to return them to the professor, with her note of warning of the stones' dangerous potential.

Her prayers also included Richard and for him to admit the truth, but knowing him, doubt clouded her faith.

Afterward, she slipped out of bed and splashed water on her face. The chill in the room hastened her decision of what to wear. She dressed and went in search of something useful to do.

She'd found keeping busy was the best way of avoiding

unhealthy thoughts. She went out to her workshop, but after she'd ruin the second iron latch, by overheating it, she set her projects aside and went to her desk. With quill in hand, she stared at a new idea she'd sketched for a cart small enough for Hanna to use with her pony, but she couldn't concentrate.

"A letter came by special messenger for you, Lady Elise." A servant curtseyed and handed Elise the letter.

"Thank you, Fiona." Elise's hand trembled when she saw her father's seal. Was it good news or bad? She slipped into her father's study to escape further interruption.

Using her father's letter opener, she carefully slit the seal and pulled out three sheets of paper with her father's distinctive handwriting. She took a deep breath and blew it out before she read his letter. For fear she had missed something, she read it through again.

"After my arrival in London, I went to the school first to conduct my own investigation of the matter. I spoke with Professor Canterbury and others, and found out everyone associated with the school, along with all of the students, had been arrested the day after the explosion. Fortunately, they were all released the same day. For the school's nightguard, Mr. Harrison, gave his testimony of the incident clearing up any misconception of what had happened that morning. He confessed that instead of waiting until after his break, he had unlocked the gate two hours earlier than normal for the tradesmen to come inside the compound. His hip was bothering him and he didn't want to walk back to the front gate later to open it as was his normal routine.

When he noticed a strange carriage in the drive, he abandoned his tea and sought out the driver. The man told him his passenger, Lord Richard Blackstone had demanded he enter the compound and wait. He exited the carriage and followed a young woman into the blacksmith's building. Mr. Harrison went to investigate and opened the door to the building. He saw Lord Richard stalking after you in spite of your demands that he leave. Before Mr. Harrison could intervene, the man swept the contents on a table into the fire, which resulted in a huge explosion. The next he knew; he was on the ground outside of the building with burning debris all around.

"The carriage belonged to Duke Archibald Blackstone. His carriage driver also confirmed he had been concerned when Lord Richard hadn't returned, because he had been drinking heavily that evening. His fear for the young lady caused him to follow the guard to the building. He confirmed the guard's story of what happened, for he was standing in the doorway when the blast threw him into a large oak, breaking his arm.

"By the two men's testimony, and others who gambled and drank with Richard that evening, and who also testified to Richard's drunkenness when he left their establishments, the charges of witchcraft brought by Lord Richard's accusations were quickly dismissed and everyone freed.

"I want to assure you that you've also been exonerated from the accusations of witchcraft, and from causing the explosion.

"I'm not sure if this missive will reach you before I return home, but I wanted to relieve your worry as soon as possible.

"Duke Blackstone and I agreed to fund the building of a new blacksmith shop, which pleased the school's administrators and staff. The school remains open, but several of the students left and fewer have enrolled for the following term, fearing they would be accosted later with false charges if they miscalculate an experiment.

"There is one area of concern. The duke has disowned Richard over his many transgressions, and has refused to pay any of his gambling debts, which are apparently extensive. According to rumors, Richard blames you for all his woes. He has made public threats against you, which I take seriously. Inform the guards and servants to be on alert to his possible appearance, though I doubt, with his lack of funds he would travel to Brighton to seek his revenge while he is being pursued by some dangerous people, whom he owes money, plotting their own form of retribution.

"I will speak with you when I return. Try not to worry.

With love, Da

Elise hugged the letter and allowed the words to comfort her. She was safe here surrounded by her friends and family, unlike Richard, who would be hard pressed to find a place of safety after his grandfather disowned him. If he would but humble himself and seek forgiveness for his sins, and turn his life around, Jesus would forgive him and perhaps so would his grandfather.

She tucked the letter in her pocket and went to sit with John. If he were asleep, she would reread the letter. It gave her comfort to know others had come forward to tell the truth even if Richard had not.

Over the last few weeks, as a form of penance, she felt a need to learn every detail she could on the healing properties of each herb and oil her mother used to cure different conditions. Approaching the compounds as scientific formulas made it possible to produce the right outcome consistently. It was important that she help her mother with her brother's care.

There remained a hush over the castle, as John hovered between life and death. Her mother split her time between his bedside and the chapel in prayer.

Elise feared for her mother's health for she looked exhausted. Dark circles appeared under her eyes as the days turned into weeks. John's fever would spike then calm, only to return in a day or so. His manservant, Chester had bathed John earlier and mentioned he seemed more alert, but he was sleeping when Elise came to sit with him to give Chester a break to eat and rest.

"How is my handsome son doing this fine morning?" Her mother came into the room with a flask. "I awoke early this morning with an idea for a new combination of herbs made into a tonic." She went to the side of John's bed and touched his forehead. "Help me lift him, Elise, so I can give him a sip."

Together they were able to lift him high enough to administer a small sip of the liquid so he wouldn't get choked. He coughed and frowned, but didn't spit it out. They lowered him back to his pillow.

"I'll stay with him. You go get some fresh air." Her mother walked Elise to the door. "I'll call you if I need you." She gave her a hug and returned to John's bedside then Elise slipped out of the room.

Elise climbed the stairs to where a large lead glass window brightened the hall. She craved the feel of sunshine on her face, but wanted to remain nearby. Without leaving the castle this place on the stairs was a good place to soak in the sunlight.

Hanna and Miss Violet walked from the kitchen to the entry and stopped. A stableman entered the hall and knelt down in front of Hanna. He was holding something and waved for Hanna to come closer. Miss Violet nudged the reluctant girl forward. When he opened his hands, Elise saw he held a little gray kitten. It wiggled and mewed in his hands.

Hanna brushed a finger over its fur. Without a word or sign of emotion, she turned and walked toward the stairs that would take her to her rooms.

A sob slipped out of Elise. She dabbed away the accompanying tears, for she was determined to be strong for her family. Hanna climbed the stairs with her gaze down and walked past Elise without a hug or word. Miss Violet followed behind the little girl, her concern evident, by her furrowed brow.

Elise's once enthusiastic, happy little sister, who was nicked named Sunshine because she always had a smile and found the good in every situation, now moped around as if lost in despair. If she couldn't find joy at the sight of a newborn kitten, then how would she survive if John's condition should take a turn for the worst?

Elise's heart broke for Hanna, for all of them.

She had to escape the gloom. After she informed one of the

servants where she'd be, she made her way outside and sought solace in castle's private garden, but even the flowers and sculpted greenery could not lighten her spirit. By the shadow on the sundial, an hour or more had slipped by. It was time for her to relieve her mother.

She started back inside, but hesitated when she saw her father, his assistant, and their guard ride into the courtyard.

Her mother would be happy he was home safely. With a wave of greeting, she didn't wait for her father to dismount, but hurried to John's room to let her mother know of his arrival so she could greet him.

As she opened the door, she heard her mother's laughter.

"Come in, Elise. Your brother is awake and hungry as a wolf, he says." Her mother's face lit with joy and relief.

"I don't know what all the fuss is about. I feel fine." John was sitting up with his back against the headboard. His intent to sound gruff fell short when his stomach growled loudly. "See? This proves the depth of my hunger."

Elise laughed and her mother motioned to the nearest servant. "Chester, ask cook to prepare John some fresh vegetable broth."

"Broth?" John's disappointment was ignored as the servant hurried away to do her bidding. "I'm starved, Mother. Please, have pity on me."

"You can't have meat or any solid foods until you've been up and able to be on your feet for at least a couple of days." She kissed him on the forehead.

Elise smiled, knowing the kiss was as much to make sure he had no fever as it was a gesture of affection.

Voices in the hall preceded the door swinging open. Their father, holding Hanna's hand, walked in and smiled.

"I've come home to some good news, I see." He crossed his arms over his chest. "It's about time."

"You're awake!" Hanna ran over to the bed and climbed in

beside her brother and touched his forehead with her hand, just like their mother taught them to check for fever. "I'm so glad you're feeling better."

John laughed and hugged her tight before allowing her to slip off the bed and head toward the door. "Hey, where you going in such a hurry?"

"To see the kittens and give them all names." She blew him a kiss and hurried out.

"Apparently, I come in second place." John winced as he tried to adjust his position.

"We all come in second place when it comes to newborn anything around here." Elise hurried to his side in case he needed help. "Remember the baby mice she found in the hayloft a few years ago?"

"Don't remind me." Her father walked to his son's side. "I had to be the one to explain why she couldn't keep them. It didn't help that her favorite barn cat was seen shortly after, carrying them off to feed to her babies. The cycle of life and death is not a concept that Hanna appreciates." Henry put a hand on John's shoulder. "Good to see you sitting up, son. How are you feeling?"

"Hungry, but Mum refuses to feed me." John gave a good imitation of Hanna's pout and glanced at his mother. She frowned and shook her finger at him, then they both chuckled.

Their father glanced from John to his wife with humor in his eyes.

Elise could feel a good portion of the heaviness she'd carried for weeks lift away. With John finally on the road to recovery, castle life would soon be back to a more normal routine. Instead of whispers and cautious muffled steps, it would resume its hurried pace with happy voices once again echoing through the halls.

"How's William?" John's voice weaker than moments ago, and his shoulders sagged. With Elise's help he scooted down.

Once he was comfortable, she adjusted his pillow beneath his head.

"Keep him in your prayers, John. Helen is fearful he's given up. He refuses to accept the loss of his leg. He says he'd be better off dead." Her mother frowned. "Helen is with child again, and I fear for her and the baby's health. She's exhausted."

Elise turned to her mother. "Since John no longer needs constant attention, perhaps I can go and relieve her this afternoon so she can rest."

"That's an excellent idea, Elise. I'll send a servant ahead with a message to expect you." Her mother put an arm around Elise's shoulder and led her to the door. "We should let the men talk—" She turned toward Father. "But not for long. John needs his rest."

Her father smiled and motioned them out. As the women left the room, John chuckled. "Maybe they'll bring enough broth for me to share with you, Father."

"No thanks." Their father groaned. "But I can keep you company until you've eaten."

Elise and her mother went down to the castle's greenhouse and gathered more herbs for Elise to take to the inn and give to Helen, who was as proficient with using them as Elise's mother.

Elise's heart fluttered at the thought of seeing William after so long a time. She hated the thought of him giving up his fight to regain his strength and health just because he'd lost his leg. Her mind buzzed with ideas to design him a new leg, even better than the one he lost. If only…

CHAPTER 7

William often heard voices whispering around him. Some days the pain was nearly unbearable. Fear tormented him with thoughts of death and worse—what use would he be if he lived?

He barely remembered the battle, only the urgency to protect John. He'd been struck off his horse—the enemy closed in with a battleax intent on delivering John a fatal blow…

William's heart raced and his leg throbbed with intensity. If he'd reacted sooner, maybe…

He took a deep breath and blew it out. It was hopeless. Nothing could undo what had happened.

His mother had tried to encourage him. She said that the king's earl constable had called him a hero and promised him a commendation for his actions.

With the proper commendations, a knight who was injured in battle earned a small pension and land. With that, he could get married, but who would want to marry a crippled soldier?

Elise?

He cast down the thought.

Turning on his side, he tried to ease the cramp in his leg by rubbing his thigh and the area above his knee. At least, he still had the knee even if the rest of the leg was gone. The grief of losing his leg had become a deep sorrow, as hard to accept as having lost a loved one.

He couldn't shake the thoughts of self-pity that questioned, *why me*, or the self-loathing of seeing the ugly stump where his leg should be. Why should he fight to get better when it would have been better for all if he'd died in battle?

His room at the top of the stairs of his family's inn had become his prison. The gloom he insisted on, by keeping the windows shaded with heavy curtains, fit his foul mood.

His mother's footsteps on the stairs were familiar, but the second person's light tread was not. The women's voices got closer, and he stilled, not wanting them to know he was awake.

Dread burned his gut. He recognized the second voice.

Elise.

The pity he saw in his family's eyes was painful enough, but for Elise to see him like this...

"I'm finding this child I'm carrying requires me to rest more often than I did with the others. Or perhaps it's just because I'm older." His mother's tone lightened as she spoke of the new baby. "Thank you for coming. I'll relieve you in a couple of hours."

"Helen," Elise said, "I will remain by his side for as long as you need me. Please, go and rest, I'll be fine. I brought some handwork and drawing paper to keep me busy." She pulled up the chair by the side of his bed and sat, placing her bag of supplies beside her on the floor.

He had dreamed of Elise so often over the last two years, he feared it was another torturous imagination, but her familiar scent of wildflowers and lavender made her presence real.

He drew in a deep breath to be reassured but kept his eyes closed, for he would not survive her pity. He must have drifted off, for he awoke when she bathed his brow with cool water.

Her voice was as soothing as the cool cloth she placed on his forehead. He listened as she prayed over him healing scriptures from the Bible, many of which he'd learned as a child and heard his mother pray often over their family.

He loved the sound of her voice. It brought peace. His heartbeat quickened as her prayers changed from prayer for his healing to more personal pleas.

She leaned closer and whispered her love for him.

His conscience stirred him with guilt for listening to her pour out her secrets. How could she still love him? If he lived, he would never be the man he used to be.

William risked a glance. He opened his eyes and stared into hers. There was no pity, only concern and love, but also something else. Her glance was that of a wounded deer. Something horrible had happened to her while he was gone. All he could think was to make it better.

"My beautiful Elise."

"Oh, William." She bent down and kissed him so deeply that he drew her down beside him and embraced her.

For that moment, she was his.

There was no dream as good as having her in his arms. She professed her love for him unashamedly, and in his weakness, he whispered, *"I love you, Elise with all that is within me"*, a secret he'd never planned to share. If he died tomorrow then he had this moment to cling to forever after.

His broken body and spirit awakened with her in his arms, as if from a deep sleep. Suddenly, it seemed his cares were lifted and he was made whole again.

"After we're married," she said, "we can build a small house near my workshop where we can invent all manner of things to help people." Elise grinned and he noticed the faraway look she always got when she was thinking of a new project. "I know I can build you a new leg, maybe even better than the one you lost."

"That's a good dream…but I can't marry you." William drew in her scent one last time, released her, and pushed her away. The surprise and hurt in her expression quickened his desire to pull her back into his arms, but with all of the strength within him, he resisted.

The familiar sound of his sisters' footsteps on the stairs and their voices drew closer.

"What? But you said…" Elise blinked. Hearing the footsteps, she slipped off the bed and stood. Her dress was wrinkled, so she smoothed her clothing and tidied her hair, which had come loose.

"You must forget what happened here. I wanted only to comfort you." He hated the lie and betrayal he saw in her gaze.

Voices and footsteps coming closer made him adjust the blanket to hide the evidence of his longing for Elise.

"Mum said we weren't to wake him." His eighteen-year-old sister, Silvia's, loud whisper could frighten roosting birds into flight. Married while he was away in the army, she and her husband, Vern, were expecting their first child in a few months.

There was no doubt Elise's visit had stirred up the love and longing within him to make her his bride and raise a family of their own. Their embrace made that need almost too strong to deny, but deny it he must. Elise was destined to marry someone with noble blood. As much as he wished it were possible, a marriage between noble and commoners was not acceptable in either quarter.

"Then you shush." Martha, his seventeen-year-old sister had his mother's coloring and softer nature. According to his mother, a young farmer had declared for her.

How would William feel if that young farmer only stirred up promises of love and marriage with no intention to fulfill them? Anger burned within him. He would take the man to task, resulting in so much pain he wouldn't soon forget.

His guilt reminded him that he had just done the same thing

with Elise. To be honest, if they had been left alone for much longer, he would have promised Elise anything, the sun and moon, and marriage.

"Oh, hello, Lady Elise, I forgot you were still here." Martha said. She and Silvia gave a little curtsey and glanced from William to Elise with raised eyebrows. "We were sent to check on William to see if he was awake and, if so, if he was ready to try some broth." Martha grinned at him as if she knew he and Elise had kissed, but there was no way she could have known.

"You are welcome to stay for the evening meal, Lady Elise." Silvia smiled as if she too knew something.

"Not today, thank you. With John feeling better, I must return home, for my family expects me to dine with them." Elise's voice was husky with emotion. She glanced down at William as if waiting for him to insist she stay and perhaps declare his intentions to his family. He clamped his jaw shut, but his chest pounded as he fought the urge to comply.

The three women watched him with expectations. He had to say something.

"Thank you, Lady Stanton, for ministering to me and allowing my mother to rest." He drew himself up until his back was against the wall, the first time he'd accomplished the task on his own since he'd been home. He focused on his sisters. "Have her driver bring her ladyship's carriage around. And tell Mum I'm starving."

His sisters glanced from Elise to him and back again as if waiting for more.

"Go." William waved them all away, but not before he noticed the tears gathering in Elise's eyes. It was all he could do not to reach out for her, but he loved her too much for that.

❡

"*O*-o-oh, that man!" After two hours of pacing and grieving, Elise's hurt turned to anger. "How dare he accept my adoration, affection, and declaration of undying love and then send me away like a—a—I don't know what." She threw herself on her bed and hugged the nearest pillow for comfort.

Crushed, she had one thought, to go far away to escape her humiliation. There was only so much rejection a woman could endure for love.

A trip would be good, but the thought of Richard finding her away from the safety of the castle made her heart pound. If she and William married, Richard wouldn't dare try and accost her when he learned of William's bravery and skill with the sword.

She'd needed to take her mind off William and Richard. John had been allowed to eat in his room this evening as a consideration of his convalescences, so she went to his room for a visit. Perhaps he could enlighten her on William's reluctance to declare for her.

"Your color is better." Elise touched her brother's forehead with the back of her hand, as has been her custom these last weeks to check for fever, but he brushed her hand away.

"I'm fine." He winced as he pushed up to lean against the headboard. "I heard you went to see William. How's he doing?"

"He's feeling better." Elise turned away so he wouldn't see the sudden tears that sprang to her eyes. Before he could question her, their mother came into the room. Elise busied herself with tidying the table lined with vials of herbs and oils.

"Elise, I see we had the same idea." Their mother walked to John's bedside. She also checked his brow for fever. He frowned at the attention but remained still.

"Your skin is cool. How do you feel?" She studied him until he squirmed.

"As I told Elise, and countless other well-wishers, I feel fine."

Pain pinched his brow when he shifted positions. "Now that I'm better, I'd like to be moved to the east tower." He raised his hand when their mother frowned and put a hand to her hip. "Before you protest, I know my nightmares disturb everyone's sleep. Until I am free of them, the tower room will keep the sound from echoing through the halls."

"Once you are on your feet and able to climb up and down those steep stairs on your own, you are free to move up there, if the need still exists." She straightened his bedcovers. "Until then, it is easier to see to your needs in this room, on the lower level."

"Then that is my goal." John straightened and smiled. His manservant came with his meal. "I hope you brought me something more substantial than broth."

"I will check you again before I retire." Their mother gave him a kiss on his cheek.

Elise waved good-bye before she left.

The lack of John's presence at dinner didn't diminish the family's joy of seeing him finally on the mend. Happy conversation displaced the heaviness and fear for his life that had hung over the meals since the news of his injuries. No longer gloomy and sullen, Hanna's gleeful chatter once again dominated the dinner.

Elise was happy to see her brother awake and sounding like his old self, but she found it hard to pretend to be joyful after her visit with William. Had she said or done something to cause his sudden change from confessing his love to abruptly dismissing her?

The few bites she managed to eat of the well-prepared food, tasted like sawdust. She ignored the efforts of her mother to be drawn into the family discussion of Hanna's latest discovery of a stray dog and her six puppies. Hanna's excuse that the poor animal was thin and had scars all over her body with signs of abuse only further ignited their mother's lecture on the dangers of approaching strange and injured animals, much less encouraging them to follow her home. Their mother raised her hands in defeat and turned to Elise's father for support. "The guard, who escorted her on her walk to pick wildflowers for her brother's room, had begged me for forgiveness, for he was unable to dissuade Hanna from her purpose of supplying the abused dog and her brood with a hearty meal and a good home."

"But Mum, she needed my help and…" Hanna's protest was interrupted when a servant entered.

The servant approached her father and leaned down to whisper something that Elise couldn't hear from where she sat. Her heart quickened. Had Richard found his way here?

A messenger dressed in full livery stood beside the doorway awaiting an audience.

Her father motioned the man inside and accepted the sealed envelope he carried. Even Hanna stilled as he silently read the letter he found inside.

"Henry?" Her mother stiffened, and her features filled with concern. Messengers had rarely brought good news of late.

"It's from Sarah." His shoulders relaxed, and he handed the note to his wife, and stood. He motioned for the messenger to follow him into the study.

"What is it, mother?" Elise feared the worse.

"It concerns you, Elise." Her mother glanced up and smiled. "I suspect this might be welcome news for a change." She stood and walked around the dinner table to where Elise remained seated, her food mostly untouched. "Here, read it for yourself and tell me what you think."

Mother signaled to the servants that the family was done. "Hanna, it's time for your bath." She raised her hand. "And no, you may not take a puppy to your room to play. You've been with the puppies all day. It's time for them to rest too." She hugged her youngest daughter and waved her nanny, Miss Violet forward to take charge of the bath and bed routine.

When they were gone, she glanced at Elise. "We'll speak after you've had time to read the letter." She left the dining hall and went to the study to meet her husband.

Elise needed privacy to read the contents of the letter and took the missive to her room. She chose her favorite chair near the fireplace, and got comfortable by pulling up her legs to tuck beneath her.

She unfolded the parchment paper and noticed a royal seal at the top.

"My dearest parents, I miss you terribly. I hope the family is well and John is healing. He is in our daily prayers.

As for me, I am beyond happy. Even after three years of marriage, Trevor continues to be a most wonderful and dutiful husband, although he has been a bit overprotective of me since we found out I am with child after all of this time. It is at his request that I am sending this letter.

His favorite aunt, Lady Clara Meriwether was injured when she was thrown off her horse while foxhunting at our estate three weeks ago. Though on the mend, she is not adjusting at all well to the seden-tary life needed for her convalescence. A very active woman for her age, she has become morose and has lost her once vigorous appetite for life and good food.

After much prayer, Trevor and I came up with the idea of Clara traveling to Spain to stay with her sister, Hazel, and her husband, Fernando, at their villa. This is the first sign of interest she's shown, so we dare not tarry.

She's not been happy with any of the companions we have hired thus far, and desires a more intelligent and creative type to accompany her to Spain.

I thought of Elise immediately. By your recent letter, I understand she has taken leave of school and is helping with John's care. If you can spare her, and she is willing, Trevor and I would be most grateful and will fully fund her trip.

In anticipation of acceptance, the messenger and the three guards are prepared to accompany Elise to a waiting ship at Sunderland. She will rendezvous with Clara and sail to Spain where Clara will have endless sunny days to regain her strength and cheerful nature. (I doubt if Elise will miss another bitter English winter.)

Tell Elise to pack light, for Clara will purchase anything of which she has need. I wish I were able to go, but at Trevor's insistence, I must remain here. I'm still having bouts of morning sickness and he fears for my health.

Elise, my dear sister, if you decide to go to Spain, Clara will make sure you have ample opportunities to satisfy your inquisitive and adventurous nature. Who knows, you might even meet a dark handsome man who'll satisfy all of those expectations on your list, which you insist are non-negotiable for an acceptable husband.

Love and prayers,

Your loving daughter, (and sister), Sarah

Her mother came to her room and took a seat near the window. "What do you think of Sarah's offer to travel to Spain?"

Elise abandoned her seat by the fireplace and took the seat next to her mum leaving a small table between them. A servant tapped on the door before being bid to come in. She carried a tea tray, which she placed on the table, curtsied and left the room.

"It is kind of Sarah and Trevor to think of me, but I'm not sure if I should go. You might need my help." Elise poured a cup of tea for each of them.

"John's fever has not returned, and from all signs, his recovery should be swift from now on." Her mother took a sip of her tea and put her cup down. "Your father and I think it would be good for you to go to Spain for a while. He had a missive come this morning from an agency he's hired while he was in London to check into Richard's whereabouts."

Elise put her hands in her lap to still the trembling. "Do you think it's safe for me to leave Brighton after Richard's threats?"

"The man in charge of the agency, Sir Elliot Wyatt has many men in his employ whose job it is to investigate such matters. One of his men spotted Richard at his grandfather's hunting lodge, which is many miles from London. The agency will continue to monitor Richard's whereabouts for as long as necessary." She stood and so did Elise. "We believe after all you've been through, this opportunity to travel to Spain will help to alleviate your bad memories and replace them with good ones." She put an arm around Elise and walked to the door. "Your father will send a message to Sir Wyatt to see you are safely aboard Lady Meriwether's ship in London where her servants will keep you both safe."

"Then I shall go. Would you send in Izzy to help me pack?" She needed to clear her mind and heart of some bitter disappoints of late. This would be a good time to keep her distance from William.

"Remember to pack light. Elise, that means take no tools." Her mother's unsmiling and pointed gaze reinforced her stern tone. She knew her too well. "I'll tell your father of your decision. He will inform the messenger and guards to make preparations for a hurried trip to the coast. They will expect you within the hour."

~

The trip to Spain was exciting and more informative than she could have hoped. There were no surprise visits from Richard, and she found the elder Lady Clara Meriwether a delight.

As Lady Clara reconnected with her sister and brother-in-law, Elise was given a carriage, a servant, and a guard to escort her around the nearby villages. She chose to visit several craftsmen to see their different techniques for forging steel and other alloys, some elements of which she'd never worked with before. She'd asked lots of questions hoping to find the right material to create a strong, yet flexible replacement for William's present pine peg. One elderly blacksmith, showed her an ornate candlestick holder made from a strange alloy, he called, *metromium,* because it came from a large meteorite, he'd found years ago. The alloy was lightweight and might work for her design for a peg.

She purchased the item with the intent to study the properties, though that would require melting it down and she loathe to destroy the lovely candlestick. She justified her decision since there wasn't enough of it to create the leg she had in mind. Yet, the possibilities stirred her imagination. Did the professor's meteorites also contain that alloy, and if so, how much would it take to complete her project?

The first month in Spain had been quiet, as Clara convalesced in the villa. The weather was sunny and pleasantly mild. Elise didn't miss the bitter English winter that had come early this year, according to her mother's letters, but she did miss her family...and William.

Christmas came accompanied with parties and merriment, but she missed her family and their traditions of hanging stockings and her father reading the Bible story of Christ's birth. Everyone she encountered in Spain was kind and respectful to her, but the days went by leaving her feeling restless and discouraged. She wanted to work on her design for William's leg even if she hadn't found the right metal, but Clara and Hazel would not have it. Women were destined to be in charge of the home, not working like a peasant in the hot blacksmith shop.

Each letter from home was a treasure, but unlike being away to school where her days were filled with learning and she was kept too busy to miss home, her duties as Clara's companion often left her idle, even in the midst of a busy household.

She missed the freedom she had at home...and her workshop.

According to her mother's last letter, John was getting stronger every day. She had visited Helen recently and she was doing well, but her pregnancy kept her exhausted. William was also on the mend, which eased Helen's worry and allowed her to rest more.

Her mother also filled each letter with updates on everyone but no mention of Richard, which Elise presumed was good news.

Over the weeks, Clara healed from her bruised hip, cracked ribs, and sprained ankle that were caused by her foxhunting accident. As she felt better, and her physician gave his approval for short outings, she and Elise visited the local market places. She and Clara were drawn to the artisans and their wares. Clara amused herself in the shops as Elise questioned the artisans about their process of creating their wares made of steel, copper, tin, gold, and silver.

Clara's sister, Hazel came with them on occasion, but her interests were more about fashion. She had insisted on buying Elise a closet full of finery, ignoring her protests.

Hazel and her husband, Ferdinando, entertained often and they were eager to introduce Elise to all of the right people. Hazel's taste in clothing ran more to exotic fabrics and designs by the local dressmaker, who shunned the simple dresses Elise had brought with her.

The matrons in Spain were not much different than the English matrons in their need to see all single women and men, of means and title, married, and Hazel was earnest in her goal to see that happen.

Elise honed her knowledge of the Spanish culture until she was able to decline the many social invitations with socially acceptable excuses that would not offend the hostess, but as the weeks went by it became more difficult to avoid the eager young men who came calling.

At the end of February Elise wrote to her mother with her

plans to return home to Brighton. Clara had joined forces with Hazel to pick out a suitable match for Elise. Their pick was a nephew of Fernando's, a young man, named Stephano. He was handsome and charming, and had some skill with bullfighting. Hazel and Fernando took her to a demonstration of Stephano's swordsmanship as he competed against ten others. The competitors rode through a difficult course filled with targets designed to prove the skill of young soldiers. He hit every target and won the competition. His prideful attitude, as he received the praise and adoration as his due, confirmed Elise's previous assessment of the demanding-type of husband he'd be to the poor girl who married him, but it wouldn't be Elise.

Elise's stay in Spain went from pleasant to unbearable with Stephano's constant presence. When Elise explained to Clara and her hosts at dinner one evening, that her family was expecting her home, they insisted Stephano accompany Elise on her journey. They assured her she would be safe for he wanted to meet her parents with the intent of declaring for her.

Why didn't people listen when she told them she wasn't ready to get married?

CHAPTER 8

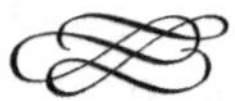

March arrived with a large amount of rain several days in a row, but the last two days were sunny and the temperatures mild, a welcome relief from the cold that chilled William to the bone and caused his leg to ache unmercifully.

The heavy rains had stranded travelers and filled the inn to overflowing. He had given up his room to a couple with three children, and gladly slept in the barn's tack room to get away from the people's stares and questions about his leg. He enjoyed watching over the animals, which accepted him without a fuss.

The last guests left early this morning fearing more rain would make the roads impassable.

William came inside the inn to help out, while his father went to meet a shipment of supplies, which they were in much need. William hobbled around a table he'd just wiped clean. He grabbed his crutches, which were propped up next to him, and headed outside for some fresh air.

The effort it took to learn to maneuver with the crutches and the new peg leg was exhausting. The pine peg he'd whittled in his spare time to replace his missing leg still didn't fit well enough and rubbed a blister on his stump even with the lamb's wool he used to cushion it. Elise could have fashioned one that fit perfectly, but she'd been gone for months, and only God knew how long it would be before she returned...if she returned. His gut clenched at the thought of never seeing her again.

Everything made him angry.

His parents and friends had gone out of their way to make life normal for him, everyone but the one he wanted most to see.

The grief in her eyes still haunted his dreams. Something horrible had happened to her in London, but he couldn't exactly demand she tell him the whole of the matter while his rejection remained a wall separating them. Even when she returned from Spain, he couldn't tell her the truth and ask for her forgiveness, for the reasons still remained.

It was hopeless.

He leaned against the porch support and threw down the crutches that identified him as a cripple. He hated them like an enemy when he had to use them to navigate around outside. Inside the inn, he had practiced walking without them, using the tables and chairs for support. One day soon, he would be able to walk without a limp or a crutch. He was determined.

"Here you go, William." His six-year-old sister, Libby, picked up the discarded crutches, handed them to him, and smiled, dispelling his anger with her eagerness to please him.

"Thanks, Libby. What's your hurry?" William had watched her from the porch, as she'd run up the road to the inn as if a predator were chasing her.

"Elise is coming home today, and she's bringing a man. I saw the fancy carriage from the tree I had climbed. She'll reach the castle soon." Libby rushed into the inn. He could hear her repeating the information to their mother, but it was as if all nature stilled around him, and the air grew heavy like before a storm.

Elise was coming home?

With a man?

William's stomach clenched with dread. What had she done? Married the first man who asked her? Had his rejection driven her into a stranger's arms?

He shouldn't care. It was none of his business. Still…

Perhaps it was time he visited John. He headed to the barn to hitch up the cart and find out for himself who exactly Elise was bringing home. Riding would have been faster, but he still had trouble mounting a horse, and once mounted, his balance was off, making staying on the horse more difficult, as his peg slipped through the stirrup.

He drove the cart out of the barn, and waved good-bye to his mother, as she stepped outside holding his newborn baby brother, Timothy, in her arms. Mum should be resting, yet she came outside to check on him. William loved her for her concern, but her hovering was growing old. She needed to be more concerned with her own health. He prayed little Timothy would grow strong and healthy, for he knew it pleased both his parents to have another son, one with two strong legs.

He stemmed the self-pity that threatened to reappear at the slightest disappointment. He was grateful that his stump had healed, but even with thicker padding, the pine peg made his leg ache if he was on it for more than a couple of hours. He had already been on it for three hours today helping out around the inn and stable.

Wearing his peg too long also caused a feeling that his missing foot was cramping, demanding to be rubbed. Since it was impossible to minister to his missing limb, the only thing he could do was massage his leg and pray for the pain to ease.

He used the shortcut to the castle from the inn, and within a half-hour, he reached Castle Brighton. He saw Elise in the courtyard. A tall, slender man with a well-trimmed beard and hair stood next to her and talked with Lord and Lady Stanton. John stood off to the side, frowning until he spotted William coming toward them. He excused himself and strolled over to where William stopped the horse and started to get out of the cart. His leg cramped up and refused to be ignored. John must have noticed his pain, for he led the horse and cart out of sight of the people whose attention was now on him.

William was humiliated and angry by the time they reached the stable.

"What can I do to help you?" John stood by waiting.

"By the saints!" William removed the peg and rubbed his stump, knee, and thigh, which helped relieve the pressure. He massaged the cramping muscles until the intense pain settled into a dull ache.

"I take it you heard about Elise's return...and her guest?" John gave William a knowing smile.

"Just overdue for our visit." William hated being so easy to read. He replaced the peg and secured the harness that kept it in place. John stepped back so William had plenty of room to get out of the cart in his own time.

"Want to come inside and meet our visitor?" John's grin proved he was enjoying this little game.

"Who is he?" William wasn't in the mood to play twenty guesses.

"Stephano Santiago. She wrote about him in her letters. Elise met him when she accompanied Trevor's aunt to Spain" John waited until William limped up beside him, and they continued out to the courtyard.

It was slow going, but without a crutch William had to concentrate on every step to avoid stumbling.

They arrived in time to see Lord and Lady Stanton usher their guest inside, but Elise lingered by the carriage as if looking for something.

"Apparently he's related to royalty and seems to have taken quite an interest in my little sister." John's voice dropped to a conspirator's whisper. "They sailed together from Spain to England, and then he insisted on escorting her all the way home—for her protection. Nice of him, don't you think?" John's grin proved he knew more.

"He's a regular humanitarian." William couldn't keep the sarcasm out of his tone. "When is he leaving?"

"Leaving? He just arrived." John slapped William on the shoulder, nearly knocking him over.

"Elise, what are you looking for? Can I help?" John put his arm around his sister and peeked past her at the open luggage inside the carriage door.

"I'm trying to find my gift for Hanna. You know that's the first thing she's going to ask about once she sees..." Elise glanced up and stopped. "Oh, hello, William. You're looking well."

William was dumbstruck. Elise had filled out in all the right places, or maybe it was the way the Spanish-styled dress, with the scooped neckline, hugged her curves. He opened his mouth, but words refused to cooperate. That and he had no legitimate reason for standing so near her and breathing in her exotic scents of jasmine and spices. He preferred her old scent of lavender and wildflowers.

She turned her attention back to her search. "Oh, here it is." She pulled a wrapped package from her things and shut the case. "I have more things for her in my trunks but wanted her to have this first."

"There you are, mi querida."

My darling. William was not amused with the stranger's familiarity.

The foreign male with dark hair and eyes who called to Elise sprinted out on two good legs and stopped beside her. He put his arm around her shoulder, his gaze roamed over William with a spark of jealousy—until he saw the pine peg. Pity crossed his features, and he reached out a hand. "I am Stefano Garcia Hernández Rodrigues Santiago, second cousin to the king of Spain. And you are?"

William accepted the man's outstretched hand.

"Sir William Degraf, Knight of King John." William choked on the title for he rarely used it. Elise's eyebrows arched in surprise at his stern tone, but she didn't say a word, only smiled and winked.

What did that mean? That woman could vex a saint.

The Spaniard's handshake was weak, as if he were afraid to put strength behind it, so William clamped down until the man winced. Satisfied he had made his point, he released him.

"Stefano was gracious enough to escort me home all the way from Spain." Elise smiled at William but allowed that Spaniard to reclaim her with a hand at her waist.

William hated the anger seething within his gut. His mind spun seeking ways of rebuking the man for his forwardness. Englishmen protected their women, and a glance at John's pinched disapproval gave him satisfaction. The man was crossing a line that would not end well if he continued to act with such familiarity toward Elise. Perhaps Spaniards were less strict with their protocols when dealing with young maidens. That was the only thought that kept William from striking the man with his fist.

"*Si*. My beautiful Elise needed an attentive escort to keep her many admirers from accosting her with their attention." He grinned as if he knew a secret. "She left many broken hearts behind. I am here until I can convince her to return with me as my bride."

"Mum said to come inside. It's time to eat." Hanna ran up to William, and he bent over, so she could give him a hug. "You can come too." She turned her attention to Elise, eyes widening at the sight of the package in her hand. "Is that for me?" Within seconds, she stood before Elise, bouncing from one foot to the other.

"It is for you, my little Sunshine, but you'll have to wait until after our meal to open it." Elise handed the gift to Hanna, who hurried inside, then turned to William. "It's a skillfully carved wooden puzzle with hand-painted pictures of baby animals on all six sides. Each side has a different picture. Once she opens it, she'll be too distracted to eat."

"I'm sure she's going to love it." William swallowed hard. There was much he wished he could say. His happiness to see her and his strong aversion of her marrying that pompous Spaniard were top on his list, but he refused the urge to speak his mind.

John kept the Spaniard busy with questions while Elise spoke to William.

"I agree with Hanna. You are most welcome to share our meal, Sir Knight." She smiled at him and his heart quickened.

Her teasing tone reminded him of when they were children, and she was the fair maiden and he was the gallant knight who rescued her from imaginary dragons. The thought lightened his heart. "Thank you for the invitation, but I must return home." William frowned as Stefano appeared at her side again.

"Good-bye, Sir Knight." The Spaniard gave William a slight nod, but his smirk suggested that he knew of William's interest in Elise. The stranger's possessive attitude toward her was an insult that should have been met with a sword, but he had not brought one, nor was he steady enough yet to wield one. Besides, John, his father, and a castle full of guards were there to intervene and put the Spaniard in his place, if necessary.

William turned away before he said something he'd regret and headed toward the barn where he'd left the cart. Anger and jealousy stiffened his posture, but somehow with a concentrated effort not to limp, he managed to avoid falling on his face.

~

*E*lise hated to see William go, for his presence had given her an opportunity to distance herself from the clingy Stephano. She'd seen the jealousy in William's eyes and it pleased her to know he still cared. She didn't want to deceive him, but she wasn't ready to tell him she had only allowed Stephano to escort her from Spain to Brighton, because of his ability to keep her safe from any chance meeting with Richard. She had tried to dissuade the self-assured Spaniard, from getting his hopes up of marriage, but he chose to believe in his power of persuasion.

Perhaps if Stephano remained at the castle, William would be moved to declare for her. It might be worth the aggravation of dealing with her pompous suitor, if it moved William to action.

CHAPTER 9

TWO WEEKS LATER

William had found numerous reasons to visit Brighton Castle since Elise had returned. When he had visited John, he had seen Elise with Stefano several times walking in the garden or riding but had never found her in her favorite place, her workshop. Even though her forge was again filled with hot coals, she was curiously missing when he came. Where was the woman who was always in or around the forge working on one thing or another? He did notice signs of a project. A piece of oak was on the work bench and carving tools.

Was she avoiding him?

William was becoming more accustomed to his peg for longer periods until, though his stump often ached in protest of a hard day, it no longer throbbed with enough intensity to keep him awake at night. It was his dreams about Elise that disturbed his slumber.

He rarely found the need to use the crutches. His balance

had improved to the point he could ride a horse without risk of falling off.

Early the in the morning, of day fifteen since Elise had arrived home with her visitor, John sent a messenger to the inn to ask William to come to the castle at once. A couple of sheep had been slain and the recent rains had wiped out most of the tracks. He needed William's expertise in tracking down the predators that killed them.

On his way to Castle Brighton, William passed a familiar ornate carriage with a uniformed driver and footmen heading in the opposite direction. The Spaniard was leaving?

He couldn't see who was inside, only a couple of shadowy figures. Had Elise succumbed to the Spaniard's charm? Stefano Garcia Hernández Rodrigues Santiago, second cousin to the king of Spain, had vowed he would not return without her as his bride.

Suddenly his heart thudded in panic.

His anticipation of the hunt turned to a chore more tedious than fun as he warred with the sudden urgency to chase down the carriage.

A woman's laughter came from the meadow to his right. Could it be? He turned his mount to investigate.

There was Elise, wearing a simple linen shift sitting cross-legged in the meadow. Hanna and a couple of the servants' children were racing around picking daisies in a child's game filled with giggles and protests when one captured another's prized flower.

Her hair was woven into two long braids, like she'd worn when she was not much older than Hanna. Elise sat in the middle of a large pile of picked flowers, where she wove chains of daisies to match the crown adorning her hair.

The relief felt as if a crushing wall of stone had been lifted off his chest. William drew in a deep breath and released it. He stopped his mount at the end of a grove of trees, so he could remain in the shadows out of sight of the group, not wanting to interrupt their carefree time.

It was enough to see Elise being her true self, not the grownup object of another man's affection.

Because of the report of a predator killing sheep, William scanned the perimeter and saw a castle guard patiently watching over the group from the shade of a large oak. He spotted William and gave a silent salute, which William returned. Confident that Elise and the children were safe and after another scan to confirm no movement that would indicate a predator in sight, he continued on to the castle. He met John, who waited for him outside the gate on his warhorse, Shadow.

"I didn't expect to see you looking so happy." John furrowed his brow as if confused. "I'm glad the expectation of a hunt has lightened your spirit...or is it that you saw the Spaniard's carriage leaving?"

"It passed me on the road." William rode beside John as he led the way to where the sheep had been slain.

"And you weren't worried..." John searched William's face. "You saw her in the meadow, didn't you?" He leaned back and gave a hearty laugh. "I was afraid my sister's ploy to make you jealous had gone to waste."

"What?" William pulled back the reins and stopped. "Elise used that man to test me?" He hated the thought of how well it had worked. He was not about to admit that when he saw the carriage and thought Elise was inside, he'd been tempted to stop it, slay the Spaniard, kidnap Elise, and take her to the priest to marry them, thereby dismissing all of the reasons that would have made that decision a bad idea. He simply couldn't bear the thought of never seeing her again.

"I suspect so." John laughed and pressed his stallion into a canter, leaving William to try and rub the expression of stupidity off his face.

William pressed his mount to catch up. They found the spot

where the carcasses remained by the carrions, which circled above. William dismounted and paced the kill site until he identified the tracks. "Two wolves by the signs. An adult and a young one, possibly a mother teaching her pup to hunt."

William hated to kill any animal. Wolves did their part to eliminate the weak and sick forest animals, allowing the stronger, healthy ones to prevail. Unfortunately, these wolves had found the sheep unattended making for an easy meal. They would not be satisfied with one kill and would surely return. By nature, they rarely hunted alone. The next time, a larger pack would come, and they could decimate an entire flock in one night.

He helped John bury the remains of the dead animals, and then they moved the rest of the flock to a closer pasture, where the stockmen could watch over them.

"Isn't Delbert the new gamekeeper? Why didn't he protect the flock or deal with the kill?" William thought the man too often slack in his duties. He should have gone or sent stockman to keep a closer eye on the sheep in that more distant field, which was close to the forest the wolves preferred for cover.

"Stefano Garcia Hernández Rodrigues Santiago, second cousin to the king of Spain, may have had to return home without a bride, but he did not go home empty handed. He filled Delbert with promises of fame and fortune if he would come and be his uncle's gamekeeper." John chuckled. "It was actually an answer to my father's prayers. He hated to dismiss the man, since his father had been such a faithful and expert herdsman and had saved my father's life on two occasions. But Delbert was lazy and lacked the instincts or passion for the job. He's caused more harm than good during the short time he was in charge after his father's death." John turned to William. "Which brings me to another reason I wanted to see you."

William frowned at the serious tone.

"My father would like you to come to the castle tomorrow

their growls were menacing, as saliva and blood, from the kill, dripped from their mouths. These beasts were much larger in length and height compared to local wolves; the men's stirrups were level with the animal's backs.

The pack circled them, as a pack used to working together. One darted forward and nipped at one huntsman's horse sending it into panic, which made the rider focus on staying mounted instead of aiming his lance at the beast. If the horse or rider fell, the pack would pounce on the victim with deadly intent.

William hadn't felt such intensity in battle since the time it cost him his leg. It took an hour before the last wolf was slain, leaving both men and horses exhausted. Hopefully, there would be no further encounters with wolves the size of those. The men skinned then buried the carcasses not wanting to draw more predators to the area. There were enough hides for each man to take one home as proof of their encounter. William claimed the largest hide to preserve and show Lord Stanton when he returned.

William brought up the rear of the group, as they traveled back to the castle. He listened to the huntsmen as they embellished the tale of their battle with the giant wolves. Every man gave a different account, each version more terrifying than the last. The youngest huntsman, still in his teens, gave his version, which was the most elaborate tale of them all.

"Me great-grandda told us stories of huge beasts they called werewolves that roamed all of England and Scotland 'afore 'is time. They were vicious man-eaters, near the size of horses, and ran in packs of at least thirty." The young hunter's voice grew solemn. "I thought they were just tales to scare wee children but these beasts are just as he described."

The guffaws from the other huntsmen didn't hinder his story as he elaborated in great graphic detail of the *mammoth* beasts coming at them from every direction.

When questioned about bringing home a lot fewer than thirty pelts, he merely shrugged. "It seemed like more of 'em when we were in the fight."

William joined their laughter at the young huntsman's determination to stand by his view of what happened. Each man's version would grow over time into a fantastic tale to assure their children and grandchildren would marvel at their ancestor's bravery. William chuckled knowing if he were ever blessed with children of his own, he too would retell this adventure over and over again, perhaps not describing the beasts as werewolves large as horses, but he could spin a good tale when given the opportunity. He could hardly wait to see the expression on Elise's face when he told her of the hunt, but when he returned to the castle, Elise and her family were gone.

The night was clear and warm, so sleeping outdoors was becoming a far more appealing option than the stuffy rooms inside the inn. Elise thought the drivers would have the better arrangement than the family this night.

The family claimed the two large benches between the inn and the barn, where they took refuge to wait until the night grew cooler and quieter, before going back to their rooms.

The drivers settled in for the night. She could hear them talking about taking shifts so each would have time to sleep and guard.

"Oh, look." Hanna stood and pointed to the sky. Elise looked up and sucked in a breath of awe.

"It's a meteorite shower, Hanna." Elise's voice was a hoarse whisper. Like flaming arrows arching through the sky reminded her of the explosion in the blacksmith's shop. Blood rushed to her head, and she swayed. She was glad she was sitting down. The dizziness passed quickly. Thankfully, everyone's eyes were on the sky and not on her.

Once her heartbeat slowed, she was able to enjoy to spectacle. She wished she had her writing materials and could capture the scene on paper, though there would never be a way to translate the true power of the moment.

The drivers came around to investigate and stood in silence as they, too, watched the fiery scene above them.

As the meteor shower streaked across the night sky, their fiery gases burned through the atmosphere like the finger of God marking their passage.

"Is it safe to be out here, m'lady?" Theodore rubbed his arms then crossed himself as if to ward off evil. He had worked for her father for as long as Elise could remember. He was a wise old man who never seemed to age beyond the gray hair and beard that had become his signature of authority as head driver.

"Aye, Theodore." Elise was glad to be able to share something she'd learned while at school. "There's no danger, for their trajectory appears to be far from here. There is nothing evil about them. They are simply stones that are drawn down from the sky to a larger body, which is our earth. Some think our world has a magnetic center which is strong enough to hold us all upon it, and the power of it pulls the stones here." Elise glanced at her family as they gazed transfixed above. "I studied meteors with Professor Lord Isaac Canterbury, who knows quite a bit about them." She rubbed the kink in her neck from staring at the sky. "He says the meteorites like those are much smaller pieces that break off of larger stones in the heavenlies. The smaller pieces mostly burn up as they fall to earth. But the professor believes that the few that survive and can be studied hold the potential for great scientific advancements."

The drivers watched for a few minutes before returning to their tasks.

Elise grew excited as she watched at least three of the larger meteorites continue to earth. They didn't appear to burn up as the others had. If she had a sexton, she might have been able to track their trajectory. She hoped the professor had been able to witness the fiery display, though she had no desire to stop at the school to inform him. Perhaps once she arrived at Sarah's, she could write him a letter and tell him of the event.

A half-hour later, the meteorite shower was over. The evening had cooled and the inn had quieted, so the family went inside to retire. Father stopped to speak with the innkeeper before following his family to their rooms.

When he joined them in their cramped and stuffy room, he said, "According to our host, we'll make better progress tomorrow, for the roads have been recently improved and are better maintained the closer we travel to London." Her father escorted Elise to her adjoining room, and waited until she locked her door before heading toward his and her mother's room.

After the incident with the potential robbers, Hanna was still too frightened to stay alone even with Elise, so her parents had a cot set up in their room for her. Elise had a room to herself, a luxury she planned to enjoy, except the day's adventure had exhausted her. She fell asleep soon after she laid her head on the pillow she'd brought in from the carriage.

CHAPTER 13

William didn't usually ride far from the castle so early in the day. There was much to be attended to for his job. As head gamekeeper watching over the two thousand acres surrounding the castle, it didn't leave him much time to ride for pleasure.

John had gone to follow his calling as a monk, leaving Shadow in William's charge, and the big stallion needed regular exercise. William had helped raise and train the warhorse and was the only one, besides John who could ride him, which left the responsibility squarely on his shoulders. Not that riding the magnificent animal was a chore. He loved every minute of it.

It had been two weeks since Elise and her family had gone. William purposed to keep busy, but every time he passed by Elise's empty workshop, he felt a deep sense of loss.

The early morning air was crisp, and the stallion was impatient to stretch its legs, so William gave him his head. If only William could outrun his regrets and shake off his past with the ease the stallion shook off his captivity.

It wasn't long before they reached the outer boundary of the two thousand acres. A lone horse stood in the middle of a meadow.

William drew his sword, for traps were often set to lure the curious within striking distance and murder them for whatever possessions they had. The perimeter appeared clear. No movement that he could see, and Shadow remained calm, something he would not be if he sensed danger.

Edging closer, William found a man face down on the ground, still gripping the horse's reins. A good thing, for if it had not been for the horse, William would never have seen the man lying in the tall grass.

He rolled him over, unsure if he was dead or alive or simply lying in wait for a victim to rob. The man had a great deal of dried blood on his torn pant leg. Had he received the wound in an accident or in battle?

"They're gonna be killed!" The man's eyes opened wide with fear as his boney fingers clutched William's tunic. "All of 'em." He struggled to get the words out between gasps for air.

"Who's going to be killed?" William pried the fingers lose one at a time. The man looked familiar. The jagged scars across his arms and face were the evidence of a hard life. After a moment of study, he thought he recognized him. "Angus?"

The man's gaunt features were almost hidden by the gray in his long hair and scraggly beard. Yet the droopy eye…

"I must…" He blinked, then his countenance lit with a momentary flicker of recognition. "Warn them." His eyes rolled back, and he went limp.

William shook him, but there was no response. By his pale, clammy skin, Angus needed help if he was to live long enough to explain who was going to be killed and why.

He pulled the man up and prepared to put him on his horse, but the horse sidestepped away, so he settled Angus onto his shoulder. The extra weight made William's peg leg sink into the soft ground. The horse sidestepped again.

"By the saints." He hated the feeling of helplessness. He was strong enough to easily handle the man's body, but the loss of his leg had changed everything when carrying a heavy load on soft ground. He shifted Angus to his left shoulder and pulled the peg free only to sink again. The imbalance threatened to throw them both to the ground.

"Lord, I could use your help." With renewed effort, he again pulled free. He took a firm hold on the horse's reins. Finding firmer ground, he managed to deposit Angus on the man's horse. "Thank you, Lord." He swiped the sweat off his brow. "Now, please keep this poor man alive long enough to deliver his message."

He remounted Shadow and led Angus's horse toward the abbey, which was the closest place to find help. The priest was a former soldier who knew a great deal about healing, both spiritual and physical.

The pace was frustratingly slow but necessary to keep Angus in the saddle. He turned to check on him, since he hadn't moved since they'd started out.

When William approached the abbey, he saw Father Alvin outside, tending his small garden and worshipping in song so loudly he hadn't heard their approach. The priest switched to an off-key homily in Latin, also at the top of his lungs, as if the volume helped it to reach the heavens.

"Father Alvin." William rode up to the garden gate. "Father!" Even his shout was not heard above the good father's recitation. William knew better than to get close enough to touch the trained fighter while he was so distracted.

He drew his short sword and touched the priest with the tip of the steel blade to get his attention. Startled, the priest swung his hoe and stuck William's sword down faster than he could withdraw it. The priest's fierce expression was that of the war-worn soldier he'd once been before he'd heeded the call of the priesthood.

"William. You could get seriously injured sneaking up on a body like that." The priest smiled and settled the hoe against the short fence that kept out the rabbits.

"I couldn't get your attention with all that caterwauling. I apologize for interrupting your...a...gardening, but I have an injured man that needs tending." William dismounted and walked around to the other horse where the priest met him.

"Who do you have with you?" Father Alvin pulled the man off the horse and slung him over his shoulder. "Let's take him into the abbey and see what ails him besides that nasty leg wound."

William walked beside the priest. "I found him unconscious. He came to in a panic claiming someone was going to be killed, but passed out again before he could tell me who." He held the door open so the priest could enter with his burden and followed him to a spare room, where he laid the injured man on a cot.

"Do you know this person?" The priest had been in Brighton for six months but was still trying to get to know everyone in the village.

"Aye, Father. He grew up around here but left about five years ago. His name is Angus." William helped the priest take off Angus's filthy clothes to check for other injuries. He had many scars on his torso in addition to the ones visible on his arms and face.

"Fetch me some water. The bucket is by the entrance." Father Alvin put a hand on Angus' forehead.

William carried the bucket into the room and sat it near the priest. "You might know his family, Father. His mother is Anna Greene. The family lives down by the glade where they raise goats and sheep."

"I do know the family. Good parishioners. So, this is the son she prays for at every mass." Father Alvin washed the blood and dirt off Angus's arms. "Did you see this?"

William leaned closer and saw a black bird tattooed on the underside of Angus's forearm above the wrist. "It's nothing I've seen before. Have you?"

"There's a secret order of assassins that uses that symbol. I've heard a few of their confessions before I was assigned here. That image is used to identify them. They expose the tattoo in battle to insure they don't fight against each other."

Before William could question the priest on how a farmer became an assassin, Angus stirred. He opened his eyes and blinked as if unable to focus. The priest propped him up to give him a sip of water, which he grabbed and drank down without taking a breath.

"More." Angus's hoarse whisper earned him another drink. "Please, Father, hear my confession." The words were weak and rushed as if he feared he would die before getting right with God.

The earnest request to repent sent William outside to give them privacy and to check on the horses, making sure each of the animals had access to water.

A half-hour later, the priest poked his head out of the abbey door and motioned to William. "Come. You need to hear this."

William hurried inside.

"He wants to see you." Father Alvin led the way to Angus's cot. "Here's William." The priest sat beside the injured man. "Angus, William brought you here and most likely saved your life."

"I'm grateful, but you must listen." Angus's words were raspy and low, making it necessary for William to lean in to hear them. "Lord and Lady Stanton." He closed his eyes and drew a ragged breath. "They and their children are on a list of the Black Guard's death squad." His eyes widened with panic. He reached up and clutched William's tunic. "You have to warn them. They must flee or they'll surely die."

Angus dropped his hand and sunk down onto the cot. His

breath came in shallow gasps. "Lady Stanton saved my life as a child." His voice grew weaker. "I have a debt to return the deed." His hand shook as he again reached out to William, but his arm fell to his side. "The Black Guard will stop at nothing—" he sucked in a ragged breath "—to track down and..." He blinked, making a concentrated effort to remain awake. "...murder each person on that list."

"But why?" William demanded.

But Angus' energy was drained. He tried to reply, but no words came out.

"I'll warn them." William could at least give him that promise.

Angus let out a sigh, closed his eyes, and his features relaxed.

"The draught I gave him will help ease his pain and let him sleep." Father Alvin rose and led the way outside. "He has lost a lot of blood. It's a miracle he made it this far. He thinks it's been at least two days since he received his injury while trying to subdue some noble women he was assigned to track down. He's been running for his life from another assassin who killed the two men he was with. I'll do my best to help him, but with so much loss of blood, he's in God's hands." He patted William's shoulder. "He risked his life to bring this warning. I would take it most seriously."

"Do you think the Black Guard's death squad will track his lordship and the family to London and beyond?" William's heart raced at the thought of them traveling into harm's way.

The priest's expression turned fierce. "I believe once those with traitorous intent and bloodlust are loosed in our land, no one on their list is safe." He rubbed a hand across his face. "I'll not violate his or any other's confessions, but I can tell you the Black Guard are ruthless killers set on taking over the realm. They plan to murder the king and any who can legally claim the throne. A hefty bounty has been set on each life of noble blood that is taken for their cause." The priest's expression grew grim.

"There is no time to waste. Their murderous plot has been set in motion as we speak."

William had to warn Elise and her family. John was on the road somewhere between here and London. Hopefully, he could track him down before he got too far away. Together, they would protect John's family. He must make haste. Preparations had to be made to defend the castle and the village. The ruthless assassins would be coming to Brighton soon. Simply telling the assassins the nobles were away would not satisfy them. They would destroy all that stood in their way.

"Father, I will leave it to you to warn the village and those remaining at the castle. They will heed your advice on what precautions to take against the assassins. I must leave immediately to warn Lord John and his family of what to expect."

"Aye. I'll have someone fetch Anna to come and sit with her son while I warn the village elders. I will let those at the castle know that you will not return until you've warned his lordship." He patted William on the shoulder. "I pray for God's hand to be upon you to accomplish what must be done."

"Thank you, Father." William felt the urgency of his quest settle across his shoulders. "I know John will be traveling on foot, for he told me so when he asked that I take charge of Shadow, but he's been gone almost two weeks." William filled his water flask, as he spoke. Knowing he would need to ride hard and fast, he did a quick check of the horse and saddle, then mounted the waiting stallion.

"You should know John will look quite different since last you saw him." The priest had William's attention. "Traveling as Brother John, he donned a monk's habit, shaved his face, and cut his hair. Oh, and he will be leading a donkey."

"What?" William found this information beyond his imagination.

"It is a long story he will have to tell you when you find him. Knowing that particular donkey, it is likely John may not have gotten as far away as he had hoped by now." Father Alvin smiled. "God be with you and keep you safe, my son." The priest made the sign of the cross in the air and turned away.

William gave the stallion his head, and it raced down the road. The warhorse could carry him as fast and far as he needed to go. He chose to follow the old road, guessing John had chosen to take it because it was less traveled and therefore less likely he would come across anyone he knew. Perhaps his friend would head over to the abbey of the Sisters of the Holy Heart to rest for a night or two.

The sun was high, but the road was shadowed by the overgrown trees and brush. It was barren of travelers, as William had suspected, so he made good time. With no sign of John, he merged onto the main road and saw a farmer with a cart.

"Good sir, have you seen a monk leading a donkey on this road in the last week or so?" When he thought of John leading a donkey the question sounded daft.

"Aye." The farmer glanced from William to his peg positioned in the special sling, Elise had designed for him. "Soldier were ye?"

"Aye." William held back the frustration for the delay.

"I recollect seeing a monk leading a donkey maybe two or three days back." He tugged on his beard. "But he weren't alone. There was a woman riding the animal and another high-born lassie in fancy dress walking beside it." He pointed to a narrow trail. "They went that way."

"Thank you." William nodded to the man and turned Shadow in that direction. He'd been right. This trail led to the abbey.

John had a donkey and female companions on his *solitary* journey? William found the thought amusing. John told him he sought to become a monk to live a simple life, while serving the Lord. Now he was escorting two women, and one was high-born and pretty. William couldn't wait to hear what his friend had to say about it all.

~

*W*illiam arrived at the abbey midafternoon, yet there was no one tending the garden, and no sounds of children playing.

He drew his short sword. What if the assassins had found John?

The stallion pranced beneath him picking up on his tension as he rode to the entrance. He reached for the bell cord, which would get the attention of those inside the closed gates. Before he could pull it, a figure swung out of the tree knocking William out of the saddle. As he reached for his fallen sword and struggled to get to his feet, a boy swung a branch and struck William in the side. The pain stole his breath.

Shadow pawed the ground, snorting and throwing his head.

The boy stumbled away from William and the horse.

The animal stood near William, ready to attack the skinny youth if he stepped near them. An effective surprise attack, but by fear in his eyes, the youth was obviously not a skilled assassin.

William raised his hand to signal the horse to hold its position. William couldn't get his breath, but he waved his short sword in warning not wanting to inflict pain on the scared boy.

As he got to his feet, the abbey's gate opened, and Sister Agnes hurried out with a hoe in her hand and several other nuns carrying various garden tools like weapons.

"William, is that you?" The nun stepped between the youth and his victim.

He nodded and held his injured side. "Could you call off your watchdog before the stallion attacks him?"

"Alfred, you did a fine job protecting us, but please put down your club. This is a friend." Sister Agnes reached out to William. "Did he hurt you badly?"

"He dinna look like no friend with that sword he's carrying." Alfred stepped back a few more steps but held onto his weapon. The branch he had used had spikes poking out all around. It looked as if it had been fashioned by trimming the smaller branches into sharp points and hardening them in a fire. William had seen that type of weapon before. Villagers often kept them for protection.

"Oh, William you're bleeding." Sister Agnes waved to the boy. "Open the bigger gate so we can bring him and his horse inside."

Alfred gave the horse and William a wide berth and hurried to get the gate open enough to admit them. As soon as they were inside, the boy closed it again and set the bolt in the lock.

"You swing a mean club, lad." William gave the youth a weak smile as the shock of the attack passed. The pain throbbed against his side, and each cut stung like fire.

"I made it myself." The boy smiled with pride and held the branch higher until the horse snorted and put back his ears. Alfred quickly dropped the weapon next to the gate. "After hardening the spikes in a fire, I painted them with wet ash to leave a sting."

"That it does." William led the horse to the water trough and tied him there. "Don't go near the horse. He's a warhorse and he won't forget those who attack him or his rider."

"Aye." Alfred kept a safe distance from the stallion as he headed to the stable.

"Have you seen Lord John, Sister Agnes?" William followed the nun into the abbey.

"He was here, but left a day ago." The nun waved William to a chair in the dining room. He heard the sound of children saying their ABC's somewhere in the distance.

"I have to find him. It is of utmost importance." William

couldn't help the blush as he pulled up his tunic for the nun to check his wounds. He winced as she cleaned them with water and dabbed witch hazel on each cut.

"He had two women with him." Sister Agnes said. "They warned us of assassins sent to keep them from getting to London to deliver an urgent message for the king." She glanced up at William. "We had just such an assassin show up yesterday afternoon. He disappeared when he found resistance. Unfortunately, one of our young charges, Thomas, also fled. I fear the child caught up with him and bartered information about John and the women to gain his promise to take him with him." She resumed her doctoring, pulling a splinter from one of the wounds, causing William to bite his tongue to keep from swearing. "Alfred has taken his job as lookout and protector very seriously since then." She wrapped a bandage tightly around his middle and tied it off. "There is bruising, and you will certainly feel worse by nightfall. The bandage should be changed tomorrow."

William stood and lowered his tunic over the bandages.

Sister Agnes frowned. "You should stay and rest for a couple of days." She smiled. "But you won't will you?"

"There is no time to rest. I need to find John." He winced at the stiffness of his wounds. "Did he or the women mention anything about the Black Guard's death squad list?" He straightened and felt the bandage shift.

"Nothing was mentioned about a death squad." Her voice rose with fear. "Are John and his family on that list?"

"Aye, Sister. They must be warned."

"The women traveling with John are now disguised as nuns and riding in a cart drawn by a rather cantankerous donkey, so they can't have gotten far. I think they were heading to Scarborough to seek passage on a boat." Sister Agnes crossed herself. "God willing, you'll find them before that assassin. The man's name is Thoreau."

"Thank you for your help. I need to leave immediately." William allowed the nun to lead the way outside.

"If you can wait, I'll gather some food for your journey." She stood by as he led the horse to the gate.

"You sent them with food?"

"Of course."

"Then I'll eat when I find them."

"But you can't be sure you'll locate them quickly." She handed him a couple of apples she picked from a bowl on her way out. "Here, at least take these." She held the gate open, and he led the stallion outside the abbey.

"Thanks." William tucked the apples inside his tunic then mounted the horse, waved, and took off at a gallop. John would take the quickest way to the coast. Leading a donkey and cart would be slow going, but that would help William reach him before he sailed for London. If the assassins were after John's passengers, then there might be more of them waiting at all ports. Hopefully, the women's disguises would help keep them all safe.

"Shadow, we need to find your master." William patted the horse's neck. "Find John." It had been a fun pastime when they were training Shadow as a colt. The stallion enjoyed the activity and became very good at finding John, no matter how well his master tried to hide. It had been years since they'd played that game, but maybe the stallion would remember.

William stopped twice to refill his water and let the horse drink its fill. The stallion seemed as restless as William to be on its way, but he kept the horse's pace slow enough to reserve its energy. Could Shadow find John's scent?

William's leg and the wound in his side ached with the constant riding. The weariness grew, but he couldn't stop while there was still daylight. Another hour, and they would stop for the night. His head nodded as sleep pulled on him. If he could rest for a short time...

Shadow's pace was a steady walk just right for a quick nap. The horse would stay on the road unless challenged. William had perfected being able to doze and remain in the saddle while in the army. Short snatches of sleep allowed him to fight with more vigor when called upon.

William was jolted out of sleep by the stallion's jerk on the reins. To his surprise, it was pitch dark and thunder rumbled all around them. It would rain soon; he could smell it in the air. Or was this a dream, too? His side ached as if he'd been stabbed multiple times. He felt hot then cold. He couldn't keep his eyes open. How far had they come? Had they missed John?

Lightning lit the sky.

He couldn't think. "Find John, Shadow." William slumped against the front of the saddle and clutched the reins to keep them from falling to the ground.

CHAPTER 14

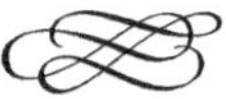

lise pulled the hood of her cloak over her head and leaned away from the window. London was a busy place, but her father was well known here. The coat of arms on the doors of their carriage would do as much to announce their presence as a town crier.

"Aren't you hot in that, Elise?" Hanna tugged on the wool cloak. "Are you hiding from someone?" Her little sister was growing up and becoming entirely too outspoken when it came to Elise's business.

"I'm fine. How about you?" Elise couldn't resist turning her sister's curiosity to other matters. "Are you sorry we couldn't stay at the Hardisty's estate longer so you could visit with your friend, Samuel?" She knew the boy had teased Hanna during their visit. Father had insisted they stop there, for he had business with Lord Hardisty.

Her mother was impatient to go to Sarah's but because the family was longtime friends of their parents, she'd agreed.

"He's a bully who has no respect for other's belongings." Hanna frowned. "He spoiled my best watercolor picture. I had worked on it for hours." She fisted her hands. "I hope I never see that boy-child again."

"Boy-child?" Mother's eyes lit with amusement as she focused on Hanna. "Where did you hear that phrase?"

"His nanny calls him that all of the time." Hanna smiled. "He hates it."

"I'm sorry he ruined your picture, but I think it was his way of getting your attention, for you had ignored him the whole visit." Mother touched Elise's cloak. "Is there more to the story of your time at the school that you'd like to share?"

"No." Elise tugged on the hood to better shade her face. "I simply prefer not to be recognized." Elise turned her attention to the people lining the streets. "We should have waited until tomorrow to come through the city. Market day is always very busy."

"I fear the crowds are there gathering what they can in case the rumors of war are true. I hope John is safe." Mother glanced out the window as if searching for the truth in the faces of those they passed. She relaxed against the seat and glanced at Elise. "According to Lord Hardisty, there have been multiple assassination attempts recently against King John, putting both nobles and the church on alert. Lord Hardisty's nephew is a captain in the royal guard and he warned his uncle to hire more men for protection in case of trouble."

"Do you believe there will be war, mother?" Elise hoped her brother would avoid London and because of their delay at the Hardisty's, he could have reached Sarah's before them.

"Lady Evelyn believes it will be worse than her husband lets on. She's listened to the gossip from the wives of the nobles who have high positions in the king's court. The whole time we were there she was preparing for her family to take an extended trip to Spain. They are leaving tomorrow, including her husband." Mother stopped when Hanna gathered her little practice sword and hugged it to her chest, her eyes wide with fear.

"Everything is going to be fine, Sunshine. Try not to worry." Elise hugged her little sister, and Hanna clung to her.

"Hanna, God will protect us and John." Mother touched Father's leg. "God also gives us wisdom, and I think it prudent to get to Sarah's as soon as possible."

"What?" The sleepy edge to his voice confirmed he had been dozing.

"I was saying I would like to arrive at Sarah's by tonight if possible. What do you think?"

"Since we've been traveling all day, I think it best if we find lodging along the way and start fresh in the morning. I'm sure the horses and drivers could use a rest by now." He yawned and stretched. "I know I could use a good night's sleep."

The three females in the carriage laughed.

"What's so funny?" He looked puzzled.

"My wonderful husband, you have been sleeping for many miles." Mother patted him on the shoulder.

"Nay. I've only been resting my eyes." His denial set off more laughter.

"Well, I pray that the rest of us are able to rest so peacefully, and the rumors and dire predictions fail to come to pass." Elise glanced from one parent to the other.

"Amen." Her parents spoke in unison. Father hugged mother, and she snuggled into his embrace.

Elise wanted that kind of relationship with a husband. Considered an old maid by twenty, and with William's stubborn determination to ignore his feelings toward her, it might not happen at all. The thought of never marrying caused a deep sorrow to settle within her. She sighed and glanced out of the window. The hood of her cloak slipped back, and she quickly tugged it back in place to hide in its shadow from the gawking passersby.

Hoping to avoid more crowds, they traveled through the

outer edges of London and further on until they were miles away by evening.

The place they found to rest was a large country estate turned into an inn. The sign over the gate read, *Hathford Farms,* and below that a smaller sign, *Hathford Inn and Stables.* Its well-maintained appearance suggested the weary travelers would find comfort and safety here.

The large home looked to have plenty of room for the drivers as well as Elise and her family. The barn was almost as spectacular as the manor.

Elise yearned to explore the beautiful estate, especially the old shed, with the large padlock on the door. She'd notice it when they drove past on their way to the manor house. What mysteries did such a building hold that made it necessary to be secured? It would not be proper for her to inquire of its contents, but if she were to take a walk, she might be able to see inside a window, just to satisfy her curiosity.

After the drivers stopped, she and her family walked up the steps to the entrance where they were met by a man in simple clothes who motioned the family inside.

"Welcome folks. Mistress Hathford will help you get settled. She'll meet you at the counter." He smiled. "I'll show your drivers where to park the carriage and wagon then help them tend to your horses."

"Thank you." Her father said. He put a hand on Hanna who abruptly stopped, fascinated by a large yellow tabby that wandered across in front of them. "Hanna, come along." He ushered the girl inside.

Elise followed her father to a large, high-ceilinged foyer where a counter dominated one end. An elderly woman wearing a simple green dress covered by a white apron greeted them with a smile of welcome. She answered her parents' questions about accommodations and assured them there was plenty of room for their family and drivers.

While her parents conversed with the woman, Elise tried to come up with a reason to explore the mysterious shed. She already knew her mother's answer—no. Elise was to remain presentable. Her clothing would be expected to remain clean and unsoiled. It was the same answer she gave whenever they stopped along the way. There would be no digging into odd places, in hopes of finding something exciting Elise could use to stir her imagination for her next project.

Maybe if she worded it just right, a walk to stretch her legs might find her near the object of her attention…

"Lady Elise." A male voice called her name and made her heart thump with fear. Her father nudged her and nodded behind them.

Elise turned and released the breath she held. "Jeremy, what are you doing here?" She turned to her father. "This is one of my fellow students from the School of Scientifica." Her voice lowered so only Jeremy and her father heard. "He was one of the nicer and smarter students I met there."

Jeremy's laugh was something she liked best about the young man, who was always polite to her and treated her with respect while listening to her ideas. They'd often worked together on projects, winning top honors, to the anger and dismay of the more competitive pursuers of science. Those students who were there for power, praise, and fast money never understood that the joy of science meant finding the truth, then sharing it freely with those whose lives could be made the better for it.

That Jeremy was a commoner and only fourteen when he first attended the school, which made him the receiver of more than his share of bullying. The sons of noblemen, who were older and better funded, thought their titles and privileged lives made them superior to commoners—and any woman, titled or not.

Elise had taken him under her wing like a little brother and made it her mission to treat him with the respect that any serious scientist deserves, for he had a quick mind and the same passion to learn as did she. He had grown in stature and had developed a more muscular physic since she had last seen him.

"This is my grandfather's estate. My father helped him turn it into an inn when…" Jeremy met his grandmother's gaze, and she frowned. He shrugged. "The details are unimportant." He glanced at her father and smiled. "Your daughter is brilliant, sir. With her innovative ideas and research, she helped me design and complete several projects at school." He turned to Elise. "I have been using some of our data on genetics to improve our flock. I've crossbred different breeds of sheep by focusing on their strongest attributes. Our genetically improved flock now produces thirty times more wool than before."

"Our Jeremy has done wonders." His grandmother smiled fondly at the young man and Elise could see the pride she had for her grandson.

"Our wool is superior to any around and greatly in demand." He glanced at his grandmother who was handing out the room keys. He leaned closer to Elise and lowered his voice. "I think she wants to continue the inn even after the farm returns to its former glory. She likes the company."

"It was nice to meet you, Jeremy." Her father shook his hand. "I think I need to intervene, lest my men bring in any more luggage. We're only staying the night." He frowned as her mother directed the men and bags toward the stairs.

"Would it be acceptable if I take Lady Elise to my workshop and show her my research?" Jeremy's tone was respectful but his expression held the same eager anticipation as Elise.

Her father glanced from the boy to Elise. "Make sure she's back in time for the evening meal…an hour at most. Agreed?" She could barely hold back a yip of excitement.

Jeremy and Elise nodded, and he grabbed her hand and led her out the side entrance.

She waited to withdraw her hand once they were outside so as not to embarrass him in front of his grandmother.

His eyes widened with the realization of what he'd done. Handholding was strictly reserved for family or properly betrothed couples.

She was glad her father was distracted or he might have withdrawn his permission or insist on coming along as chaperone. Her and Jeremy's relationship at school was less formal because of the necessity of working so closely together on projects, but there was always a teacher or professor around to maintain the air of propriety.

"I'm truly sorry, Lady Elise. I was so excited to see you that I forgot my place."

She nodded her acceptance and motioned him on. He led the way to the small building she had noticed on the way to the manor. After taking a large steel key from his pocket, he unlocked the padlock and pushed open the door. She could hardly wait to see what was inside.

"Oh, Jeremy, you've been busy." Elise went from one area of beakers and test tubes to another. The workbench was covered in drawings and formulas. A large board covered one wall that also had drawings and pictures of a parasite in different states of development. His notes identified this particular parasite as one that hindered the health of an entire flock. "These drawings are exquisite works of art." She leaned closer and saw the minute detail captured.

"I knew you would appreciate them." He touched the last drawing on the right. "You were my inspiration."

"Ha!" Elise's laughter startled him until he realized what he'd pointed to, and he laughed.

"Not because you remind me of the parasite. Your determination to find a solution to a problem and follow your scientific instincts kept me working when it seemed all of my efforts were for naught." He frowned. "I'm sorry you left school."

Elise recognized the pain in his expression as similar to the one she saw in the mirror whenever she thought of her last day in London.

"I'm sorry for all of the trouble I caused the school," she said. "I don't know what you heard of the matter, but an unwanted suitor showed up with nefarious intentions, and when I wouldn't consent to his demands, he destroyed the blacksmith shop then blamed it on me and the school. I feel awful that his lies led to the students and professors being arrested."

"Actually, that part was rather exciting. I felt very important to have people run when they saw me." A slight chuckle escaped. "It was afterward that I found overwhelming. Those who had made it difficult for you and I to work in peace continued their torments. In fact, it became even more difficult for me to do my experiments after you'd gone. They called you bad names, and I received more than one black eye because of my objections."

"Oh, Jeremy, I'm so sorry, you found it necessary to defend me." Tears gathered in Elise's eyes". "If I had only waited on the guard…"

"All was not lost. Because of their confrontations, I became quite skilled with my fists. Eventually, I was able to gift the worst of the tormentors with a busted lip and black eye, which kept the rest of them at bay."

"You took on Chester Field?" Elise's eyes widened. Also, a student, he was big, mean-spirited, and jealous of Jeremy's intelligence. He played cruel pranks on Elise and Jeremy by spoiling their experiments and stealing their work and claiming it as his until he was caught by Professor Dexter, the dean of the school. But for Chester's father's influence, he would have been arrested, or at the very least expelled.

"Aye." His grin was contagious. "One day I'd had enough and asked around until I found a former knight who was recommended to me as a good instructor. He allowed me to trade my knowledge and abilities with the forge for his many years' experience in the service of the king. He taught me how to find the opponent's weakness, which is almost as important as the physical act of self-defense and the use of weaponry. In exchange, I designed for him a one-of-a-kind sword that was weighted and balanced just for him. He had lost three fingers in battle and needed something he could wield with only his thumb and little finger." Jeremy opened a closet door. Inside were several types of swords, bows, and maces. And hung on the inside of the door was a drawing of her. "I did that one of you by memory." He moved a few sheets of paper on his desk, which revealed another drawing of her smiling and another of her with an intent expression as she bent over an experiment. "I did those while you were still at school."

"You are a very good artist and flatter me with your renditions." She turned to draw attention away from her and back to his weapons. "Did you design and make each of these?"

"I did. While I heated the metal and pounded each blade into shape, I thought of how many ways I could pay Chester Field and his friends back for the harm they'd done to so many. I thought after I bested him in combat, he would leave the school or stop his tormenting but he seemed more intent to cause trouble. Several students, including myself, finally had enough and dropped out of school." His expression of anger smoothed until a smile replaced the frown. "Because of the trouble, I drew closer to the Lord. After much prayer, I was finally able to forgive them. It was not an easy decision, I must admit." He waved a hand over the room. "I've found my place here, and my parents and grandparents are happy I'm home. I only wish..." He glanced shyly at her. "I've thought often of you. I'll be eighteen in two months, and one day all of this land and everything on it shall be mine." He blinked and drew a deep breath. "If you are not married, I would like to offer you my hand." He hurried on, not waiting for her response. "We could create all manner of beneficial things together." He waved a hand toward the closet.

"I'm getting better at making, as well as, wielding all manner of weapons, so I could protect you properly if the need should ever arise."

"Oh, Jeremy, how kind and generous you are." She hugged him and kissed his cheek. "I'm not married at this time, but I must decline. I am completely in love with another."

"Why has he not declared for you?" His innocent surprise mocked her declaration of love for a man who may never declare for her.

The fear of growing old and alone swirled and rose again from deep within her, like a premonition of the death of a dream.

"I will promise you this. If my William has not declared for me and made me his bride in one year's time, then I shall return here. If you are not married and your parents agree, then I shall gladly become your wife, and we shall invent all manner of wondrous things together. How's that?" She curtsied. The words had rushed out before she could stop them.

"I shall hold you to that promise, fair maiden. Until then, I shall make myself worthy of such a vow." He bowed then raised her hand and kissed it.

The door slammed open.

"What are you two doing? Conspiring to make more black magic to destroy your enemies?" A young man, a drunkard by his slurred speech, stench, and filthy condition, stumbled and fell hard against the doorframe, jarring the frame building. A glass beaker fell and crashed on the stone floor.

"Out with you, Markus Reed. You're drunk, again." Jeremy shoved the ruddy-faced lad back outside before he caused more destruction. Jeremy raised his hand as a gesture for Elise to stay where she was. "You know you are not allowed anywhere near this building. My father can fire your da for such disobedience. Where would your family live then? How would they survive?"

"I knowed her. Ain't she that witch who that lord posted a

reward for? I seen it in the pub." Markus scrubbed a dirty fist over his eyes and tried to focus on Elise. "I'll get that reward and runaway from this place." His face paled as the ill effects of whatever he had consumed fought back. He turned and staggered toward the four small houses off in the distance.

Jeremy turned toward Elise when she joined him. "I was concerned Markus might show up. I saw him looking our way, as we headed toward the workshop. He's a ne'er-do-well who has cost his poor hardworking parents many jobs because of his drunken lifestyle. He's their only child, which is the reason they keep taking him in after he's run off for being in one scrape or another." Jeremy shook his head as he watched the boy stumble, fall, get up and stumble again. "If he remembers seeing you when he comes to, he'll certainly follow through with trying to earn that reward."

"Don't let it vex you, Jeremy. I am well able to defend myself, and my father and mother are both experts with the sword. Besides, we shall be leaving here in the morning and be a long way off before he comes to his senses. Surely, he will forget me." She watched him frown. "But I shan't forget you."

"Or your promise to me?" Jeremy's gaze was steady as he met hers. He may not have been the vision of the brawny knight that she expected to wed, yet after her impulsive declaration, he fully expected to make her his bride in one year if she had not married.

The promise lodged in her chest, for the ill-advised commitment she'd made would hold up in a court of law if he chose to pursue it.

What had she done?

"Jeremy, you are handsome and smart." She raised her hand to stop him from interrupting. "You are not to wait for me if a young maiden takes your fancy. I'm considered by many to be too old to subject you to such a promise or commitment, and I'll be even older next year. I—"

"It is done. Your promise was made freely, and I've accepted it." He beamed as if he won a most wonderful prize.

"If that's what you truly want, then I will honor my pledge, but you must make me a promise."

His eyes narrowed with suspicion. "Tell me first before I agree."

"Let us keep this our secret until that time." Elise panicked at the thought of her parents finding out. Jeremy's parents and grandparents were wealthy landowners but held no title or noble blood, not that it would bother her, but her parents would find her declaration reckless without consulting them first, and they might challenge it before it was necessary. It was her prayer that William declared for her. His kiss and words of love were as good as a promise of marriage, whether he chose to admit it or not. She may have to insist he fulfill his promise, though she would rather he did so on his own.

"Why keep it a secret?" Jeremy watched her expression, and the intelligent man he was drew his own conclusions. "I understand. I, nor my parents, are of noble blood and that could present a problem for your parents. I hope to eliminate that obstacle by next year." He smiled as if he knew something she did not. "If my experiments are successful in finding a cure for that parasite, it will gain me fame and fortune. I fully expect the king to make me an earl at the very least for my accomplishments for the crown." He grinned and drew her into a hug. "Fear not, my fair maiden. All will work itself out in due time." He laughed at her surprised expression.

"Indeed." Elise joined his laughter.

He locked his shop, and they walked back to the manor. It would be hard to look upon Jeremy as anything more than a sweet younger brother. God's mercy, she would wed William and never have to adjust her thoughts of her friend as husband.

CHAPTER 15

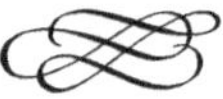

"Elise, you've been very quiet since we left the inn." Lady Evangeline touched Elise's knee, and she jumped. "Did young Jeremy say or do anything that you need to tell us about?

"He was a perfect gentleman, just as he was at school. You would like him if you had time to get to know him." She rubbed her face, knowing she should prepare her parents for the possibility of Richard, or someone looking to earn the reward he promised on the posters, showing up and making trouble. "There was an incident at the inn that may or may not be a problem in the future." She hated to spoil the last part of their journey to Sarah's, but Hanna was asleep and her father was awake, which made for the right opportunity to bring up the matter.

"There are a few details I left out in the telling of what happened before the explosion in the blacksmith shop at school." She withheld nothing in her description of the events after Richard followed her into the building.

Her father stiffened to attention. "He said he intended soil you in that filthy place so no other could wed you?" His fury was like a thunderstorm building until it could pour its wrath on any in its path. "I'll have him horsewhipped or better, I'll…"

"Henry, you'll wake Hanna." Mother put her hand on her father's arm. "Besides, don't you think stirring up your wrath is part of the reason Elise hesitated to tell us this in the first place?" Her gaze met Elise's. "As much as I agree with your father's instinct to punish the young man, you must tell us the rest. Your father will hold his peace until you're done, won't you, dear?"

"It's a father's duty to protect his daughters—" Another pat caused him to concede. "Fine."

By the time Elise was finished, her father's face had turned two shades of crimson. She had never seen him so angry, and she had certainly given him cause on several occasions whenever one of her experiments had gone awry. The last thing she wanted was to ruin their journey by stirring up the past.

"Please, I told you the whole of it only because I must tell you what happened at the inn." Elise had both of her parents' attention. "Jeremy showed me his ongoing experiments." She raised her hand before her father spoke. "As I said before, he was a perfect gentleman. He's a brilliant scientist and remains a true believer in Christ. While we were visiting, the son of one of their workers showed up in a drunken state. Jeremy pushed him outside, but before he left, the drunkard claimed he recognized a sketch of me on a poster he'd seen in the local pub and threatened to seek the reward promised on it for finding me. Surely Richard knew he could find me at Brighton whenever he had a mind. It seems he wants to know when I'm away from home and unprotected. What he plans to do with that information is beyond me, but I thought you should know in case he should make an appearance at Sarah's."

"Your father and I were acquainted with Richard Blackstone's parents before their deaths. We've only met his grandfather, Duke Blackstone a few times since then at an occasional social event. Richard comes from a good family. Such a shame he's grown into such a troubled young man." Her mother shook her head and frowned.

"He planned to marry me to appease his grandfather, and he expected you"—she nodded to her father—"to barter me off for whatever his grandfather thought I'd be worth to you to be rid of me. Richard fully expected you to accept the proposal and demand I wed him, since he would one day have the duke's wealth and title. Richard planned to use me and my good name as a pawn to stay in his grandfather's good graces until he died." Elise stiffened and her face flushed with anger. "I love you, but I would have runaway, if you'd chosen to accept Duke Blackstone's contract of marriage on behalf of Richard." She crossed her arms and seethed with the memory of his threats.

"I did get a glimpse of that contract from the usually frugal duke. It was very generous, considering your advanced age and all." Her father's chuckle broke the despair that hung over them. Elise hugged him.

"In spite of my *advanced age*, I still hope to wed a good man." Elise sat back. A flash of guilt flushed her skin. She had no plans to tell her parents of her arrangement with Jeremy until absolutely necessary. By her mother's surprised expression, Elise needed to turn her parents' attention away from her situation. "Sarah was years older than I when she finally married Trevor. He seems to adores her, but from her comments, it wasn't always so."

"By her admission, Sarah spent many sleepless nights after meeting Trevor." Lady Evangeline leaned back and relaxed, glad to relay a happier turn of events. "With him being the only male heir, his family was pressuring him to marry before he left to study archaeology in Egypt and Israel. He was gone for years and his family feared he would never marry or return to England." Her mother frowned. "Trevor was forced to return home by a mysterious illness that almost took his life."

Elise had read the letters from Sarah written during the time before her marriage.

"Two professors hired by the Egyptian government arrived the day after Trevor announced his discovery of an ancient tomb. They were the ones who arranged for him to be sent home to heal or die, not wanting to risk the integrity of the dig if what he had was contagious." Her father seemed relieved to talk of other matters than what Elise had revealed.

"Thankfully, Sarah had always been interested in what I taught her about the Biblical and healing properties of herbs and oils." Lady Evangeline leaned forward and tugged the lap blanket up over Hanna, which had slipped down. "Sarah had helped your father's cousin so much that Trevor's mother insisted she come and see what she could do for him, for the doctors had given up and told his family to prepare for his funeral."

"According to Sarah's letters, Trevor was not a good patient, which made helping him an unbearable chore." Elise chuckled. "I don't know how she persisted."

"After Sarah had done all, she could do for him, she threatened to leave him to his own devices unless he became more cooperative. He did and eventually got better physically, but his attitude remained surly for having been shipped home unconscious while others took credit for his years of hard work."

"He'd just uncovered a tomb of great importance." Lord Stanton's voice lowered but couldn't hide the anger his tone conveyed. "From what he described to me, it was filled with vast historical wealth, as well as riches to rival any of the Egyptian Pharaoh's tombs. The day after the announcement, two officials from the Egyptian government arrived. The following morning Trevor awoke very ill. It is thought they poisoned his food or drink, but when questioned, they claimed it was the curse of that ancient pharaoh. Such nonsense for none of them or the workers became ill."

"I sent Sarah a list of herbs best used for ridding the body of poison and to restore his system to normal, and included a package that contained the special herbs I grow that are hard to find elsewhere." Lady Evangeline sat back with the look of satisfaction, having been right in her diagnosis and treatment.

"I remember the excitement of that discovery, though Trevor's name was never mentioned. Even the king sent an emissary to confirm the evidence." Elise had been at the school in London at the time. "The school also sent two students and a professor to see the dig for themselves—and to confirm it wasn't a hoax, as often happened when someone appealed to the king for funds. The sketches the students brought back were first class with their detailed descriptions." Elise cringed at thought of what else they'd found. "The horrors of finding poisonous scorpions in their bedding and the deadly snakes of which they drew detailed pictures, still sends chills down my spine. Their guide was bitten and died the day before they returned home to England." She felt sorry for Trevor for having his life's work stolen from him. "Father, perhaps you can get the school to share the drawings with Trevor so he can compare them with what he remembers of seeing at the dig."

"That's a good idea, Elise. I shall inquire once we've reached Sarah's." Her father pulled a sheet of paper from his satchel and made a note. "After he and Sarah were first married, they spent a lot of time in London appealing to the government to give him the credit for the tomb's discovery."

While in London as Trevor spent countless hours in meetings, Sarah had insisted Elise attend those awful parties in hopes of finding her a husband. Elise's memory was probably faulty because she was counting the minutes until she could leave those parties without offending the hostess or her sister. "I can't remember how Sarah and Trevor fell in love."

"Trevor admitted later it was love at first sight, which grew deeper as she ministered to him, but, according to Sarah, he was too engrossed with sulking over his misfortune to acknowledge their mutual attraction." By her mother's happy expression, she enjoyed retelling the story. "As he was healing and regaining his strength, he refused, with a grand gesture of dismissal, the last dose of herbs she tried to give him to clear up a cough. He yelled at her. She yelled right back at him, declaring that she was through with his bad attitude and lack of gratitude for what he did have, and stomped out. She was so angry that she packed her things and had a carriage brought around before he could reconcile in his mind that she wasn't coming back." Her mother paused. "If I remember each of their versions of the event correctly, she'd made it back to London and booked passage on the first boat headed toward home before he gathered his wits and decided no other would wed her but he. He found her, and they reconciled, so he came with her to Brighton. He spoke with us about the marriage contract the two of them devised on the trip, to wed as soon as the bans could be published and read, so his family's priest could perform the official ceremony." Her mother's expression turned solemn. "They would not be swayed to wait for me and his mother to organize a proper wedding. It would only have taken a few weeks."

Lord Stanton cleared his throat.

"Fine, perhaps a bit longer. A few months at most." Her mother closed her eyes as if visualizing the grandeur of the imaginary event. "They were eager to begin their married life, so I could not stand in their way with my wishes for a grand ceremony fitting their noble heritages." Her mother glanced out the window.

"My darling, as I remember, we were wed within days of our first meeting and I don't remember anyone trying to get us to wait...not that I would have allowed such a delay." He chuckled when she blushed at the remembrance. "I do admit, it was a grand celebration with many important people there to witness our vows." He caught Elise's gaze and winked.

"True." She sighed. "I just wanted my daughter to experience the same."

Elise recognized the disappointment her mother still harbored for being unable to give Sarah the same type of wedding she'd had.

As much as Elise would hate to disappoint her mother again, she had no wish for such pomp and circumstance, nor would William.

"Sarah and Trevor were a good match, and now we are about to be grandparents." Her father's chest puffed out in his pride and put his arm around his wife. "Their wedding may have been small, but you made sure it was memorable."

The driver shouted at someone ahead.

Hanna sat up and rubbed her eyes. "Are we there yet? I'm hungry."

Elise glanced out. "I believe so."

They were at the gates of Trevor's country home, Barrington Manor. The stone-covered structure looked as big as Brighton Castle. It also appeared as well-fortified. If trouble should come seeking Elise here, it wouldn't have an easy entry.

Peace settled over her heart with that thought.

CHAPTER 16

William awoke with a start. A strange nun was scowling at him as if he might be a killer or thief. He hurt everywhere, and he was so thirsty he couldn't remember the last time he had tasted water. Pushing his elbow into the straw beneath him, he tried to rise, but the angry nun put a hand on his shoulder and, with the slightest pressure, caused him to surrender and lie flat.

"He's awake, Brother John."

"William." It was John's voice, but he looked vastly different. His face was shaved clean and his hair cut high above his ears.

"John?" A whisper was the best William could produce. Where was he? Was this a bad dream too? He had something important to tell him. Rubbing his temple, he tried to jog his memory. A picture flashed in his mind of a wounded man lying on the ground and his desperate warning.

"They're going to be killed." William needed to protect John, but his strength failed him and he slipped back into sleep.

The next he remembered he was in a cart parked under a large shade tree. With John's help William slid out of the cart and limped to a clearing.

"Who's going to be killed, William?" John helped him to a log beside the fire, a welcome site, for his energy was spent.

"Brother John, can't you see he hasn't the strength to answer your questions now? Wait until he's had a drink of water and some soup." A pretty nun busied herself with filling a cup with water and handed it to William.

"Thank you, Sister." William drank that water and another until he had his fill. "I found Angus Greene lying in a field, badly injured." William's voice was still hoarse and his hand shook as he was given a bowl of watery, but acceptable soup. He drank it down. It was the second bowl when he felt his strength beginning to return.

John's impatience was evident by his rubbing his bare chin, where he used to tug on his beard.

William sat straighter feeling the pull of his wounded side. "He was unconscious and in bad shape, so I took him to Father Alvin to doctor his wounds. When Angus came to, he told the priest that he was a member of a group of assassins who have been hired to kill the king and any nobles who could vie for the crown after his death."

The two nuns exchanged glances.

"You mean the Black Guard?" The older nun, whom John called Lois, spoke with a voice of one experienced in dealing with such.

"Aye." William turned to John. "Angus risked his life to warn your parents of the danger."

"What of the village and the castle? Have they been warned?" John stood and gripped the handle of the dagger at his side.

"Father Alvin has taken care of that." William said. "I'm confident he will do a good job for he has more time in service to the king as a soldier than our time combined." William stood and waited for the strength to return to his limbs then limped up to the cart where the warhorse was tied. He examined the stallion, speaking softly his praise. "You found your master and kept me safe." William's concern over Shadow was replaced with guilt, as the horse must have traveled all night in the storm to find John. There was no sign of injuries, only exhaustion, which will pass after rest and care.

When the nuns had cleaned and replaced the utensils, the group again resumed their trip. William rode in the back of the cart alone, relieved that he didn't have to endure the older woman's scowl whenever she glanced at him, for she had moved to the driver's seat. His side still ached from the wound, but the salve John gave him to put on the cuts eased the pain.

The warhorse was obviously exhausted by the way the stallion walked behind the cart with its head down. As long as John stayed near the stallion, it remained calm, which meant the younger nun had to lead the donkey. Shadow would require at least a day or two to fully recover his strength, otherwise, William or John would have ridden ahead to the nearest port to secure passage to London. The urgency of their mission made for short tempers but there was nothing that could be done to hasten their journey. The donkey refused to be rushed.

"I'm sorry about Shadow. I remember telling him to find you then I fell asleep in the saddle." William was proud of the horse for finding John but hated the perilous journey that almost killed the courageous stallion.

"He'll recover, as I trust, will you." John reached over and slapped William on the shoulder to show he held no hard feelings.

"Oh, I remember something else. I stopped at the abbey hoping to find you there and that's where I received the wound in my side." He rubbed his wound. "It's a story for another day." His voice lowered not to carry to the women. "Sister Agnes told me that an assassin by the name of Thoreau, had stopped there, but when he couldn't gain entrance, he moved on, most likely because a young runaway named, Thomas may have bargained bits of information for his promise to take him to London with him."

"We must stay diligent, if that man is on our trail. I wonder why he's not overtaken us by now." John hurried forward to speak with the two women before he returned to put a hand on the agitated stallion. "Perhaps Thomas didn't give him the right information."

The trip to the port was impossibly slow. None they encountered on the road was willing to loan, rent, or sell them their horses to get them there faster. Every minute they were delayed worried William. He needed to get to Elise and her family to warn them.

When they got close enough to the port to smell the salt air, John took off on Shadow to make the arrangements to sail as soon as possible.

When their little group were within minutes of the port, a small boy jumped out of the shadows and waved for them to stop.

"Thomas!" The pretty nun, whom John had called Julianna, rushed over to the boy.

"He made me do it." The boy cried.

William scooted out of the cart to investigate, when something hit him. He awoke with a throbbing headache, the screams of women, and the donkey's loud bray practically in his ears.

"Are you badly injured?" John lifted William up and turned him over.

"What did I miss?" William rubbed the dirt off his face and scrubbed his hands down his tunic.

"Here." The little boy he had seen in the road handed him his peg leg. "I's sorry ye was hurt."

"Thank you." William quickly attached it and took John's hand, extended to help him rise. "Is the man, who is bound up tight like a Christmas ham to the wheel of the cart, the assassin, Thoreau, Sister Agnes mentioned?"

"Aye. He's part of the Black Guard. His attack on us was to keep us from warning the king. After he knocked you out, he brought the lot of you to this abandon shed." John walked over to check the rope tying Thoreau to the cart. "The man didn't realize what a group of warriors he was dealing with." John glanced at the women and patted the donkey. "Enough to say we won the battle and he is now our prisoner."

William glanced at the boy. "And you must be Thomas. Sister Agnes was very worried about you." The boy nodded and big tears dripped from his eyes.

"I lefts a note. I has to find me gran'da." He dropped his gaze to the dirt and kicked it, stirring up the dust. "I's sorry." He raised his face. "Ye ain't goin' to leave me here, are ye?"

William pointed to John. "Ask him your fate. It is his expedition, and he's in charge of such decisions.

"We're all going. You included…if you obey my orders." John knelt down at the boy's level and reached out his hand. "A man never makes a vow he can't honor." The boy slipped his hand into John's and shook it.

"Aye, monk." He blinked back more tears. "But can ye help me to find me gran'da?"

"We'll see what can be done about that once we get to London." John readied the group and with William's help, put the injured assassin in the cart. The older nun guarded him, sitting nearby, with her dagger trained on his heart, should he rally and make trouble.

William also rode in the cart but ignored them, only making sure the assassin didn't try to escape. By his observation, Sister Lois seemed to know the prisoner extremely well, for after he came to, they argued off and on about their pasts or some such nonsense.

The ship John had engaged was owned by soldiers with whom William and John had served in the king's army.

"Good to see ya lookin' so alive." Captain Keet had a hook to replace his missing hand and looked none the worse for wear since they'd last met.

"It is good to be alive." William shook the captain's good hand and slapped him on the shoulder. "Thanks for taking us aboard. It will shave several days off our trip to London."

"Glad to help." Captain Keet smiled as John hurried past heading down to the cargo hole to be there when the donkey was let down inside. "Looks like the commander's got his hands full with the lot of you."

"Aye, and I best go and help him, at least with the animals." William listened to Captain Keet's laughter as William followed John down into the hold of the ship, where the animals would ride out the trip. Not a place William would want to take up residence. The pungent smell of the last catch of fish, and the animal's fresh deposit of manure, the stench was near unbearable.

Their trip was not without trials, but during the journey he found out Elise had also sailed with Captain Keet. The man seemed a bit closed mouthed about the reason she and her handmaiden left London in such a hurry, which only confirmed to William something terrible had happened to Elise to make her flee the school and not want to return.

Through the crew, he found out Elise's handmaiden, Isabella had later married the captain and was probably the reason he had not chucked John and the lot of them overboard for the trouble they stirred up during the voyage.

William was never more grateful to reach a port. The docking took time then the crew had to unload the animals. He paced the dock, for he could do nothing to hurry things along. His fear and impatience grew. He needed to leave and warn John's family of the impending threat from the Black Guard.

"I'll see these women reach the king, while you warn my family. Tell them I'll come there as soon as I can." John waited on the dock with William as the crew unloaded the animals and cart. "Once Shadow has limbered up from the trip, he'll be ready to run. You should reach the duke's manor within a day, two at the most, if the weather remains good and the roads are clear."

"Aye, John. I trust we'll see you soon." William saddled the stallion, then made his way out of London, hindered by the crowded streets. Once out of the city, he let the stallion have his head and they sailed over the road, eating up the miles.

Dark clouds formed and thunder rumbled in the distance. He hoped to be somewhere dry before the storm hit.

Near evening, the temperature had turned hot and muggy and the air smelled of rain. Thunder grew closer and louder.

With no farms or shelter in sight, William allowed the horse his head until he felt Shadow tire. He drew the stallion back to a walk to rest before another push. William felt the horse's gait change and become uneven, which indicated a problem. He dismounted and confirmed Shadow had thrown a shoe. The warhorse had special shoes made for his large size, making it necessary for William to backtrack until he found it. Fortunately, it wasn't far and easily visible on the road.

The scenery he'd passed had been wide open fields for miles, so he had no choice but to continue on. They needed to find shelter soon.

He led the stallion for over an hour, when he saw fenced pastures and a large, stone house in the distance. Even though it wasn't the duke's grand manor that he sought, he might find a hot meal and the tools needed to replace the shoe.

Shadow pranced beside William. Only the stallion's training kept him from bolting when a loud rumble of thunder erupted almost on top of them.

"Easy, boy." William kept a running dialog of comforting

words and scriptures of protection to keep the horse calm, as well as himself.

When he got closer, he saw the sign. *Hathford Farms.* He led the horse up the long drive to the stables and left him secure, in an empty stall to find the owner. He wouldn't unsaddle Shadow until he knew it was safe to bed him down. It would be dark before he could get the horseshoe replaced, and it wasn't safe to travel at night and in the middle of a storm. He would have to secure a room for the night, or sleep in the barn with the stallion. Either would do as long as they were safe and dry.

Large rain drops began to fall, as he left the barn and hurried to the manor.

A sign hung on the wall beside the front door inviting whoever approached to come inside. The entrance had once been grand, with high ceilings and polished walnut floors, which still shone from someone's loving care. The scent of hot apple pie made his stomach growl. It had been a long time since he'd had tasted one, or had a good meal, for that matter.

"Hello?" William called. There was no response. He saw a brass bell on the counter and a sign to ring it for service, so he did.

A woman hurried into the room. "I'm Mistress Emiline Hathford. How can I help you, sir?" She wiped her hands on a towel. "Sorry, to keep you waiting. I had pies to take out so as not to burn them."

"They smell delicious." He could almost taste the cinnamon and sugary treat. "I'm Sir William Degraf. My horse threw a shoe, so I'm in need of a room for the night for me and a stall and grain for my horse."

"Certainly." Thunder and heavy rain echoed around them. "Looks like you made it here just in time." She smiled and told him the cost, and he paid it from the funds John had insisted he take with him—something about it being part of a benevolence fund to be used for such emergencies. "The night's lodging includes dinner and breakfast. Dinner will be served in two hours."

"If that means sampling some of that apple pie, I can hardly wait." William heard the door open and close behind him. "If it's possible, I'd like to replace my horse's shoe tonight, but I'll need to borrow some tools."

"I can help you with whatever tools you'll need."

William turned to face the young man approaching behind him.

"We have a few standard size horseshoes in stock, but I'm sure there's none to fit the horse I saw in the barn. We do have a good forge and enough iron to fashion what you need." The young man reached out his hand and looked William in the eye. "I'm Jeremy Hathford." His handshake was firm. He gave William's peg leg a casual glance, but didn't mention it.

William lifted the horseshoe he'd carried inside. "Aye, it's a bit larger than most. I'll need to do a little work on the hoof and shoe before I can replace it."

"Let's see what we can do." Jeremy led the way out a side door.

Staying close behind the young man, heading to the barn, William got a good soaking along the way. With a firm hold, he led the still agitated Shadow out of the stall and crossed an open court to the farrier shop a short distance away. The rain had slowed but not stopped. Though considerably smaller than the main barn, the farrier's shop had thick stone walls like the main barn and the manor house, which muffled the thunder.

William tied the stallion to the hitching post, near enough to the tools but far enough away from the hot forge not to interfere with working with the iron if need be. The tools were clean and lined up in the order in which they would be needed to replace a shoe. "Looks like a knowledgeable farrier lives here and takes pride in his tools."

"That would be my da." Jeremy smiled. "He's in the next shire helping a friend, otherwise he would have been glad to help." He walked toward the big stallion and the horse snorted and pawed the ground. "Not a fan of strangers, I take." He backed off giving the horse some space.

"And the storm has him on edge. That's the reason I need to do the work myself." William unsaddled the horse and placed the gear on a rack nearby. He signaled the horse by a light tap on the leg and it picked up its front left hoof for William to inspect.

"He's well trained." The lad stood nearby watching.

"It makes life easier for both horse and farrier." Facing toward the rear of the horse, William pressed his shoulder against Shadow's chest, bent over, and drew the front hoof between his knees to steady it. Working with the horse made him ever grateful that he still had both knees. The missing portion required the peg to steady him while he worked.

With a small curved pick, with a dull pointed end, he cleaned the hoof and checked for cracks, chips, and tender spots. Once satisfied that the horse hadn't sustained any injury, he used a steel rasp to smooth the edges and readied it for the shoe.

"I recognize this mark on the cone-shaped leather boot hanging over the stirrup." Jeremy rubbed his hand across the small letters stamped along the top edge. "*LES*. Lady Elise Stanton puts this mark on all of her creations. Did she create this special piece to hold your peg to stabilize you in the saddle?" When William ignored the question, Jeremy went on with his inspection. "It is ingenious in its simplicity." Jeremy fingered the mark and smiled with obvious affection.

William felt a flame of jealousy at the young man's knowledge of Elise's work. He released Shadow's hoof and straightened, so he could focus on the lad.

"How do you know Lady Stanton?" William tried to keep his tone even, but he couldn't keep it from reflecting his displeasure.

"We met at the School of Scientifica in London. We became very close over the months she was there. We…" Jeremy's face flushed as if he'd said too much. "How do you know Lady Elise? Are you pursuing her?" He tried to look casual by leaning against a post with arms crossed, but his glance never wavered from William.

"I've known her and her family all my life." William had no intention of explaining more. "Now, since this not the proper place or time to discuss a fine lady, I must return to my work." He smiled to take the sting off his gruff reprimand and resumed his work. He heard Jeremy leave shortly after. The young man obviously had feelings for Elise, and he couldn't fault him. She had an innocent way about her that stirred a man's imagination of what might be, if only…

As William worked on replacing Shadow's shoe and checking the other shoes to make sure none needed attention, his thoughts were on Elise. He needed to get to her to make sure she was safe and to deliver the warning about the Black Guard. The storm had again increased in velocity and he and the horse were tired from pushing hard to get this far. The stallion needed a good night's rest almost as much as William. Refreshed, he would make better time in the morning. As much as the urgency of his mission continued to worry him, for safety's sake he would wait and leave at first dawn. He led the stallion back into his stall and noticed a good measure of feed and clean water. Jeremy must have tended to that before he left.

William ate dinner in a communal dining room. The only other diners were a couple with two small children, who retired to their room.

It was a simple but delicious meal of fried chicken, fresh vegetables from the manor garden, and apple pie, which tasted better than it had smelled.

Jeremy made a short appearance, and gave him a nod before disappearing into the family's private quarters. William suspected he wanted to press for more information about Elise, but by his hesitancy, he wasn't ready to risk another rebuff.

After the meal, William headed to the main barn to check on Shadow and to walk off the fine meal. The stalls were dry even after the heavy downpour and the other out buildings looked well-maintained. He hadn't seen but a few staff about the estate, which meant the family was mainly in charge of the work. They took pride in their labors, knowing they were leaving a legacy for future generations.

That was what he wanted. A place of his own that he could develop and improve until it was something he could proudly leave to his children.

He walked to the stallion's stall. The horse stood at rest. Upon sensing William's presence, he raised his head as if waiting for a command.

"Rest, my friend. We have a long journey tomorrow." William kept his voice low and calm. The stallion snorted and closed its eyes.

"Sorry to disturb you." Jeremy walked into the barn wearing a look of determination as if he had something on his mind that he couldn't wait to unload.

William turned and leaned against Shadow's stall.

"I just realized who you are." His eyes narrowed and his tone accusatory. "You're *her* William."

William straightened and frowned. "Whom do you refer?"

"Lady Elise. She promised she would marry me if she was still single next year, unless one named William declared for her."

"She promised what?" William's loud tone startled Shadow. On battle alert, the warhorse pawed the ground and paced his stall. William's skin flushed hot. "You have no noble blood nor title, do ye?"

"Nay, I come from humble but hardworking people, but I plan to have the title of earl bestowed on me before the year is out for my scientific achievements in service to the crown." Jeremy scowled and moved to the opposite side of the hall. He rubbed a hand across his mouth, as if he'd said more than he intended and had no idea how to fix it. He faced William. "She's unconcerned about such hindrances as titles and bloodlines, but I want to honor her by obtaining a title and my own land to start our marriage."

William's gaze narrowed. He wanted to shout, but lowered his voice to allow the stallion to calm. "Do her parents know what she's promised you?"

"Nay, for I promised to keep her vow a secret until that time." Jeremy rubbed his face again and looked anguished. "I've failed that promise by telling you, but I had to know." He glanced up at William, his scowl changed to an expression of open curiosity. "You have had all this time and never declared for her. Why should she believe that you would do so now?"

William was furious. Why had he been so certain that by sacrificing his love for Elise, she would wed someone with noble blood, as was her birthright? Instead, she would be expected to honor her pledge to this adolescent commoner if William didn't marry her.

"My reasons for not declaring for her before now are unimportant. I love her and shall marry her before the year is over, so you mustn't expect her to return to you." It was William's turn to pace from one side of the wide hall to the other. How was he going to approach her father with his declaration when he was still without a title or lands of his own? Even this young upstart had a legacy of land and money, if not a title.

Instead of anger or censure, Jeremy smiled and slapped William on the shoulder. "I believe that to wed you is what she's wanted all along. I care for her deeply, but I want her to be happy." He frowned. "But if you do not do what you say or cause her to reject your hand in marriage, then I will honor my pledge. I'll make her a good husband and provider for all of our children." He smiled. "She told me once that she wanted a large family of at least seven children." His smile faded when he saw the scowl on William's face.

William hated that Jeremy knew more about Elise's dreams of a family than him. He managed to grumble, *"Goodnight",* before they parted and William sought solace in his room.

Though the bed was comfortable, he tossed and turned most of the night. His first responsibility was to warn her family of the Black Guard then perhaps find a way to see if she was still of like mind to wed him. If so, then he must find a way to approach her father with his request. There was no clear solution to the problem so he prayed and sought wisdom and favor. God was his only hope.

At first light, William saddled Shadow, led him outside, and was ready to mount when Jeremy came out of the inn and hurried toward him.

"I failed to tell you something important last evening. I couldn't let you leave without warning you of a possible danger." He told William about a drunkard who had seen Elise and threatened to tell her whereabouts to Lord Richard Blackstone who had offered a hefty reward for information about her current location. "I removed this from our local pub so no others shall see it." He unfolded the poster and handed it to William.

"So, this is what gives her nightmares and haunts her days." William refolded the poster and shoved it inside his tunic to read again later. "Thank ye. And I should warn you of another potential danger to Lady Stanton and all nobles. If your family is one of faith, please pray for our nation. There are a band of evil men intent on overthrowing the king and murdering any of noble birth that might claim the throne. They are ruthless assassins, so take whatever precautions you think necessary to protect your family and hers in case they should come this way. They can be recognized by a black bird tattoo on their wrists."

With a nod and a salute, he mounted the stallion and gave him his head, allowing the warhorse to stretch his legs.

When the horse had his run, William pulled him back to a slower pace. By late afternoon he saw the duke's manor by John's description. There were people working in the fields but the gates to the manor were closed.

"Who goes there?" The guard at the tower shouted down to William.

"I'm Sir William Degraf. I've come with an urgent message for Lord and Lady Stanton. Please tell them I'm here with news of their son, John."

"Dismount. Wait while I send someone to alert his lordships." The guard on the second tower trained his bow at William.

Soon the gate was opened only far enough to admit William and the stallion before it was closed and locked again.

Declining a servant's offer to take care of the stallion, William tended to Shadow and secured him in a large box stall. A servant showed William to a place where he washed the dirt off his hands and face before he went into the manor to meet the family.

"William, it is good to see you." Lord Stanton met him in the entry and led him to the dining hall. He waved to a servant. "Bring food and drink for I'm sure Sir William is hungry, am I right?"

William nodded, but before he could say anything, Lord Stanton raised his hand and waited until the servant had gone before he relaxed and focused on William.

"I assume this is urgent business that brought you all this way?" Lord Stanton tensed. "You told the guard that you have news of John?" Sending away the servant first was a way to keep any bad news from escaping the room.

"John is fine. I met with him on the way here." William could see the relief in Lord Stanton's face. William spent the next half-hour eating boiled lamb and bread spread with thick slabs of butter and honey, while explaining between bites what he had learned about the Black Guard and John's mission to warn the king of their plot. He avoided mentioning the nuns traveling with John. Their presence on his journey and their prisoner were stories for John to tell when he arrived.

William answered every question asked of him until the lack of sleep from the previous night, and the long journey caught up with him. Well fed, he couldn't hide the yawns or exhaustion that made it hard to focus on the conversation.

"We'll talk again once you've rested." Lord Stanton motioned for a servant to come near. "Take Sir William to a quiet room where he can sleep. He is not to be disturbed until morning."

William followed the servant to a room with a small window and a large bed. He undressed, washed, took off his pegleg and slipped under the covers. He barely closed his eyes when he succumbed to a deep and dreamless sleep.

The door opened to his room and he stirred awake. He grabbed the dagger from under his pillow and waited. Sunlight streamed into the room from the solitary window, declaring a new day.

"His Lordship feared you would sleep away the day and sent me to fetch you so you can get dressed for the midday meal in but an hour." A manservant waited until William swung his legs out of bed before he came forward. "I have clean clothes for you and if you wish, a bath can be brought up." He hung the clothing in an ornate cabinet.

William yawned and stretched. "A bath is fitting, for my journey has been long and arduous." Relieved there was no danger, he withdrew his hand from the dagger tucked beneath the bedding, ready if needed.

Once the bath was brought and filled, the servants left. He checked the wounds in his side. No redness, only a slight scar marked the injury. The slightest tenderness remained when he stretched. He noticed his own discarded clothing had been removed, probably to be washed. After the bath he dressed in the borrowed tunic and pants, which were of superior quality. His peg and only boot had been buffed and polished until they looked considerably better, too.

He'd finished his ablutions by the time the servant came back and led him to the main dining hall. Lord and Lady Stanton and their daughter, Hanna sat around the table talking. They all glanced up when he took a seat.

"Sir William. I'm glad you're here." Hanna gave him her biggest smile, making him feel more like family than a stranger.

"I'm glad I'm here, too, Sunshine." William winked at her sending her into a fit of giggles until her mother put a hand on her shoulder.

"I take it you rested well, William." Lord Stanton nodded to a servant standing nearby. "You may serve."

"Yes, thank you. I'm sorry I've delayed your meal. I don't usually sleep so late." William leaned back so a servant could serve him. The roasted turkey and vegetables looked and smelled delicious.

"Henry said you've seen John." Lady Stanton turned her attention on William. "We had expected him to arrive days ago."

"He's well and told me to tell you he would arrive here as soon as he completed some business in London. I'm sure he'll explain all when he arrives." William glanced down to focus on his food, lest they see the guilt in his eyes and suspect there was more to tell of John's *business*. Their only male heir's decision to become a monk would be hard for them to bear. Thankfully, it was not his secret to reveal.

"Trevor sends his regrets that he couldn't greet you properly. He's with Sarah." Lady Evangeline smiled. "All is well, but he's anxious. He rarely leaves her side of late, in spite of Sarah and I assuring him everything is as it should be." Her smile revealed tolerance and acceptance. "It could be weeks before the child is born."

The family conversed about the storm damage seen around the countryside, until the last course was served. Hanna's chatter eliminated any lulls in the conversation with details of a litter of six puppies born at the manor during the storm. She went into great detail to describe them and the names she'd given each one.

Elise had yet to arrive? Working on a project, which had often made her late or kept her from sharing a family meal? Anger warred with urgency to tell her that he knew about her vow with the young farmer. Should he demand an explanation and her reasoning behind that foolish promise, or beg for her hand in marriage. Dare he risk her rejection, as he had once rejected her, or simply carry her off to the nearest priest to wed? An anxious thump in his chest came with the thought of how to ask Lord Stanton for his permission to wed his daughter.

"Elise went away with some people. Mum says she hopes she'll find a good husband along the way."

William choked on his wine.

"Hanna, it's time for your nap." Lady Evangeline motioned a servant to her and ask they fetch Hanna's nanny. "Elise's trip had nothing to do with finding a husband." She shushed Hanna when the little girl protested.

William coughed again, then dabbed his mouth A small sip of wine helped to ease his distress, but not his embarrassment.

"Elise has gone on an expedition with an old friend of Henry's and her former professor, Lord Isaac Canterbury and his wife, Caroline, along with two other scientists. One was a former student, I believe. They're hoping to find a few of the meteorites that fell some days back." Lord Stanton leaned back and allowed a servant to take away his empty dinner plate. Another servant came with a bowl of brandied peaches for each of the three adults.

The now pouting Hanna was led away by her nanny with the promise of a sweet treat if she took a nap without a fuss.

"Elise has gone on an expedition?" William tensed and turned towards Lord Stanton. "She could be in great danger." It wasn't only the Black Guard who could put her at risk. There was a madman who sought her and was willing to pay a reward to find her. Had he mentioned that to Lord Stanton when they'd talked? He'd been so tired, he couldn't remember. "Shall I fetch her back here for her safety? I can leave immediately." He stood, anxious to be on his way.

"With the recent developments, Henry, bringing her back here might be a prudent plan." Lady Stanton glanced at her husband and stood. "I shall have the servants pack supplies for your journey, William."

Lord Stanton remained seated and tented his fingers in thought. "After the completed repair on their wagon wheel, Isaac was most eager to reach the coordinates of the meteor strike. Elise and the professor's party left three days ago. Depending on no further delays, they could be at their destination by now." His brow furrowed, as if pondering his next words. "Elise appeared the happiest I've seen her in a long time to be included in the expedition. I'd hate to ruin her trip unless it's absolutely necessary." He stood, as if he'd come to a decision. "I believe, my friend and his party are experienced scientists and explorers who are used to dealing with danger and harsh conditions." He made eye contact with William. "However, once you've found them, I trust you to assess the situation. If you judge it secure where they've set up camp, stay with her there and allow her time to participate in the dig, while guarding her safety. If you deem it potentially dangerous for her to remain with the expedition, by all means bring her back here to the manor." Lord Stanton led the way to a study. "Isaac gave me a general direction they intended to travel, but he was unclear how long it would take to arrive at their destination." He gave

William a written note with the professor's vague destination, and a pouch with a hefty sum of money, enough to cover whatever expenses he'd need for lodging and food, whether he stayed at the camp site or returned Elise to the manor.

William gathered the supplies needed and headed to the barn. He hoped Shadow had also rested sufficiently to make another long trip.

CHAPTER 17

he road was bumpy and rutted from recent rains, but
the carriage drivers kept a steady pace.

She could hardly believe it. Only three days before, Elise had
been invited to join Professor Lord Isaac and Lady Caroline
Canterbury's expedition to search for the meteorites that struck
the earth some days ago. Excitement grew as their group journeyed closer to their destination. The talk around the evening
campfire had, at first, centered on some of the professor's more
challenging former expeditions. Rather than being deterred by
the hard work, rough living, and possible danger, the stories
stirred joyful anticipation within Elise. Like a child's impatience
for Christmas, she wanted to find her first meteorite.

Only by divine intervention, she had met the professor and
his party in the village nearest Sarah and Trevor's manor. The
professor's drivers were dealing with some repairs to the
carriage wheel when Elise and her father came upon them at the
local blacksmith shop.

Since her mother seemed to think Sarah still had a while
before she delivered, her parents decided it would be a good
opportunity for Elise to go and further her education with the

learned professor and his wife. She planned to be back in plenty of time for Sarah's delivery.

The trip would also put her far away, if Richard sought her at the manor.

Elise glanced over at her fellow occupants in the carriage. The professor continued making calculations in his notebook and his wife, Caroline leaned over to him periodically to read what he'd written and occasionally pointed out something in his notes. He'd nod and make a correction or disagree with her observation, which led to a lively discussion.

Fortunately, Elise was not required to give her opinion. Instead, she turned her attention to their fellow travelers. From Elise's seat in the carriage looking behind, she could observe the men driving the supply wagon following close behind, who were well known to the professor and his wife. According to Caroline, who'd given Elise a little background on their fellow travelers, Lord Michael Sebastian was in his mid-twenties. He'd attended the School of Scientifica to study astronomy as well as other sciences, but due to a family emergency, he left the school before Elise had arrived. He was polite, but his focus was obviously on science not romance, for he barely glanced her way, which was a relief. On the other hand, Lord Avery Smithe seemed to show up at her side whenever they stopped along the way. The eighteen-year-old son of close friends of Caroline and the professor, he appeared to be without any worthwhile goals for his life. His parents had urged the professor to take Avery along and teach him about science in hope of stirring his interest in more worthwhile endeavors than going to pubs and associating with some very unsavory types. According to Caroline, who had known him most of his life, Avery was strong, intelligent, and an eager learner if the subject interested him. After hearing about the professor's expedition, he readily agreed to join. The two men took turns driving the wagon that hauled the tents, tools, equipment, and supplies, which contained enough to allow their group to stay for a month, if needed, to locate the meteorites.

The carriage drivers, Desmond and Clarence have been employed by the Canterburys' for years, and appear competent in their many duties, which included everything from caring for the livestock to setting up the camp, when they stopped for the evening.

"The reports have been sketchy on the exact location of the primary stone, but from my calculations we should start our search somewhere near the Wales border." The professor consulted his sextant and wrote more notes in his journal. "Because of the trajectory of the shower, we'll make a preliminary search just beyond the next village. We'll set up camp there."

"Why do you think so many people are going in the opposite direction?" Elise glanced out the carriage window and saw a family of four leading a donkey and cart filled with household belongs.

"The last time we stopped to water the animals, I asked a farmer who was watering his stock about the suspicious migration." Professor Canterbury stopped his writing and glanced out the window. "The old man said he and his family came from a small village called Breconshire. A pagan cult leader appeared after the meteor shower and told the villagers that he alone had called the fires down from the sky."

"By his description of the pagan's evil markings covering his face and threats of all manner of evil to befall the villagers if they didn't bow down and serve him, it could be a sect of Druids, I've investigated in our travels." Caroline's tone suggested the news was quite disturbing.

"The farmer looked frightened when he mentioned the followers the man had convinced to join his cause." The professor frowned. "We need to be on alert in case we encounter those pagans, but we have more than earthly weapons with which to fight our battle, we have the Blood of Jesus and the Word of God to deal with those unholy heathens."

Caroline stroked her cat, Tabitha, on her lap. "Amen." The woman seemed unafraid and content to be riding along to who-knew-where the expedition might lead.

"We've been able to glean from witnesses that several balls of fires streaked across the night sky in silence. After several minutes, they heard a loud explosion, and the ground shook hard enough to cause landslides and toppled small buildings." The professor glanced up from his notes and closed the book. "According to my calculations, we should be arriving in that village in an hour or so." He leaned back against the cushioned seat, crossed his arms, and closed his eyes. A gentle snoring followed within minutes.

Caroline's chuckled making Elise smile.

"We've been married fifteen years, and I still cannot figure out how he can fall asleep so quickly." Caroline's expression held affection for her husband.

"My father and brother can do the same. I'm certain there is a scientific reason, but I've no idea what that might be." Elise chuckled.

Caroline attention turned to Elise. "I'm surprised you haven't married. Aren't your parents intent on finding you a husband?"

"My scientific interests have been a hindrance to that process." Elise glanced out the carriage window. "I've had several opportunities to be courted, but my heart is given to one who cannot seem to understand that I care more for him than his lack of title or wealth." She returned her gaze to the woman sitting across from her and saw tears in Caroline's eyes. "You understand?"

"Yes, I do." She straightened and glanced at her husband, whose snores remained steady. "I once actively studied as an astronomer and can prove the earth is round, not flat, a heretic's view if you'd heard my father." The cat wiggled free and dropped to the floor of the carriage as if her mistress's hold had become too firm.

Caroline continued. "He was so angry with my choice of study that he signed me to a marriage contract without my consent, to an elderly duke whose property adjoined his. What he really wanted was access to the man's land when he died." She glanced down at her hands and clasped them in her lap. "Terrance was a nice old man whose two sons died in infancy and his wife of thirty-seven years, whom he adored, had died two years before we wed. Still grieving her loss, he had no wish to replace her in his affections and didn't expect more of me than to be his hostess when businessmen brought their wives with them to the manor. He wanted me to take charge of his home, and in turn, he gave me a great deal of freedom, far more than my father ever had. He too was an amateur astronomer, so we found we had many things in common. I was happy there.

"When he died ten months after our wedding, my father demanded I return home and told me he planned to take control of my assets and contract me to another man immediately." She took a deep breath and let it out. "I refused. Having experienced freedom from his control, I was determined not to allow his interference in dealing with my husband's estate. Father was furious at my rebellion and my solicitor's confirmation that he had no legal right to make me do his bidding. During a drunken rage, his servants witnessed my father fall down the steps into the wine cellar and hit his head on the stone floor. His death left me, as his only heir, with two estates to manage. I sold them both, retaining certain investments for continual income, and decided to move somewhere I could freely study. With the wealth and freedom of widowhood, no one questioned my decisions to go where I wanted. I determined that I would never again allow a man to rule over me." Caroline's expression turned pensive. "On reflection, I don't believe there is such a place where women are not considered in need of a man to tell them what to do."

"I understand, although I believe my father has been the exception, since he hasn't demanded I marry…so far." Elise had given thanks daily in her prayers for such grace and tolerance.

Caroline's story explained why the professor never seemed in need of funds, which allowed him time away from the school on his sabbaticals, to pursue hunting down meteorites at his leisure.

"I was fortunate to be able to go anywhere I chose to study." Caroline said. "I found a school in Switzerland that allowed women to be taught alongside the men, as their equals. That's where I met Isaac." She glanced at her sleeping husband, whose snores had increased in volume. "I didn't like him at first…too bossy." With a slight tug, she pulled up his lap blanket that had slipped down. "We have very strong opinions about how to approach a scientific equation, and they're not always the same, as you might have heard." She smiled, but didn't apologize. "Because of his love of the Bible and its history, I found what I'd been missing, a loving Savior through Jesus Christ. I think it was not long afterward that I realized how much I also loved Isaac. The day after graduation, we married."

"So, you have the same degree of education as he?" Elise was surprised she had never guessed the truth. "I must assume you are on this expedition because you're also interested in the science and the meteorites?"

"I earned my degree alongside Isaac and would be considered his equal, if I were a man." The cat jumped back into Caroline's lap and she settled it next to her. "I'm as earnest as he to uncover the potential of the meteorites. Our studies have led to some interesting discoveries, but our research is far from conclusive. We need to locate more meteorites to compare our findings." She pointed to the professor's notebook. A page had fallen open on the seat between them, and Elise could see the flowery scroll of feminine handwriting next to the professor's bolder strokes. "We had decided I should keep a low profile at the school because of some very powerful men who believe a woman is only good for one thing and science isn't it. Becoming less of a threat to their narrow view of science, I was able to aid him at night when we could experiment alone." She winked. "The shopping and fake arguments about my spending were merely distractions to keep those same people from making trouble until we decide whether or not we want to purchase the school."

"You want to buy the school?" Elise grinned. "That could change everything."

"We're still praying about the decision, but having a school where the students are free to explore the world of science without certain people in authority demanding control over the latest inventions and technology, is our ultimate plan. We want it to be more like the school in Switzerland, where female scientists are treated with the same respect and given the same opportunity as the men." Caroline reached over to pat Elise's hand. "We know the destruction of the old outbuilding was not your fault. Thank you for saving and returning the meteorites and the notes on your experiment. We were impressed with what you accomplished under the circumstances, and we're pleased to have you with us on this scientific expedition."

"I wish there had been a better outcome than what happened." Even before the explosion sent her home, Elise's time at the school had been a constant challenge to be taken serious as a scientist. If the professors purchased the School of Scientifica things would be different. As quickly as excitement stirred within her, dread took its place. What of Richard's threats? Would he grow tired of hunting her and turn his attentions elsewhere? If only God could open Richard's heart to the wrongs he'd caused. It was never too late for someone to repent and ask for forgiveness and accept Jesus as Savior. She would continue to pray for him.

By evening of the next day, they arrived at the location the professor had plotted. It was an empty field surrounded by tall trees that grew along the perimeter, as if planted to mark the property lines or as a windbreak.

"Let's spread out and see if we can find any points of impact." Professor Canterbury took off in one direction without waiting to see if anyone else followed his instructions. Michael and Avery left the wagon's team to the drivers of the carriage and spread out to search in different directions.

Caroline walked to the tree line and Elise followed.

"If we could get higher, we might be able to see a spot where the meteorites hit the earth. Look for a scorched or bare spot, or a place where the earth has been disturbed." Caroline glanced around but nothing appeared out of place. It had been several days and it had rained since the event, so grass could have sprung back up and covered the stones.

Elise approached a tall oak. "If you give me a boost, so I can reach that lower limb, I think I can climb high enough to see if there has been any disturbance in this field." Elise was amused at Caroline's surprised expression.

"I, too, was once a good tree climber in my youth." Caroline leaned over and cupped her hands.

Elise tucked the front of her dress into her belt and took advantage of the make-shift step to grab the nearest limb and pull herself up. She climbed, higher and higher, until she had a good view of most of the meadow.

"I see a significant indentation, like a gopher mound, where the grass is scorched all around it." Elise pointed to the area.

"Freeettttt!" The loud whistle startled Elise, and she grabbed the limb tighter to regain her balance. She glanced down and saw Caroline with two fingers in her mouth, which was the source of the sound. Again, the refined lady whistled like a dockworker, making Elise giggle.

Caroline waved at her husband who had looked up. He saw Elise in the tree and turned in the direction where she was pointing.

The professor started off, occasionally glancing up so Elise could convey the direction with hand signals. Finally, he found the scorched plants and followed the path to a mound of dirt. Caroline's whistle had also drawn the attention of the two students who found their way to the professor.

Elise climbed down and straightened her dress. She and Caroline made their way to the professor.

"Avery, fetch the shovels. Michael, have Clarence and Desmond come and help." Professor Canterbury slowly circled and studied the spot.

"Good job, Elise." Caroline gave her a pat on the back as they joined the men.

After three hours of digging, the only treasure they'd uncovered was a rusted ax head.

"Aye! What ye doin' diggin' up me field? Yur ruinin' me hay meadow." A man with a pitchfork limped toward them. His boots were worn and the leather on the right toe was twisted and scarred, as if it had been caught in something.

"I'm Professor Isaac Canterbury. I deeply apologize for our intrusion, and will gladly compensate you for any damage we may have caused. We were hoping to find one of those stones that fell from the sky a few days ago." The tall, lean professor towered over the shorter, rounder farmer. Professor Canterbury reached out and the man lowered his pitchfork to shake his hand.

"Me name's Garrison Alford." He studied the rest of the group with an expression of suspicion.

"Did you witness the meteorite shower?" The professor could barely restrain his excitement.

"Aye, and most the county saw the sky ablaze with 'em. It be a miracle none hit me buildings or animals, though the chickens quit laying eggs for two days." He crossed himself. "There's some what say it's a bad omen from God and where the stones fall the land will be cursed." He held the pitchfork like a scepter of authority. "I don't take to that nonsense, for me and mine are Christians."

"Good to meet an intelligent man." The professor patted the man on the shoulder. "We are also Christians and scientists who have come to recover the stones to study their composition. As a student of God's Word, I can guarantee you that their presence is not a bad omen sent from God. As a scientist, I can tell you the stones are simply small pieces of rocks broken off of a much larger stone called an asteroid, which is floating in space. The meteor shower occurs when two asteroids collide and the pieces come close to our planet. Gravity pulls them into our atmosphere and then to the ground." His expression changed slightly as he glanced to his wife who shook her head slightly.

Elise understood their silent communication. The farmer would not understand that much information.

Caroline stepped up to the man and smiled. "We would be most grateful for your help in finding any stones that fell on your property. We are willing to pay you for them and to camp here while we search."

The man blushed and tugged on his shirt collar as if it were suddenly too tight. "I dug up one of 'em about the size of me fist from that hole you were poking in. I put it over there, where I discard all the stones that I harvested from this field." He pointed to a stacked rock fence behind them.

"Would you mind if I sent one of my men to fetch it?" Professor Isaac kept his gaze on the stone hedge.

"You can have it if you can tell it from the other rocks." He frowned, as if in thought. "Ye say it's nary a curse from God? Would you mind taking the bigger one away with you, too?"

The professor gasped. "You mean there are more?"

"Aye, follow me." The man's limp increased with the added activity but he didn't complain. He led them to a different location about a quarter mile away. "There it be." The farmer sat on a fallen tree, which had recently been felled along a path leading up to a large, deeply pitted stone. The diameter was such that a man with long arms might be able to embrace it and touch his fingertips.

Nearby, a rock formation rose from the ground like a miniature mountain range, which stretched beyond the field for a long distance. The nearest section had a tall cathedral-like arch that dominated the ancient landscape and towered above the field with grass and moss growing on it until it blended into the background. It was a stone's throw from the site making a formidable backdrop for the meteorite.

The farmer rubbed his knee and propped his right foot up on the log. By his grimace he was in considerable pain.

"I tried to dig it out, but me tools stuck to it. Got me foot caught between the stone and me shovel when I tried to push the rock loose." He pointed to an assortment of farm tools covering the stone's surface as if it were a curious art project. "I'd be stuck there still if it weren't for me wife. She sent me boys to find me when I didn't show up for our evening meal. They worked for over an hour before they could get the shovel to move enough to get me free."

"It's magnetized!" The professor hurried toward the rock and circled it in slow steps. He bent over, grasped the shovel handle, and pulled to no avail. "Give me a hand, Michael."

While the men worked to dislodge the farm tools, Elise knelt in front of the farmer.

"Is your foot injured? Can I take a look?"

"Are ye a healer?" The farmer met her gaze.

"My mother is a healer and she taught me and my siblings many things about healing." With the man's nod, she removed the mangled shoe. His foot was swollen and bruised, but nothing appeared broken. "I have some medicine that will help with the healing. When we get back to the carriage, I'll give you something to mix with water to drink for the pain and a salve to massage into the foot to ease the soreness."

"Thank ye, lassie. Me wife and sons' been havin' a time of it tryin' to do me chores as well as theirs, since me injury."

Elise studied the shoe before she replaced it on his foot. She could repair and reinforce the shoe's toe and insole to straighten it, and make it more comfortable, as well as support his injured foot while it healed.

The sun was about to set by the time the men finished removing the tools and made camp near the second meteorite site. Their host bid them a good-night and carried his recovered tools home.

Elise started a charcoal drawing of the improvements she wanted to make on the farmer's shoe while she listened to the group expound on the wonders of their find.

"That it still holds a magnetic charge after impacting the earth is quite unusual." Professor Canterbury drew pictures and made notes in his book as he spoke. "It must mean it contains a large number of metallic compounds, for the force of the ground-penetrating impact should have dispersed the charge into the earth, rendering it neutral. We need to take a sample to analyze it." He could barely contain his excitement. "Two meteorites from the same shower. A rare find."

Caroline studied the smaller meteorite that Michael had retrieved from the stone hedge by the light of their campfire. "By appearance and lighter weight, this smaller one isn't of the same composition." She handed it to the professor and he nodded his agreement.

"How can a sample be gathered from the larger stone when the hammerhead is steel and everything metal is captured by it?" Michael rubbed his beard in thought.

Avery positioned his camp chair near Elise making her frown. There was something about him. Perhaps it was his privileged upbringing that lent an air of frivolous arrogance that annoyed her.

"Why not use a wooden mallet?" Avery surprised her with a possible solution, for she didn't think he was paying attention to the conversation. She gave him a smile, which seemed to please him. He sat straighter and leaned toward the professor.

"The mallet might work, but we still need to apply a steel chisel to the stone to take a sample." Professor Canterbury was a good teacher who made his students work for the answer to problems he presented them.

Elise stopped sketching the shoe, and on a clean piece of paper, she drew the stone, searching her mind for an answer to the problem. "The magnetism could be used to keep the steel chisel in place if we can position the sharp end against a flaw in the stone."

"Yes, but its very composition could defeat our efforts to remove a sample. For now, we will need to experiment to see what will work." The professor glanced at her, a teasing twinkle in his eyes. "If all else fails we could add black powder around the perimeter to dislodge the whole thing out of the earth and take it back to London to do a full analysis."

"Please, professor, don't even jest about such things." Elise voice rose in concern. "After my disastrous experiment, I fear even the smallest amount of black powder ignited anywhere near the meteorite could have catastrophic consequences." Elise heartbeat quickened with fear remembering what a small amount of crushed meteorite mixed with black powder had caused. The size of this rock combined with an equally produced charge could cause destruction for miles around.

"Only if this meteorite has similar alloys of the one used in your experiment." He referred to his notebook. "We found a compound called magnesium in that sample, which was probably what intensified the explosive force of the black powder and superheated it enough to blow out the back of the forge." He set aside his notebook and paced to the edge of their camp. "That's the reason we need a good sample from this stone to confirm its mineral composition." He glanced back at their group. "Did Mr. Alford say anything about others wanting to look at the stone?"

The group joined the professor to see what had drawn his attention. There were several torches at the site of the meteorite.

Something about the torches bobbing around the stone ignited fear within Elise. She rubbed her arms to eliminate the sudden chill that pebbled her skin.

"According to him," Caroline said. "No one but us has even come to see it. It is highly unlikely those torches are wielded by curious villagers, because of their fear of being cursed. No matter who it is, why would they come at night?" She put an arm around her husband's waist. "What do you suppose they want?"

"I have no desire to confront strangers in the dark. Let's wait until daylight to see if they've left. There's no harm they can do to the meteorite. Perhaps we're concerned for no reason, but it's best we take precautions. Avery, warn Clarence and Desmond of possible intruders, then take the first watch. Give alarm if anyone comes near our camp. Michael, relieve him in three hours, then I'll relieve you for the next three." The professor led his wife to their tent, and Elise went to hers. Since she had been added to their number, Michael and Avery had to share a tent. The drivers had their own, which were smaller and placed near the livestock to keep watch over the animals and the supplies.

Elise said her prayers and prepared for bed, taking her shoes off and loosening her clothing, but because of her fear, she remained dressed. If a problem arose, she wouldn't face it in her nightgown. She settled onto her cot and slipped her dagger under her pillow. A feeling of unrest hadn't left since they'd spotted the torches.

When the drums began, the normal night sounds silenced, and an eerie feeling of evil hovered over the camp. She could hardly wait for dawn.

The next morning, she awoke early from a fitful night, as unrelenting echoes of beating drums and unintelligent chanting filled her dream with images from the cave of long ago. The drawings she'd seen there had come alive and chased her until she quoted Second Timothy. *I have not been given a spirit of fear but of power, love and a sound mind.* She'd repeated the scripture until the evil disappeared. She hadn't had that dream for years.

Rummaging through her trunk, she found the least wrinkled dress and changed. A quick splash of cold water on her face helped to chase away the last of the nightmare. When she stepped out of her tent, the others were already gathered at the fire pit, deep in conversation.

"What's going on?" Elise heard the tension in their voices.

The shadows under professor's eyes and his pinched lips suggested he hadn't slept well either.

"It appears our visitors set up camp at the meteorite sight." Caroline poured a cup of hot tea and handed it to Elise, who gladly accepted it.

"They were responsible for the chanting and pounding that drum all night?" She sipped the hot beverage and allowed it to awaken her fully.

"At first light I ventured close enough to their camp to recognize their body markings, costumes, and chants." The professor took a sip from his cup of tea. "From my studies of cults, they're probably one of the many sects of Druids, though I thought that particular sect had been banished from the all of England decades ago because of their violence and practice of blood sacrifice." He shook his head in disbelief. "I'll go down and speak to them in a bit."

"Not alone, Isaac." Caroline put a hand on her husband's arm in protest.

"No, my dear. I'll take Michael, Avery, and Clarence with me." He turned to the other driver. "Desmond, since your people are from around these parts, I would appreciate it if you would contact Mr. Alford and make sure he hasn't given permission for those pagans to camp there, before we make a fuss and demand they move on."

"Aye, professor. I'll ride one of the horses, so I can make a quick trip of it."

"Would it be all right if I go with Desmond?" Elise asked the professor. "I want to see how he's doing, and maybe, while I'm there I can fix his shoe, which could aid in his healing." At the professor's nod of approval, she gathered her tool kit and followed the stockman to where the horses were tied.

The professor had the forethought to bring a couple of saddles, though no sidesaddles, to use as needed. She had ridden astride many times, so at least she wouldn't have to ride behind Desmond.

They passed the farmer's sons out in the pasture tending the livestock. When they arrived at the farmhouse and dismounted, Mr. Alford limped toward them from the barn with a pail of milk in each hand. Desmond hurried over. "Can I carry those for you?"

"Thank ye, but nay. I'll carry them to the house so me wife won't think I've gone soft." He grinned and limped to the kitchen to deliver the buckets, then returned to the porch where Elise and Desmond waited. He set down a crock of cool spring water. The long-handled dipper made it easy to quench their thirst.

"Glad to see ye, but figure you've got something on yur mind." The farmer sat and waited, resting his foot on a stool next to his chair.

Desmond remained standing but leaned against the porch

post. "Several people arrived last night and set up camp near the mound. Did you give permission for them to be there?"

"Nay, neither I nor my sons would do so. Did they pound a drum all night and chant nonsense?"

Desmond and Elise nodded.

"We've dealt with their kind afore. They're here to make trouble, and they're not welcome on me land." The farmer stood. "About ten years before, they first showed up at the mound. They were a bunch of odd folks with tattooed faces and arms claiming that land was a sacred place where their kind used to worship." His voice grew louder. "My family has owned this land for many generations, so any such claim is false." He fisted his hands. "We be Christians, and I'll not have those heathens cursing my land with their demon worship." His lips pinched into an angry line. "Me, my kin, the villagers, and the king's men ran them off, but they show up again every few years spoutin' the same lies, probably hopin' I'd died." His wife stepped out on the porch to check on him. He waved her back inside. "I'm fine, woman. It's those heathens again." She nodded and went back inside. "If you need help running them off, let us know and we'll add our numbers to yourn. If they resist, I'll send for my neighbors, and we'll have an army of fifty or more to send them on their way. The law is on me side, so get rid of them how best you see fit."

"We'll see to it. Hopefully, we can do it peacefully." Desmond shook the man's hand then glanced at Elise, who had remained silent.

"I'll stay here and see if I can fix Mr. Alford's shoe—" Elise turned to the farmer "—if that's all right with you."

"That would be kind of ye, lassie." He turned to Desmond. "I'll see her safe to yur camp."

Desmond rode away to give the professor the information.

"Let's check your foot and then see if I can repair your shoe."

The farmer again took a seat and put his foot up. Elise spent the afternoon working on the shoe until she had the toe reinforced and an insert in the sole made from a piece of willow bark shaved thin to fit his foot perfectly. As his foot sweated, the bark would heat and help heal his injury.

When she was in the work shed, she saw a cracked plow blade and started the forge. It heated as she completed her project on the shoe.

"Here, try this on for comfort. I can make adjustments until its right." She slipped the shoe on his foot and laced it up.

"Me foot feels better already." He stood and took a few steps. "Ye know yur stuff, lassie."

"I noticed a cracked plow blade in the work shed. Would it be all right for me to fix it, too?"

"What would a wee lass like ye know about mending iron?" Mr. Alford asked her.

"I have several talents besides healing and repairing shoes." She grinned. "One of them is mending iron. Would you like me to show you?"

"Aye. The blade on the plow broke three months ago when I hit a large rock, which be the reason we need the field cleared of that one that fell from the sky. The last blacksmith, who could mend it, left two years ago." He walked with her toward the shed. "The plow be already broken so not likely ye can do it harm." He walked with barely a limp.

"I'd hoped you'd say that," she said as they approached the shed, "for I started a fire in the forge. It should be almost ready." She repaired the plow and reinforced several stress points using their homemade forge. It took several hours, but by their looks of gratitude, it had been worth every minute. She was also able to show the oldest son how to mend other items as they became worn or broke. The farmer and his two sons were keen students, which made the effort worthwhile.

It was growing dark by the time she set out for camp. The oldest son accompanied her until she reached the perimeter.

The farmer's wife had sent homemade bread and butter enough for their group as a thank you for her help. A treat indeed and Elise was eager to surprise them.

When she dismounted and secured her horse to the wagon for the stockmen to tend to, the camp was abuzz with loud voices. Clarence came toward her from behind the wagon holding a short sword and didn't lower it until he recognized her.

"Lady Elise. I'm glad you've safely returned. The professor was about to send me to fetch you." He glanced about as if searching for something.

"What's going on?" Elise saw the concern etched on his face. His knuckles were white as he gripped the sword hilt. She walked with him to the center of the camp. The fire pit was blazing and her fellow campers were milling about.

The professor's expression was angry, which wasn't like him. She couldn't remember ever having seen him in such a state. "Our visitors were neither cordial, nor do they intend to allow anyone but them to remove the meteorite. They were actually worshipping the rock and cutting themselves as they chanted and danced around it."

"We have been given the stone by the owner of the land. They have no right to barge in and declare it a sacred thing." Avery shouted and paced away. "I've decided I shall study law when I return home. This would be a perfect situation to call upon those in authority to remove those heathens under the penalty of death." He mumbled something about one of them calling a curse down on him, which seemed to infuriate him even more.

"They cursed you?" Elise put the bread and butter on a make-shift table fashion from the tailgate off the wagon and covered with a cloth. She saw the worry in Avery's expression that seemed to be at least part of the catalyst for his rage. Fear furrowed his brow, and he swiped the sweat off his face as he paced away.

"Desmond, you'd better warn the farmer and his sons to post guards on his livestock, for the leader had to get those chickens he sacrificed from somewhere." Michael's gaze met Elise's. "That barbarian sprinkled the chicken's blood on everything and everyone within reach. It was ghastly." He shook his head. "There's no reasoning with those people." Michael had been quiet and observant during their trip, but now his cheeks were flush with anger. Elise noticed a bloodstain on the neck of his tunic.

"I'm afraid Michael was in the wrong place at the wrong time and part of their ritual blood landed on him." Avery grimaced in sympathy.

"Aye, but I landed a punch to the man's jaw that knocked him to the ground." Michael frowned. "The stupid man didn't have the good sense to be quiet. He cursed in whatever diabolical language they were spouting, so I gave him another smack to shut him up."

"Good thing we had swords and the experience to use them. It showed we were the superior force. Otherwise, I suspect they might have tried to fight." Avery paced to the edge of the camp and gazed out to the place of the meteorite, now dark and quiet.

"Mr. Alford said he and his neighbors would help you deal with those people. Why didn't you send word?" Elise turned to the professor for the answer.

"We managed on our own to send those heathens on their way, but I'm unsure for how long?" The professor rubbed his hand across his face, his expression weary. "The dilemma remains. Do we risk the lives and wellbeing of untrained villagers and farmers in a more volatile confrontation with the pagans? I'd prefer to remove the stone and leave here before the pagans return with more disciples of their cause and take up arms against us."

Caroline stepped near her husband and hugged him from

the side. "Knowing something about that type of crazed radicals, from our travels, they may try and stir up the ignorant with vile threats and return with them to fight their cause."

The professor put an arm around his wife. "It may not be so easy to get rid of them the next time." He turned to Michael. "First thing in the morning, see if there are any men left in the village who would want to make some money to help us dig. Those pagans will have tried to spread their threats of retribution by the demons, so it may be difficult. Hire anyone with a strong back and the desire to work."

"And what would you like the rest of us to do, darling?" Caroline gazed up at her husband.

"Pray for God's mighty protection around all of us and our project." He hugged his wife close. "What those poor lost souls don't understand is that our God is far more powerful than their demons, which have deceived them into believing a horrible lie. Pray for their salvation lest it be too late to repent and they are lost to suffer the consequences of their evil and end up in a fiery hell for eternity."

CHAPTER 18

$\mathcal{A}$s William journeyed on his quest to find Elise, he prayed for God's safety over Lord and Lady Stanton and their family, for if the king's army is unable to squelch the uprising, the Black Guard might make their way as far as the duke's manor. No deaths had been reported, as of yet, but that could change at any time. William feared for Elise's safety, since she had no idea of the impending danger.

After leaving the manor, William had ridden for three days stopping only long enough to rest the horse and himself. Since Lord Stanton didn't know the exact location of the professor's destination, only the general direction, it was necessary for William to inquire of travelers along the way if they'd noticed a carriage and wagon traveling together.

Several folks had seen the professor's party, but they always pointed farther on. On the eve of the third day of his journey, he passed some peasants who refused to stop long enough to answer his questions. They had wagons filled with household items leading goats and cows. An older man leading a donkey and cart stopped at William's inquiry.

"Have you seen a carriage being followed by a wagon headed

the way you've just come in the last few days?" William's tone reflected his impatience.

The older man wiped his brow with the sleeve of his tunic. "Aye. Two days, ago, about this time, a fancy carriage with three passengers and a wagon followin' close behind. They were headed in that direction." He pointed the way, confirming William was still on the right track. "I tried to warn 'em to turn around and come with us before it's too late, but they kept goin'."

"Why? What's happened to cause you to leave?" William was relieved to hear Elise and the expedition weren't far ahead, but he feared they were heading into some kind of danger. Why hadn't the professor heeded the warning?

The old man's voice rose in anger. "Two days past, a group of heathens wearin' long cloaks, with wicked signs markin' their faces, came to our village talkin' daft. Their leader tried to scare God-fearin' folks into worshippin' him by threatenin' to call down fire from heaven and kill any who won't do his biddin'." The old man spat on the ground. "Smart folks are leavin'." He tugged on the rope to get the donkey moving again. "Ye be warned."

William had to keep tight control on the warhorse, for it sensed the fear of the fleeing villagers. The stallion snorted a warning to any who wandered too close.

Impatient to get to Elise, it took a half-hour before he reached a place on the road that was free of refugees and their flocks and could give the stallion his head. By the old man's description of the men who had come to his village, they could be a fanatical druid cult he had dealings with while in the army. If so, danger was headed Elise's way and there was nothing he could do to stop it, except pray.

William was hungry and bone weary of travel when he arrived at the next village. It was obvious, by the poor state of the buildings that this place had come on hard times.

Several villagers were milling about. No one appeared fearful or in a hurry to leave. It was a possible the pagans hadn't reached this place, since he hadn't passed anyone on the road for several hours.

William dismounted and tied Shadow to a hitching post near a watering trough. He stood beside the stallion and studied the few businesses that appeared opened, trying to decide where he might find a bit of food and information. Hopefully, what he learned could lead him to Elise.

He couldn't be that far behind, calculating the amount of time it took for a carriage and a wagon to travel in a day.

He watched as a man of some importance, according to his confident stride, fine tunic and pants, approached every man he met along the road. William couldn't hear the words, but by the shaking of the heads, the men weren't interested in whatever the man had to say.

He caught William's gaze and came toward him.

"Sir, you look like a hearty sort. Would you be interested in a job? We'll pay a good wage for any willing to work." He stepped closer and saw William's peg leg.

William ignored the man's stare. "Are you part of Professor Canterbury's party?"

"Who might you be?" The stranger stiffened and put his hand on the hilt of his short sword.

"I'm Sir William Degraf. I've been given the task of locating Lady Elise Stanton." William walked around Shadow. "It's of utmost importance. Do you know her?"

"Aye, she's safe at our camp." He glanced past William and frowned. "The timing of your arrival is most fortunate. We may have need of your sword, Sir Knight."

William turned to see what the man was looking at so intensely. Six men dressed in dark cloaks, with the hoods covering their heads, headed toward them. Their strides were stiff with determination. They had strange symbols tattooed on their faces and hands. The leader's eyes were black with hatred and evil intent. His hands were fisted at his sides.

William pulled his short sword from the scabbard on the saddle and prepared for battle. If this was the druid who had threatened all of the folks fleeing on the road, William would gladly send him into eternity. Sensing danger, Shadow snorted and pawed the ground.

"I take it you've dealt with these pagans before?" William put a hand on Shadow to calm him. With one glance, he assessed the group, but saw no visible weapons. They could have them hidden beneath their robes and pull them once they were closer, a tactic he had seen before.

"They invaded our research site last night. This morning when we commanded them to leave, they slaughtered two live chickens and flung the blood at us, all the while chanting some sort of nonsense before we ran them off with our swords." The stranger stepped up beside William to face the group and held his sword in ready.

From between two tall oaks, on the opposite side of the road from William, a man dressed as a monk stepped out into the middle of the road, positioning himself between William and the cloaked pagans. The monk held his staff at an angle with a firm grip, as someone in charge. "You people need to leave this land before the One True God and the king's soldiers put an end to you and your unholy acts."

"The fires in the sky called us here. We're on a pilgrimage to gather converts and worship at the sacred ground of our forefathers, as demanded by our religion." The leader's menacing tone was meant to intimidate. He stopped a few feet from the monk. He signaled his followers to wait behind him. "The stones were sent to us from our gods as proof of our calling. We want them."

"There's nothing around here calling you, only the one true God of all heaven and earth who calls all sinners to repentance." The monk raised his staff and spoke with authority that could be felt by William and the villagers, who'd stepped out of their homes and businesses to watch and listen. "Repent and be saved or leave and don't return. If you remain, you'll face the consequences of all of your evil lies and deeds." The monk lowered his voice but his words rang clear, as if they were spoken from on high.

William and the stranger, from the professor's party, moved up beside the monk and raised their swords. The druid leader shouted something that sounded like a curse, spat on the ground, then turned and walked away, followed by the other five.

William watched until the group was no longer in view.

"I'm Brother Peter." The monk turned toward them, and reached out to shake each man's hand. "I'm a traveling clergy who goes from village to village to marry, bury, heal the sick, and give spiritual guidance to the lost."

"I'm Lord Michael Sebastian." He lowered his sword. "I am one of the scientists who have come to research the meteorites that fell near here some nights past.

"I witnessed that spectacular display. It was a glorious reminder of God's creation." The monk turned to William. "And you are?"

"I'm Sir William Degraf, former knight in the king's army. I'm only here to locate someone." William glanced around at the people watching making sure none with hostile intent were among the gathering crowd.

Michael focused on the monk. "We have need of your services, Brother Peter. Those pagans made a big production of cursing the land and threatening folks with death, declaring they had caused the meteors to fall." The scientist rubbed his face, an expression of weariness reflexed in his voice. "Our group found a large meteorite that we're willing to remove at the owner's request. Though the farmer and his family are Christians, they fear that cult leader will continue to stir up trouble until the stones are taken away. Would you return with me and bless the land, as we make our way back to the research site?"

The monk closed his eyes and raised his face toward heaven, as if accepting the assignment from on high. "Tis my duty to speak God's truth and correct any misconception and lies told to these good folk by that emissary of the devil."

William glanced around and saw the villagers step into the road. They were hesitant at first.

"Come. You're safe. Fear not for the Lord is mightier than the evil those men preach." The monk motioned for the people to come forward. He turned to Michael. "I heard you have need of some strong backs and are willing to pay?"

"Indeed. We need to dig up the meteorites and remove them for scientific study." Michael glanced over the gathering crowd. "I fear if those pagans get possession of those rocks, they'll use them to try and torment these good people into doing their evil biding."

"If you plan to help our village stand against them heathens, then I'll work for ye." A young man with a scraggly beard stepped forward and six other men of various ages joined him.

"That should be enough to do the job." Michael gestured to the men to follow him. "Brother Peter, are you coming?"

"Aye. I'll get my kit and follow you." The monk walked to the small chapel. He returned with a knapsack slung over his shoulder and followed the procession.

William wanted to mount and ride hard to the camp but stayed behind to guard the rear. He would rather fight here if the druids chose to attack, than bring the fight into the camp and put Elise in more danger.

"That's a fine animal, Sir Knight." The monk studied the stallion.

"Shadow comes from a strong bloodline and has been proven worthy in many battles." William remained alert for signs of the enemy. He was sure the druids had no intention of leaving without a fight.

"Did you lose your leg in battle?" The monk glanced at William's pine peg.

"Aye." William was used to people's curiosity. Brother Peter was no different, but William didn't elaborate and the monk didn't press the matter.

"It's just like God to send a seasoned warrior when the people have need of one." The monk wasted no more time on idle chatter. He reached out and blessed the land as they walked and spoke God's protection over all believers who dwelled here.

When they reached the camp, there were three men already digging around the perimeter of a stone, which could be seen sticking out of the earth. The scientist led the monk and the men from the village out to the site and made introductions.

William rode on to the camp and dismounted when he spotted Elise tending a fire. A large iron pot hung over it, and the smell of a hearty soup bubbled from the top.

"Elise." Relief rushed over him, until he barely suppressed the urge to sweep her into his arms.

She turned toward him. "William!" Surprise, then joy lit her face, as she started toward him. After a few steps, she stopped. "What are you doing here?" Worry furrowed her brow. "Is everyone all right?" Worry furrowed her brow. "You have Shadow. Is John, okay?"

"Your family is all safe, but you might not be." He told her the story of the Black Guard and watched as fear widened her eyes. The other matters he had to discuss with her required privacy.

"We'll need to tell the professor, for he, his wife, and two others on the expedition are of noble blood and could also be on the assassin's list." She motioned toward the busy worksite and frowned. "The professor won't leave until he gets the meteorite out of the ground and back to the school in London."

"I'm sorry, but we can't wait." William stepped forward. He regretted she would have to leave, but the added threat of warring pagans, her safety was at stake. "Your father sent me to bring you back immediately. Gather only what possessions will fit in a knapsack. The rest you'll have to trust the professor to return later." Declaring it was at her parent's request to return her to the manor, he expected her to do his bidding, but she didn't move.

"Since my family is safe, and I'm out of harm's way, I'd rather stay here, at least for the time being. I've come to help with the excavation and research of this site." The familiar expression of determination was evident by her raised chin and stiff posture. "There's so much to learn from these meteorites." She relaxed her stance and gave him a beseeching smile. "Besides, you're here now, so I'm perfectly safe."

"There are no fortress walls or trained soldiers to keep you safe in this place." William couldn't keep the anger from lacing his tone at her lack of concern for the possible danger. "It looks to me like you're doing the cooking and not helping with the research."

"We each have to take turns preparing the meal. Today is my day. Even the professor contributed on his day." She stirred the soup with a long handled wooden spoon.

"The Black Guard are trained assassins who will not spare you because you are a woman." He waved his hand toward the group in the distance. "I doubt if any of those men could survive a confrontation with one of them." He recognized her expression of stubborn intent. He rubbed a hand over his face to calm the argument stirring within him. Hauling her over his shoulder and taking her against her will wouldn't work, but he was sorely tempted.

"William, I'm not going anywhere until the project is complete." She always tilted her head whenever she was ready to meet any opposition with a lengthy argument to have her way. Her gaze met his and stirred his heart with love. In spite of his better judgment, he submitted to her will, as often happened in the past.

"Then I should see how I can help secure your safety." With a glance around the camp, he saw areas where he could make a few improvements. By arranging the tents in a circle around the fire, with the openings pointing towards the center, it would be easier to keep track of everyone and less likely the camp could be surprised by an intruder.

"Thank you, William." Her smile reminded him of his next mission. He needed to confess his love and ask her to marry him. If Jeremy was right, Elise still loved him. But what if she spoke of another William? He had to know.

He stepped closer and lowered his voice. "It's important that I speak to you privately." Before William could say more, Brother Peter came into camp carrying an empty water crock.

"Where do I find fresh water to fill this? Digging is hard work and the men have need of a good supply." He glanced from William to Elise. "I take it this is that *someone* you've been commissioned to find?"

"Brother Peter, this is Lady Elise Stanton." William stepped closer to Elise without touching her, though he ached to pull her into his arms to declare openly his intent to wed her.

"Brother Peter, I'm so glad you're here." She greeted the monk with a welcoming smile and motioned for him to follow her. "Perhaps you could hold a service this evening to fill this place with the Word of God and worship. It would be a lovely way to wash away the evil chants those pagans spouted over this area."

William led Shadow and followed, as Elise guided the monk to the water barrels, which were attached to a wagon parked behind the tents. William watered the stallion and found a place with tall grass away from the other horses and traded the bridle for a halter. He staked the warhorse out with enough rope to graze. Once Shadow was settled, William removed the saddle, his sword, and supplies.

"I'll share my best sermon." The monk filled the crock and heaved it onto his shoulder with little effort and returned to the men.

William walked with Elise back to the camp. Alone again, William dropped off his things beside the tent she said was hers. He opened his mouth to tell Elise what was burning within him, when a tall woman with blond hair approached them.

"William, this is Lady Caroline, the professor, Lord Isaac Canterbury's wife." Elise barely got the words out when a workman walked into camp.

"I was sent up 'ere to get this cut tended." The workman extended his injured hand toward them.

"Sit down and I'll get my supplies." Elise hurried to her tent and came back with what she needed.

Outnumbered, William left the camp to check out the perimeter. He needed to see what could be done to better secure the camp and meteorite site. The pagan leader didn't strike him as someone who would give up his goal without a fight. He would need a plan to protect Elise when that happened.

The evening meal was full of chatter and good humor. Elise's soup was hearty and enjoyed by all, if the empty bowls were any indication. William got a chance to meet and observe the rest of those included in the expedition. The professor insisted no one in their immediate group be addressed by their title. They were all equals in this place, as far as he and the others were concerned. The informality would be hard for William, as a commoner, when speaking to these nobles, who were strangers.

William dealt with the interest he saw in the people's eyes when they stared at his peg leg. "I lost my leg in a great battle, against a hoard of French invaders, while in service to the king." He made eye contact with Avery. His youth made it easy to read the question on his mind. "Yes. It hurt when the enemy's battle ax came smashing down on me." His tone was jovial to lighten his words and the group laughed at Avery's surprise. The mystery of William's missing leg dealt with, the people visibly relaxed in his presence and returned to their conversations concerning their project.

Following William's suggestions, the professor appointed each man their time and place at guard duty before anyone retired for the night.

William made his pallet next to Elise's tent opening. He tied Shadow close by. The stallion would let him know if a stranger approached.

He sat cross-legged on his mat and waited until the camp quieted.

"Are you going to sleep there all night?" Elise stepped out of her tent. Her tone was soft and intimate, not to disturb the others trying to rest.

The campfire glistened gold against her dark hair, which was loose and hanging down over her shoulders and down her back.

William stood and his heart sped up. "That's my plan." He needed to tell her that he knew of the wanted poster and of her vow to Jeremy, but his thoughts were consumed with a need to embrace her and tell her of his love.

Desmond walked by on his guard duty, drawing William back to reality.

"Tell me about your trip here. Since you're riding Shadow, you must have seen John along the way." Her gaze soft and inviting. She made herself comfortable on a campstool she'd carried from her tent and placed at the opening.

"I traveled with your brother to London. It's an interesting story, which I'll gladly tell you another time when it's not so late." William would enjoy telling her the highlights of the trip, leaving out John's vow to become a monk. By the interaction he witnessed between John and the nun called, Julianna, William doubted either would become wards of the church.

"I have guard duty soon. We need to be rested to face whatever tomorrow brings." He waited for her to step back inside her tent.

"Thank you, William for coming." She released the flap of the tent, and soon the glow of her candle ceased when she blew it out.

When convinced all was well, he stretched out on his mat and slept.

CHAPTER 19

*E*lise slept soundly knowing William was close by and awoke refreshed and more hopeful for a good outcome for the expedition than she'd felt since the pagans had first appeared.

She knew William well enough to realize there was something weighing on his mind. He would speak of it when he was ready. She washed her face and would have changed clothes, but she hadn't anything fresh to wear and wouldn't until she did some wash, so she put on the tunic and pants she'd saved for when she worked with the forge. She could almost hear William's censor, as the time he'd found her wearing the same type of *peasant* clothes when he'd rescued her from the flying wing.

When she stepped out of her tent, William's mat was gone and she couldn't see him anywhere. Her heart raced. Had he changed his mind and decided to return without her?

"Did you think I'd abandoned you?" William's voice startled her and she turned to see him approaching from behind her tent. His hair was damp and his beard freshly trimmed.

"I did wonder where you'd gone." Her racing heart calmed to

a flutter of relief, releasing a silly grin of appreciation, for he was very handsome.

"I've been given charge over filling the barrels with fresh water." He glanced at her attire but other than raising his eyebrows, kept his thoughts to himself.

"Mr. Alford came to visit yesterday to look at the progress we're making. I heard him tell Desmond that there is a spring of clear water located near a shallow river not far from here." Hopefully she could go along. Depending on what chores the professor assigned her, she might have enough time to address the washing. Caroline had complained yesterday about her lack of fresh clothing too.

It was a chore neither of them relished, but it would have to be done soon, for once the stone was removed, they would be striking camp and heading back to London without further delay.

"Could I go to the stream with you? None are allowed out of camp alone, and I really need to tend to some wash. I have nothing clean to wear." She brushed a hand down her tunic as a way of explanation for her current attire.

"Aye." William glanced around the camp, as if checking for any breech in the security. "I'd prefer to keep you with me. Gather your items and meet me near the wagon after the morning meal."

The farmer's wife supplied bread and fresh churned butter every morning for a fee, which was gladly paid, for she was a good cook. The farmer supplied fresh meat for their noon meal.

Their group was eating well, which made the workmen happy. No one expressed surprise when she showed up at the meal in her tunic and pants. Perhaps it was the primitive conditions and lack of servants to keep up the laundry, but not even the professor or Caroline appeared shocked or dismayed.

After helping Caroline clean up the remnants of the meal, Elise gathered the items she needed to wash. She could hear the workmen joking with one another down at the worksite, probably to dispel the heaviness that remained over the area even after a hearty sermon by Brother Peter last evening.

"Yea!" Voices raised in triumph. They must have succeeded in finding the bottom of the stone, which was the task they'd set themselves at breakfast.

The load of wash she'd gathered was abandoned in a heap on her cot. She had to see what the excitement was about. Leaving her tent, she headed cross the camp toward the worksite.

"Where are you going?" William appeared at her elbow.

"You could give a body warning if you're going to sneak up on them." Elise released her grip on the dagger at her waist.

"I waited for you by the wagon, but when you didn't show, I came to see what was keeping you." He walked beside her as they approached the excited workmen.

"I couldn't wait to see what they'd found." She was surprised that the size of the stone wasn't as big as the professor had expected.

As they approached the site, the farmer arrived leading a team of stout workhorses. Someone must have sent for him to help with the excavation, since the professor's team was needed to pull the wagon with the water barrels and the carriage horses were both saddled waiting to be used for other purposes.

Their audience listened to the shouts of instructions as the harness, worn by the farmer's draft horses, was readied to be attached to the stone by ropes and chains. The meteorite needed to be removed from the hole before the workmen erected an A-frame to hoist the stone into the air high enough to back the professor's wagon beneath it. Then, as requested by the farmer, the hired help from town would fill in the hole so the farmer could work the land without difficulty.

Elise and William met Caroline at the work site.

"Isn't it exciting?" Caroline had circled the activity at a safe distance, before stopping near Elise. "It will take time to get the stone ready to put on the wagon." She glanced at Elise. "Are two going to get water? I need to go too, if I or Isaac are to have anything clean to wear." She smiled at William. "I suspect you've volunteered to be our escort."

William glanced over the site where the men worked. "Do you know exactly where we'll find this river?"

"Mr. Alford or his sons have always brought us fresh water, but since he and his sons are here helping, my husband said we'd have to do this chore ourselves this time." Caroline glanced around and saw her husband. He was too busy with the workmen for her to get his attention. "I know we need to return with the wagon before they're ready to load the stone, so we shouldn't delay. I was there when Mr. Alford told my husband the best way to get to the river is a shortcut, which is less than a quarter mile that way. See the tree line?" Caroline pointed to a thick copse of trees. "I think it's that way."

"I thought I saw a wagon trail when I was last on top of the hill." Elise headed to the rocky mound. "I'll climb up to confirm its location." She glanced at William and raised a hand to halt his protest. "I've climbed it several times since we've arrived, and I've found the quickest way up and down." She gave William a teasing grin. "I won't be long, since what I'm wearing will make the climb much easier and faster."

❧

Before he could stop her, Elise started her climb, and as she said, she was at the top in a few minutes. She put her hand up to shade against the sun and pointed toward the grove of trees. "You're right. The wagon trail leads to the river, that way, beyond those trees."

"Fine. Now come down." William had a bad feeling in the pit of his stomach.

Several friends and family members of the workmen, by the

jovial calls back and forth, arrived to watch the excitement of the stone's removal. An adventurous youth climbed up the opposite side of the rocky mound from Elise, to watch as the team of horses hauled the stone from its resting place. A great cheer erupted from everyone present as the meteorite was pulled several feet away from the sizeable crater made necessary to unearth it.

The ground began to rumble, slowly at first. The sound grew to a roar and the earth heaved and moved, as if a monster within the mound had been awakened by the activity. Rocks slipped down the side of it and the mound began to crumble. People screamed and the youth standing at the top, scrambled down, causing more rocks to shift. A workman grabbed the boy and pulled him to safety as huge boulder gathered momentum behind him.

William watched in horror. Elise struggled to keep her footing as the ground beneath her shifted.

"Help!" She threw out her arms to keep her balance then disappeared from sight.

"Elise!" William's heart pounded with fear. He started up the crumbling sides in a desperate need to get to where he'd last seen her.

Men from the worksite and visiting villagers rushed forward to help, but backed off as several large boulders shifted and rolled down, smashing anything it their path.

William's peg slipped against the shifting soil, as the rocky landscape rumbled beneath him. He struggled to find solid ground to push his way up. Dirt clung to his body, face, and hands, but he managed to reach the place where Elise had disappeared from sight.

A large black hole was all that remained.

"Elise!" He couldn't see any movement inside. His heart pounded with the fear of losing her. "Oh, God, we need a miracle."

"What happened?" Below him the professor shouted to be heard, then started to climb, but backed down when the mound shook again, sending more rocks tumbling down.

"She fell into a large cavern, professor!" William shouted. "Keep everyone away, until I can make sure they won't put Elise in more danger."

The professor moved a safe distance away and issued orders in preparations for a rescue.

"I can't see inside to tell if she's hurt." William yelled down at the crowd staring up at him. "Desmond, bring me a long rope and a torch. No one else should attempt to come up here. It isn't safe." Besides being strong and fit, William had overheard Desmond tell another man of how he'd climbed mountains and helped rescue fellow rock climbers in his youth. William hoped Desmond was a man of his word, for Elise's life depended on him to do what was needed.

There was a mad dash by two workmen to get the rope needed as William hovered over the open hole.

"Elise, are you okay?" William's voice held a hint of panic. He fought to gain control, for from his experience, those who had survived being injured in battle were the ones who had remained calm. He needed her to survive.

He called down to her again but couldn't hear a response. There was too much noise coming from excited shouts on the ground. He waved his hand for attention. "Quiet." When a hush finally fell over the group, he again, called down into the darkness. This time he heard a faint whimper.

William called to the professor. "She's alive." He watched as the professor started workmen clearing a path near the mound.

The ground rumbled again, and the workmen stepped back.

With a pack on his back, Desmond made his way up to William's position and held out a rope. William grabbed it and threw one end over the ledge of the hole while Desmond tied the other end to a large granite boulder away from the opening.

"Step back while I lower myself down." William walked up to the edge of the cavern.

"I'll stay nearby so I can hear you if you call for help." Desmond handed him a leather pouch. "This contains water and here is cloth for bandages if needed." William gave him a nod of appreciation and tucked the cloth into his tunic then turned his attention to the task at hand.

Desmond positioned himself beside the boulder. "Let me know when you've reached the bottom, and I'll drop down a torch." The driver, and one-time mountain climber, knelt and pulled out a flint from his pack, then a smoothed piece of oak with moss wrapped tightly around one end.

Relieved that Desmond had proved himself a good choice, William tucked the long strap of the water pouch over his shoulder resting it across his chest to leave his hands free. He tugged the rope to make sure it was secure then lowered himself into the dark abyss.

The musty stench reminded him of the old cave he, John, and Elise had found with they were children. He hoped it didn't have the same evil relics inside. A knot of fear clenched his insides for Elise's safety.

He landed on the floor and stumbled over a large rock. As he fought to get his balance, his peg slipped on the loose stones that littered the bottom of the cavern. He grabbed hold of the rope and regained his footing. The close call reminded him to take his time. If he were injured, it could risk both his and Elise's life.

As his eyes adjusted to the darkness, he glanced around until he spotted a dark figure just out of the muted light seeping in from above. It had to be Elise. "I'm ready. Send me the torch."

A torch arced down toward him. He caught it before it hit the floor.

"Elise?" He picked his way to where she lay in a crumbled heap, and knelt by her side. When he touched her face, his fingers came back wet and sticky. The copper smell of blood was potent. He wedged the torch between two large rocks to free his hands.

"Please, God help her." He quoted the same healing scriptures that had been spoken over him, as he ran his hands across her head, shoulders, and down each arm and leg, making note of every place she winced or moaned at his touch. "Elise."

She blinked and reached out and touched his face. "William." It was a hoarse whisper. "You're real."

"Aye, my love." He wanted to crush her within his embrace, but feared to move her. He raised her only enough to give her a drink of water.

"Help me." She stirred, and he supported her enough to sit.

She put an arm around his waist and hugged him tight. "I knew you'd save me." He wiped the blood off of her forehead with the sleeve of his tunic. It didn't seem to be but a scratch, but, as with most head wounds, it had bled enough to soak the front of her tunic. He pulled the cloth from his tunic and tore a section off to wrap around her head wound. She stiffened but didn't cry out.

"Where do you hurt?" He watched for signs of shock, but her pupils remained even. "Does you head hurt?"

"A little, but my arm aches like the time I felt out of the hayloft." Her voice grew stronger.

"If I remember correctly, you fell on top of me or you would have been seriously injured."

She winced but managed a wisp of a smile. "I was spying on you and John because you wouldn't let me help train Shadow."

She allowed him to help her stand, but cried out when she put pressure on her right foot.

"It's my ankle." She swiveled her foot and sucked in a deep breath at the motion. "Full range, so no break."

"Sit and let me wrap your ankle." He helped her to sit.

She gasped as he tied the remaining cloth, tightly to stabilize it.

"I'm sorry I hurt you, but it has to be tight to avoid further injury." His voice repentant, but he completed his ministrations. "It's time to get you out of here."

She leaned against William, and he supported her weight easily.

"This reminds me of that cave we found." Elise's voice lowered to a whisper when she glanced around the dusty tomb-like room.

He felt her shiver and pulled her tighter against his side. "We're far from that evil place. You're safe." Or so he prayed. He looked around and spotted something unusual.

"Wait. Look at that." He retrieved the torch and pointed it toward some objects near the wall. There were six large clay jars lined up in a row. A wave of the torch revealed many symbols painted on the walls. Christian symbols by the signs of the cross and images of halos over the heads of certain figures.

"Oh, William, it's beautiful." In the single torch light, it was barely visible. A large picture, with faded colors depicted a large cloud with lightning coming from the sky and touching a mountain. There were words, as if being etched by the light-ning. Below the picture was a wall painting of the Ten Commandments written in Latin.

The first commandment caught William's attention by its bold colors. *Thou shalt have no other gods before me.*

Elise released him and touched other symbols on the wall, tracing them with her fingertips. "I think this is Aramaic." She limped a few feet further. "And these are Hebrew. The professor or Caroline should be able to translate them."

A sudden scattering of rocks fell into the cavern from above getting their attention and reminding them of the danger. There was no more time to investigate their surroundings.

"First, we need to get out of here, so we're able to report our discovery, then we'll find a way to stabilize the opening lest the whole thing comes down and buries this chamber and its treasures." William gathered her in his arms and carried her back to the rope dangling from the opening. He set her on her feet long enough to tie a loop in the end of the rope. "Put your uninjured foot in there and hang on."

"Wait. Shine the torch there." Elise pointed to something reflecting in the torch light. It was a large metal cross partly hidden beneath the rocks.

"Elise." William tone was not to be ignored.

"I'm ready." She hugged the rope with one arm and held on tightly.

"Desmond she's ready to come out. Take it slow." William lifted her as far as he could reach and watched her disappear out of the opening. He left the torch propped up between two large rocks to leave his hands free. The rope dropped down, and he climbed out. There was no reason for Desmond to have to pull him out like an invalid.

With the mound unstable, he had Desmond carry Elise down the slippery path dodging rocks and boulders, for fear his peg would slip and send them both plunging to the ground below.

Nearer to the bottom, the workmen had cleared the path. William followed Desmond as he deposited Elise at the campsite then left to help where he was needed.

Elise's excited demands to speak with the professor and Caroline, brought them hurrying to her side. They listened in awed silence to her observations of what she'd seen within the cavern. Their excitement grew as William confirmed her observations and added his own account.

When Elise winced in pain, William insisted that was enough information for now. He carried her inside her tent so Caroline could tend to her injuries and help her to bed.

Once the women disappeared into the tent, the professor hurried off to explore the cavern for himself.

William hovered outside Elise's tent, leaving only long enough to fetch Caroline a bucket of water. When he took a seat by the campfire, William noticed his wooden peg had sustained several chips and a substantial crack in the process of rescuing Elise. He would need to ask around to see if there were a carpenter in their midst who could fashion him a new one and soon or he would need to find a staff to keep his balance.

Two days later

*W*illiam remained in camp, wanting to stay near Elise in case he was needed. The accident put him on edge.

Too much attention had been given to the discovery and he noticed the guards assigned to patrol the camp's perimeter were often gathered at the mound. The professor shouted orders and got them back on the job, but for how long? These were not trained, professional soldiers used to following orders, but villagers and farmers who were being paid for their help.

During the instruction of their duties, William had warned each of them to call out if they saw any strangers, but their willingness and ability to fight remained in question.

Dirty and tired, the professor returned in time for the evening meal. He was followed by workmen leading the two carriage horses. Each horse had two large baskets strapped to their backs. The baskets were filled to overflowing with artifacts. He supervised the delivery of the baskets to his tent before he came out and joined their group. Professor Canterbury held up a large cross, the one Elise had noticed in the cavern. Their group's excited chatter surrounding the day's events hushed as their attention was drawn to the ancient piece.

Caroline helped Elise from her tent to join them. Elise's ankle was bound tightly and instead of a shoe, her foot was covered with a piece of oil cloth to keep it clean. William stood and helped her to a stool next to the one he'd vacated.

The professor sat near his wife and tilted the cross towards the evening sun. "The simple straight lines of the design are highly unusual. But its simplicity draws attention to the more decorative markings on both sides." He ran his thumb across the symbols etched in its smooth surface. "It's Hebrew and on one side the translation reads, *Jesus is Lord.* He flipped it over. "The other side reads, *All Hail King Jesus.*" He studied the metal with a magnifying glass. "It's made from an alloy I'm unfamiliar, but based on dates noted on some of the other artifacts within the cavern, the cross is at least four hundred years old." He handed it to his wife, who hovered near his elbow. "Feel how light-weight, but strong it is."

"Could it be forged from metal gleaned from the meteorites, or perhaps an ore-rich mineral once mined around here?" Lady Caroline handed it to Elise. "A large deposit of iron ore deep beneath the earth in this location could be the reason the stones are drawn here on a regular basis."

Elise inspected the cross with one hand. Her sprained and bruised shoulder and left arm were confined to a sling to immobilize them. "This reminds me of a candlestick I purchase in Spain. The metal had a similar composition." She ran a finger across the surface of the cross, and then balanced it on two fingers as if weighing it. "The craftsman who made the candlestick called it *metromium.*" She glanced at the professor. "He said the element came from a meteorite he'd found when he was a boy. Hopefully, we can find more of this special metal, for I need it for a special project I have in mind."

William cringed when the sunlight highlighted the bruising

on Elise's beautiful face. Left uncovered, the scratch on her forehead had stopped bleeding, but a purple bruise surrounded it. Her movements were slow and stiff indicating sore muscles and many more scrapes and bruises sustained in her fall.

He felt sick inside knowing she could have died in that cave-in as he watched helplessly from the ground. She required rest and time to heal before she could travel. He feared, as she felt better, she might still refuse to return to the manor. He'd heard the excitement in her voice, as she examined the cross, and there were many antiquities yet to be uncovered.

A dread stirred within him. He couldn't shake the feeling of impending danger.

As the news spread of a cavern filled with valuable treasure, it will attract more unsavory people and could embolden the pagans to cause more trouble.

He needed to persuade Elise to leave this place. Perhaps he could borrow the professor's carriage, if he promised to return it once he delivered her safely to her parents.

His stern warnings to the guards and the scientists couldn't stem the excitement generated by the find. Their joy was contagious, once the workers realized something historically good and not evil had been found inside the mound. All afternoon the workmen remained busy filling in the hole left by the meteorite, to keep distracted workers from falling into it. They used rocks and boulders removed from the landslide, which blocked the paths up to the top of the mound. As a finishing touch they used the earth from the dig to smooth it off.

The meteorite that was once the main focus of this expedition remained where it had been abandoned after the cave-in. The farmer took his horses and harness home to use on the farm.

As the people worked, they sang songs of celebration, which were often sung at weddings and the birth of a child. The tune carried up to the camp.

William took charge of the food Mr. Alford brought for the afternoon meal, releasing the farmer to converse with the professor and his wife.

"There is a treasure trove of history and artifacts in that cavern, which could take months if not years to catalog." The professor ushered his wife and Mr. Alford toward their tent. "Normally the artifacts would have been left in place until each item was thoroughly documented, but regrettably, the site is still too unstable. Forsaking the usual stringent protocol, I've made as many notes as possible and carefully brought up several of the more important artifacts, for fear of them being destroyed or lost forever in another cave-in." The three disappeared inside Lord and Lady Canterbury's tent.

William spread out the food and served Elise a portion before helping himself to the lamb stew. Elise picked at her food.

"William, I'm not very hungry, could you help me back to my tent?" After making sure she had developed a fever, he helped her to her cot. Weary and in pain, he left her to her ablutions.

He asked around and found a carpenter who assured William that he could make him an identical peg in a couple of hours. William offered to help, but the man insisted he could work faster on his own. After taking several measurements, he left.

With four men assigned to guard the camp, William rode Shadow to escort Desmond and Clarence, as they drove the wagon to the river to fill the water barrels. William planned to surprise Elise with freshly laundered clothes. He'd hired two women, from the village, eager to earn a good wage, while their husbands worked on the mound. While the women did the wash in the river, the men went up stream to fill the water barrels.

William remained on guard, for he couldn't shake the feeling of impending trouble.

An hour later, he escorted the village women and the water wagon back to the camp.

After a long rest, Elise awoke, for he heard her squeal with delight to find clean clothes waiting for her.

"Thank you, William!" She poked her head out of the tent then retreated to change into more proper attire.

The carpenter delivered the new peg for William. The only problem was it was a fraction too long, making it impossible for William to walk without a limp. The man warned him the wood was still green and would shrink in time, which he allowed for in the extra length. William paid the man and not willing to offend the craftsman, waited until he'd gone to make the necessary adjustments with a sharp ax.

That evening the professor and Caroline waited until after the evening meal then asked for everyone's attention.

"We have an exciting announcement." He put his arm around his wife and grinned like a man with a secret too big to keep to himself. "Mr. Alford has agreed to sell us this eighty-acre plot of land. He and his family are to retain equal rights to the historic artifacts from the cavern. In exchange, my wife and I are going to build a school of science and technology here on this site. It will be a place to learn without the hypocrisy and limitations in science. The building and maintenance of the school will put many villagers to work for a long while."

"Aye!" The workers who had been invited to the meal, cheered and someone with a lute played a happy tune.

William hated to put a damper on the festivities, but for safety's sake he had to say something. He ushered the professor aside.

"I must remind you that there are some evil people still out there wishing you harm." He saw he had the professor's full attention. "If the Black Guard venture this far, you must know what to do. They are trained assassins, who are willing to commit the most heinous crimes to earn their blood money."

William hated to see his words steal the joy of the professor's recent good news and replace it with fear. "You can't let your passion for this project to distract you from an even more imminent threat. Those pagans you encountered, before I arrived, are not gone, according to some of the villagers who have seen their camp not two miles away, near the river." He lowered his voice to keep it from carrying to the others still celebrating the good news. "I met their leader the day I arrived. He had the look of a zealot. It's been my experience those types are not easily deterred from their goal. The druid leader proclaimed they intended to possess that large meteorite you just unearthed. Now that it's free, they may try to steal it by gathering more people to their cause. These threats must be taken seriously."

The professor stared at the ground, as if in thought. "I will do whatever you think is necessary to protect our encampment, and since we've made a pledge to buy this land, we'll stay and protect it and our discovery. Tomorrow, I'll send Michael to the nearest outpost to bring trained soldiers here."

"Since that could take days if not weeks, there are things that must be done immediately." Until Elise was well enough to travel, he would need to keep her safe. To do that William needed to secure the camp beginning with training more villagers as guard and instructing workmen where to build gates and fences at every access point.

William gathered the men of their group and Brother Peter to inform them of his plan and get their input. It would be a long night.

CHAPTER 20

$\mathcal{E}$lise woke stiff and everything hurt, even after three days. Her heart still raced at the memory of falling into the cavern, though knowing William was nearby gave her a measure of comfort.

He had come in to check on her in the night when she cried out from a bad dream where she was falling and falling. After he gave a drink of water, he spoke softly of home and family, until she fell back to sleep.

Something was different about him, since he arrived here. She no longer had the feeling he was trying to escape being alone with her, instead there was boldness when he smiled at her, sending warmth within her being. He made eye contact without glancing away, as he used to do.

She rubbed her temple trying to remember something he said last night. She'd been so weary, for Caroline had given her a draught to help her sleep.

Had he said he loved her? Her heart thudded with the possibility. Though, it might have been another dream. But what if he had declared his love and she was too sleepy to acknowledge it? What did he expect to do about it? Before she had him bound to a pledge of marriage, she'd better ask him to repeat what he said. The sooner, the better.

Getting out of her cot without Caroline's help was a challenge, but by gritting her teeth against the pain she managed to sit up. She was determined not to be a burden to Caroline, who had tended to her needs, when she was needed to help the professor with cataloging the artifacts.

Elise swung her legs over the side of her cot and tried to rise but fell back with a muffled screech of pain. The bandage had been removed last night to care for her swollen ankle, now it throbbed from lack of support. She tried again and managed to make it to her feet. With effort that left her weak and sweating, she managed to get through her ablutions. Removing her nightgown required trial and error with only one arm. She winced when she saw the dark bruising on her face and body reflected in a mirror, Caroline had loaned her. At least, she hadn't broken any bones, for which she gave thanks to God. She'd heal…eventually.

Elise had one dress that fastened in the front making it possible to dress herself, but not without muffled cries. She adjusted the sling, which hung over her neck and across her shoulder to protect and rest her arm. Being unable to use that arm was fast becoming annoying.

Caroline slipped into Elise's tent. "I see you're up and dressed." Her tone relayed her concern. "You should've waited for me to help you. If you overdo, it can take you longer to heal." She rewrapped Elise's ankle and put a hand under Elise's uninjured arm to help her out of the tent.

William was there waiting. "How are you?"

"I'll live." Elise tried to keep her tone light and cheerful but every step took concentration. His gaze searched hers and she blushed. His expression revealed surprise then question. As others came to inquire of her condition, William waited nearby until the well-wishers moved off.

He handed her a crutch made out of a sturdy branch. "This might help you get around while your ankle heals." The V at the top was padded with lamb's wool. "Let's make sure it fits." He waited while she slipped the crutch under her uninjured arm. "It's a bit long."

He cut a small piece off the bottom several times until it fit perfectly.

One of the workmen came into the camp and waved William over. He walked off with the man deep in conversation.

The crutch helped to steady her while standing but taking a step, was awkward. It would take time to gain confidence and balance. It gave her a deeper insight into what William had faced on a daily basis. She marveled at how effortlessly he made it look to walk on the pine peg without the aid of any support.

She kept her movements to a minimum, but made it to the professor's tent to help Caroline catalog several more recent items brought up from the cavern. When Caroline left to help supervise the afternoon meal, Elise had time to examine the cross again.

Without a doubt, the lightweight metal was similar to the candlestick she purchased in Spain. The metal would be perfect to use to fashion William a better leg to replace the pine peg. Hope rekindled made her determined to find more of that alloy.

Once the school was built and the right equipment was brought here and set up, they'd be able to simplify the process of testing the meteorites.

She had been working out the design for his new leg for over a year. It would be flat, with a slight curve, more like a carriage spring, so it would flex when he walked, absorbing more of the force, as it struck the ground.

She grew excited whenever she thought of the possibilities. The invention could help countless other amputees, if it worked for William.

Elise heard the worker's chatter, as they passed the camp.

The villagers that had come to see the meteorite removed and were witness to the discovery of the cavern also heard of the plans for a school of science. They headed home to spread the good news of prosperity coming to their village.

That evening after a simple meal of roasted mutton and fruit, Caroline shared the sketches of the artifacts she and Elise had cataloged, releasing a fresh wave of excitement around the campfire among their group.

Elise was amused to see, Avery's determination to learn more about rock climbing. He and Desmond spent hours practicing knots and expounding on rescue techniques, since the catastrophe.

In spite of the good news, Elise couldn't ignore the feeling that something bad was coming. Richard could find her here as the news spread about the discovery and her part in it. She didn't like feeling helpless and a burden. Perhaps it would be better for all if she returned with William to Sarah's and rejoined her family, at least until such matters were resolved.

The scientists sat around the firepit and rambled on about each new discovery.

"As I explored the mound after the cave-in, I found evidence that this site is rich with numerous meteorites strikes. I think once we start to analyze the rocks that make up the stone hedge, we'll find many more." The professor set his tea aside and stood as if he couldn't sit still another moment.

"Tell them, Isaac." Caroline's tone held excitement.

"Even though it wasn't the ideal conditions, I risked opening two of the clay urns and found one held many scrolls in Hebrew and Aramaic. The other held scrolls with pagan symbols, which Caroline interpreted. Since this is her expertise, it is best she explains what she found.

Caroline stood so everyone could see her.

"I've studied ancient cultures, languages and symbols for many years." She closed her eyes as if recalling the story before she continued. "I dared not bring the scroll out of the safety of the tent, so bear with me as I recall the text." She gazed into the fire. "This land was once ruled by a powerful pagan priest, called Mather, which interpreted in English means, *a mighty army*. He killed…" She paused. "I think it is more accurate to say he tortured and sacrificed to his gods any who opposed him or his pagan practices until none dared come into this land without paying homage and tribute to him and his rule."

Caroline strolled around the campfire with her hands clasped before her. "Mather became very ill and no amount of chants or sacrifices made a difference. He only grew worse as the growth on his side enlarged, turned black and foul. One day a man showed up to their camp boldly declaring, the Most High God, creator of heaven and earth, had sent him from a far land to speak to a man named, Mather." Caroline waved her hand in a manner of dismissal. "The story is much longer and far more detailed, but the short version is the holy man led the pagan leader to Jesus. After he renounced all of his pagan gods and practices, the growth miraculously disappeared. He was healed and restored to health." When her audience clapped, she raised her hand for silence. "There's more. As a new Christian, one night Mather was wakened by three mighty angels who told him secret things about him, only God could know, confirming the power of the one true God who created heaven and earth." Caroline's voice carried her excitement, as she shared the amazing story of the wicked man's redemption.

Elise glanced around the firepit at the listeners and noticed they sat as enthralled as she. Even Brother Peter's eyes glistened with tears of joy at the testimony of a lost soul saved from an eternity in hell.

The discovery of these documents revealed Mather's legacy of salvation continued to bless the lives of many generations later.

Caroline's tone grew serious. "Being the leader of the cult,

Mather's conversion caused all matter of upheaval by his followers, splitting the group. After a failed attempt to overthrow him, the rebelling pagans declared they would one day return and reclaim the land." She paused and took a drink of tea the professor handed her before she continued. "I assume our recent visitors are descendants of those pagans who departed." Her expression remained somber. "According to the Mather's notes, those who remained, which he numbered at over one thousand, denounced the old ways and accepted Christ Jesus as their Savior. The holy man remained to teach them the Word of God until the end of his days. Mr. Alford is most likely a descendant of those early Christians whose legacy lives on." She bowed her head and swept her hand out and curtseyed, as an actor might at the end a performance. "And that, my friends, was merely a brief summary from the notes I finished documenting." The group clapped their appreciation. She took a seat next to her husband. "From what I gleaned from the scrolls and cave painting, the story is extensive as it documents many testimonies of God's supernatural healing and redemption within their group. I dare not do more in-depth research, until I have better facilities to protect the integrity of the artifacts and scrolls."

The professor stood. "Therefore, with Mr. Alford's help, we've chosen a location for the first structure. I've commissioned a local builder to start immediately preparing the ground for our temporary quarters to be constructed. Then we will send for a well-known architect, whom we know, to come. He will design and build the main school building and others."

"So, you'll not be going back to London?" Elise stretched her tired and achy limbs and turned her attention to Caroline.

"We'll remain here until the building is well underway, then we'll go to London to complete some business and gather our belongings and supplies. Michael has also offered to remain here and supervise the project until our return." Caroline moved her stool closer to Elise. "I realize good news travels fast, but our plan is to keep the depth of our discovery as quiet as possible. We'll soon have all the proper papers of ownership completed and filed. Isaac has asked William with his military experience to write out a plan to improve our defenses. We've asked Mr. Alford to be our liaison with the villagers, to ask for their help in protecting our site from intruders." She grew serious. "We would greatly appreciate your discretion in the matter, since you're returning home soon. We're asking everyone to keep secret what we found." Caroline stroked her cat, Tabitha, which had been strangely absent most of their time here.

"As much as I would like to tell my family of the amazing artifacts, I'll keep the story of how I sustained my injuries to a minimum. I won't mention the cavern's contents until you deem it safe to share." After what happened to Trevor, Elise understood better than most the importance of keeping such matters secret, after finding an historical site of such magnitude.

The cat blinked and jumped down from her owner's lap to rub against Elise's leg. It was too painful for Elise to lean over and pet her, so the feline sauntered off behind the tent. "Tabitha appears to enjoy the newfound freedom of country life." Elise had seen the cat prowling about the woods but it always reappeared at evening to the safety of the professor and Caroline's tent. At least, the feline had remained out of harm's way and hadn't interfered with the dig...so far.

"I've never seen her so content, therefore, I intend to leave her here when we return to London. Michael has grown very fond of her, so he promised to see to her care while we're away." Caroline dusted the cat hair off her dress. "Occasionally, Isaac and I will have to travel to London and elsewhere to purchase the finest equipment and supplies for the school and to further our studies." Caroline grinned. "I'll gladly be done with the subservient act of clueless debutante, and finally assume my role as, professor, scientist, and teacher."

"I'm glad for you both. I fear those who run the school in London, would never give you the respect and freedom this remote countryside and villagers will provide."

"Isaac and I arrived at that same conclusion." Caroline tensed as an angry screech was followed by the familiar yowl of cat that had been stepped on, followed by a man's vicious curse. Before Caroline could rise to investigate, Tabitha rushed back to the tent, and reclaimed her mistress's lap. "What mischief have you found now?" Caroline examined the cat for injury but found none. She kept a firm hand on the tabby, for the cat was agitated, and growled at everyone who walked by.

"Who are you?" A loud shout came from Desmond, and another by Ed, a local villager hired to help guard the camp. "Stop!"

William immediately rose from his seated position near the fire and drew his short sword. He made eye contact with Elise, as he hurried past. "Stay here."

She hated it when he ordered her about, but in this case, she withheld her protest.

As dusk darkened into night, with potential deadly enemies roaming about, she touched the dagger at her waist to confirm its presence. Not that she was in any condition to be much of a help.

All were on alert. The men in the camp grabbed shovels and staffs as weapons and kept them ready. No one spoke, as they waited to hear the call to arms.

Cursing and the sound of a scuffle brought the men to the edge of the camp.

William and Desmond hauled a man into the camp's fire-light, keeping a tight hold, for he jerked and twisted like a madman trying to get free. His stench was overwhelming.

"Richard?" Elise could hardly believe the man's appearance.

He was unkempt, his clothing ragged and filthy. His hair was matted and long enough to cover his shoulders, and his beard hung in dirty ringlets to the middle of his chest. His once haughty, but flawless face was marred by ugly scars. Apparently, he had not found peace nor closure in the many months since she'd last seen him.

"You!" He growled and lunged for Elise, but was held firmly by his captures. His eyes glinted with madness. "Witch!" He twisted and tried to claw at her. "You cost me everything."

"Take him to the wagon and fasten him securely to the wheel." The professor escorted William, Desmond, and their intruder out of sight.

"He's obviously crazed, poor man." Caroline put her arm around Elise. "I take it this is the man who caused the explosion?"

Elise nodded. Her hands shook with the shock of his presence in the camp. "I can't imagine what has happened to him."

"Guilt and sin, whether acknowledged or not, weighs heavily on a soul." Caroline led Elise closer to the fire to warm her.

William and the professor returned. By their frowns, both appeared disturbed by their encounter.

"I don't think that young man has had anything to eat for days." The professor filled a bowl with soup from the iron pot. "I'll take this to him and have Desmond guard him while he eats."

William stood near Elise, gazing into the fire.

She touched his arm, but he didn't turn her way, just shook his head.

"That man was raised with title, privilege, wealth, and a future a commoner like me could never dream of having." William frowned as he stirred the fire. Sparks rose into the night sky.

"Because he believed he was owed those privileges, he wasted his life on gambling, drink, and other bad choices."

Elise rubbed her injured arm, wincing when she touched the bruises.

"Was he the one who caused the explosion that almost killed you?" William stared at her with a silent demand to know it all.

Elise dropped her gaze and nodded.

"What else?" William's anger drew curious glances from those in the camp.

"Please, William, not here." Elise hated that he found out in front of everyone.

His hand trembled as he took her arm and ushered her into the darkness. The moon was bright enough to see the path. Someone had built a bench between the camp and the dig. He stopped there and helped her take a seat, but he remained standing, his fists clenched at his side. "Did that filthy animal touch you?"

"He was drunk and unreasonable. When I ignored his attention, he seemed even more determined to get what he wanted, which was me as his bride. It was after I refused his offer of marriage that he threatened to make me marry him to insure his inheritance. He was sure no one else would want me after he..." Elise rubbed her temples to try to dismiss the memory the terror of Richard's grasp so long ago.

"I'll make him regret he ever..." The intensity of William's anger frightened Elise. It gave her a glimpse of the fierce, battle-trained warrior he once was.

"William, he didn't get his way." Her voice was soft. She stood and put a hand to his chest. His heart pounded beneath her touch. "It's in the past." She slipped her uninjured arm around his waist and laid her head on his chest. He moaned and crushed her to him. It was a joyous pain, for she was where she always wanted to be...in his arms.

"I thought I'd lost you when you disappeared into the cavern." His voice wavered with emotion. With a deep breath, he released her and stepped back. "I need to tell you..."

"Who's there?" Avery came up from behind them and waved his torch in their direction. "Oh, it's you." His voice hardened with accusation. "No one is to leave the camp after dark, unless assigned guard duty." He stepped closer. "Lady Elise, would you like me to escort you back to camp?"

"I'll see that Lady Elise arrives safely to her tent." William stepped between Avery and Elise. He picked her up in his arms and started back.

"You have the next watch." Avery called after them. "After our surprise visitor, you wouldn't want to be responsible for another breach in our defenses by ignoring your duty, *Sir Knight.*"

"He'd better be glad I have my hands full." William grumbled.

"He's young and unworthy of your attention, *Sir Knight.*" Elise rested her head against him and chuckled.

When he set her down at her tent, he brushed his lips across hers, stirring the longing to be back in his arms.

"We need to talk." His intimate tone held a promise.

Loud curses set him off toward the wagon and the prisoner.

Brother Peter stepped inside the camp with the pieces of a broken bowl. "The prisoner finished the contents before he broke the bowl against a rock. He tried to use the sharp pieces to cut his ropes. When Desmond intervened, the man tried to cut him, which earned the crazed man a swift punch to his jaw. The blow knocked him out." The monk dropped the larger pieces of the broken bowl into the fire, his expression grim. "Hopefully, the poor man will remain unconscious until morning, but I'll sleep nearby in case I'm needed. Perhaps he'll awake in a more reasonable mood, so I can better assess his condition." He wiped his hands on a towel. "I bid you all a good night." He headed back toward the wagon and his sleeping mat.

"It's been a very eventful day. Goodnight, all." The professor reached for his wife's hand, and they disappeared into their tent.

"Why don't you try to get some sleep?" William returned

and faced Elise. "I'll be on guard duty for the next few hours. You'll be safe." He reached out, but dropped his hand when Michael walked by heading to his tent. "We'll talk again in the morning."

"Goodnight." Elise hesitated hoping for another kiss, but he turned and disappeared into the night. With the aid of her crutch, she hobbled inside and prepared for bed. Her whole body ached and she smeared a healing ointment everywhere reachable before struggling into her nightgown. An extra blanket added to her bedding softened the cot and allowed her to relax into its comfort.

Poor Richard. He'd once enjoyed the best of everything, now he slept on the hard ground, tied to a wagon wheel, like a common criminal. By what she'd witnessed, he was in great need of healing, spirit, soul, and body. She prayed he would allow Brother Peter to minister to all. She continued her prayers for their group and everyone that worked at the campsite, before succumbing to sleep.

Elise awoke to voices and sounds of activity in the camp. Slow moving, she did her best to ignore her aches and pains, as she managed her ablutions and dressed.

She hobbled out of the tent and found the camp surprisingly quiet. William was nowhere to be seen, though she had peace knowing he would not abandon her.

The sounds of men at work, carried up from a secondary camp, which had been made so more workers could spread out and remain close to the new building project. Another cook was hired to feed them.

The professor's group continued to have their meals within the primary camp, before going out to give assignments and supervise the activities of the day.

"Good morning, Elise." Caroline greeted her with a cheerful tone. "William went to help Clarence take our troubled guest to the river to clean him up." She waited until Elise took a seat and then handed her a bowl of boiled oats with honey and plenty of butter and cream on the top.

"This looks delicious. Thank you. I'm surprisingly hungry this morning." She said a quick blessing over the food before taking a bite of the creamy mixture, which warmed her all over.

William returned to camp with a scowl on his face, and water soaked, from head to toe.

"I take it our guest resisted your help to bathe him?" Caroline handed William a dry towel.

"It wasn't until I threatened to drown him that he made an effort to cooperate and use the soap to bathe properly." He dried his face and went to his kit to pick out dry clothes. "It took multiple scrubbings to get the worst of the stench off of him, then we realized the smell was coming from the man's hair." He tucked his clothes under his arm. "Desmond took his knife to the matted mess, threatening to slit Lord Richard's throat if he didn't cooperate. After our guest was shaved and clean, he was given dry clothes to wear, which Desmond generously donated from his kit. His Lordship objected vehemently, declaring the garments not worthy of his station." He smiled. "Desmond shoved the rags Richard had been wearing into his face and told him he could wash them and put them back on, if he preferred." William turned to Elise's tent with his dry clothes in hand and disappeared. He returned and hung his wet things on a line strung for that purpose.

"I need to relieve Desmond of guarding the prisoner so he too, can get into some dry clothes." William winked at Elise before he left.

With one arm in a sling even the simple task of washing her dish became awkward. The wet bowl slipped from her fingers and broke.

"I'm so sorry." Elise teared up with frustration. "I hate this feeling of uselessness." She recognized the self-pity in her voice.

"It's just a bowl, Elise." Caroline picked up the pieces and dropped them into the fire. Nothing was wasted on such an expedition. The clay pieces from the broken bowl would heat and help keep the coals hot. "Besides, I've hired a woman from the village to do the cooking and cleaning up from now on. She'll start tomorrow." She patted Elise on the shoulder and smiled. "Try not to be discouraged, for you'll soon heal and be back to normal. It just takes time."

"Well, I admit, I won't miss the cooking and washing, but I'd prefer to stay busy."

William and the professor returned from checking on Richard. Caroline poured them, each a cup of tea.

"Thank you, my dear. It's just what I need." The professor turned to William. "And thank you for your assistance with our uninvited guest." He took a long sip of his drink and sat beside his wife. "I fear the poor man's mental state is beyond reason at the moment. I hope with rest and proper nutrition he'll regain a good measure of his faculties."

"Ye'll be a proper gentleman, if ye know what's good for ye." Desmond's warning preceded the prisoner's appearance. Richard's hands and ankles were tied with ropes. Desmond and another man clung to each arm, as they entered the camp to eat.

With the filth gone, Elise could see that his skin had a yellowish cast, which did not bode well for the state of his health. He had lost so much weight he was but skin and bones.

Elise limped away, using the tents as cover, before she was notice hoping not to incite Richard into another crazed fit that would result in his being returned to his prison by the wagon. Maybe without her presence, he could eat in peace. She headed to the bench to watch the activity around the building site and stayed out of the way.

William was again at her elbow, giving her a sense of safety and peace.

"What do you think we should to do with him? I can't allow

him to wander free and continue to risk your life." William stepped before her blocking her view.

"I don't know. I've prayed for his soul and have tried to forgive him, but I'm having trouble forgetting what he did." She glanced up to meet William's gaze. "I want to do what is right. I'm just not sure what that is considering the state he's in. He needs help."

"Come with me." William reached out and scooped her up in his arms, along with her crutch.

"Where are you taking me?" Not that she cared. Her place was with him, no matter where they went.

"You'll see." He headed toward the cavern. The workmen had removed decades of earth and rocks to open the original ground-level entrance, though it remained a narrow passage to keep from weakening the area and causing further rockslides. The workmen had secured the opening with timber and added a heavy oak door, fashioned to the opening to keep it secure.

"Sir William, do you an' Lady Stanton wish to enter?" The guard stepped aside.

"Thank you, Jimmy. We won't be long." William set Elise on her feet and waited until she gained her balance with the crutch. He motioned for her to go inside.

"William." She hesitated; her heart pounded with the fear.

"It's not as you remember. I'll go first and we'll leave when you say." William had to slip in sideways because of his broad shoulders. "It's important."

She whispered scriptures to fight the fear, took a deep breath and limped through the narrow opening, toward him as he held out his hand to help her hobble inside.

The room was lit by three torches set in holders fastened on three separate walls. The air still had a musty smell, for the opening at the top, where she'd fallen through, had been covered with tarps, and a wood platform had been built to hold the tarps in place to keep out the weather, varmints, and any curious trespassers. A chill of remembrance skidded down her spine. But by God's grace, she had survived the fall and she would heal.

She leaned against the crutch and turned her focus on the wonders revealed in the chamber. With most of the debris removed, the space appeared much larger than she remembered.

"According to the professor and Caroline, this place belonged to a learned man of God." Elise felt suddenly shy, with the need of idle chatter.

William's intense gaze sent swirls of giddy anticipation fueling her words.

"Aye. The man who built this room had need of privacy, too." William helped her to stone bench that had been uncovered. Its curved design had been fashioned by a talented stonemason. She sat, but he remained standing. "I needed to speak to you privately, and the camp is growing in numbers by the day."

"Is my family truly well?" She found it hard to sit still.

"Your family was fine when last I saw them. The manor and those inside are well protected from any threat, including the Black Guard." William backed away, as if he needed distance. "On my way here, I stopped at an inn for the night, where I met a young commoner, named Jeremy."

"And?" The dread of what he may have found out pooled in her gut. Her breath quickened.

"He told me you promised to marry him in one year." William's gaze narrowed, and his hands fisted at his side. "Is that true?"

"He asked for my hand in marriage, since I was still unwed, and we have much in common, I..." She paused, realizing how foolish it sounded. William's gaze remained fixed on her. "With no other prospects, I did promise Jeremy, I'd marry him in one year's time, on the condition I had not wed by then." Elise stood, raised her chin, and glared back at him. She pointed her finger at his chest. Anger gave strength to her voice. "I have loved you for as long as I can remember, William Degraf, and I know you love me. What I can't understand is your obsession with me marrying a nobleman, a stranger whom I do not love." Her raised tone echoed in the chamber. "That is your problem not mine, so since you're not interested in marrying me, I shall wed whomever I wish." Her gaze narrowed. "And I'm sure my father will approve the union, as long as the man's heart is noble, if not his bloodline."

"I won't allow you to marry that young man." William's tone lowered, but still reflected his anger. He rubbed a hand across his face in frustration.

"You have no say in the matter." Elise hated the tears that blurred her eyes. This conversation hurt more than her injuries.

"I do have a say." He reached her in two strides. "You were always John's annoying younger sister, until one day John mentioned in passing, that your father was already receiving requests from interested noblemen to meet you with the purpose of courting you. He repeated your mother saying, she felt you were still too young and they should wait a year or so before entertaining such offers." He brushed his fingers across her cheek. "At the thought of losing you—I suddenly realized that you had grown up, as had my feelings for you. You had become my one true love." His hand dropped to his side. "My only hope of being worthy of your hand was to join the king's army. My purpose was to gain a title by serving valiantly and earning many honors. If that didn't happen, then I vowed to forget you." He pulled her into his arms. "An impossible vow to keep, since I still can't close my eyes at night without seeing your smile and hearing your voice in my dreams." His voice lower and the sadness she glimpsed in his face silenced her anger, giving way to hope. "When I lost my leg, my plans of earning a title and lands died. I found out the king's earl constable, who had vowed to submit my commendation to the king, had perished when his ship sunk during a terrible storm." His words softened to a whisper. "I didn't want your pity as a reason to marry me, when there were men of noble blood and title who had two good legs wanting to declare for you."

"Oh, you make me so angry." She pushed him away. "That day when I came to sit with you and you pulled me onto your bed, you kissed me senseless and told me that you loved me. Our future together was settled in my heart then, but you denied the truth of the matter." She put her hand on her hip, her tone lowered to convey her hurt and anger. "You've wasted all this time because of what? Your pride? Your stubbornness?"

"Yes." William tugged her back within his arms. "It took a young commoner's bold declaration to release me from every reason to protect you from my love." His gaze was unwavering. "Is it too late? If your father accepts my declaration for you, will you marry me?"

"I'm of age. I will choose whom I wed." She snuggled deeper into his embrace. "Besides, our parents will welcome the chance of having our families united by marriage, as well as respect." She leaned back and touched his cheek. He turned his face to kiss her palm sending a flurry of butterflies brushing her skin. "We have a man of the church here who can perform the ceremony today. I see no reason to delay and allow you to change your mind." She laughed when his eyes widened in surprise at her boldness.

"Then I shall ask Brother Peter to perform the wedding immediately." William touched his forehead to hers, then gently raised her face to his and kissed her. The kiss deepened until they were weak-kneed and breathless. "I have dreamed of you so often, I needed to make sure you are real."

"I'm real, and with the exception of a few bumps and bruises, I'm more than ready to be your bride." Elise heart still raced leaving her near speechless. The glow of the moment dimmed knowing the regret her parents would have that she didn't wait for their formal permission. She dreaded to see her mother's disappointment that she was again denied the opportunity to make a fuss over the ceremony, but Elise refused to wait a moment more than necessary to wed the man she loved.

"Today, I shall become the wife of the brave and gallant knight, Sir William Degraf." She leaned away from him and frowned. "Oh, William. I packed nothing suitable to be married in, and there's not a dress maker within a two day's ride of here."

"With the exception of the peasant's tunic and pants, you seem so fond, I care not what you're wearing, my beloved, only that you'll speak the vows to make you mine forever." He pulled her into his arms and kissed her again, until they were both short of breath. "Enough. I've waited far too long to make you my bride. Let's go." He opened the door and ushered her out following close behind.

He started to gather her into his arms to carry her back to camp, but she stepped back.

"The symbols in the cavern reminded me. I insist you solve a mystery for me before we can wed." Elise picked up a stick near the entrance of the cavern and drew some symbols in the dirt. "You wrote these on the back of your note, when you brought back my wing. I completed the picture of the knight saving the fair maiden from the dragon, but could never decipher what these other squiggles meant."

William gave her a shy grin. "You weren't meant to be able to decipher them." He took the stick and completed the broken lines. It read, *I shall.* That was all.

"You shall what?" Elise straightened, and her brow furrowed with frustration.

He glanced over at the workmen busy about the site and brushed the message away with the end of the stick. "I made up a language to tell you a secret." He raised his hand to stop her protest. "I shall, is all I dared reveal. That I couldn't wed you didn't mean I couldn't stop how I felt about you."

"William, what were you trying to tell me?" She gazed into his eyes.

"Those words meant, and still mean, *I shall* love you all the days of my life. *I shall* protect you until my dying breath. *I shall...*"

She put her hand to his heart. "I *shall* wed you tonight and *we shall* have the rest of our lives to fulfill those promises and more."

He scooped her up into his arms and headed back to camp.

CHAPTER 21

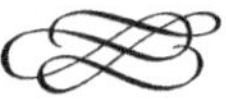

William made the necessary arrangements with Brother Peter, and then sought out the professor to discuss the need to keep Richard confined until they were safely away.

William and Elise had discussed the issue of Richard on their return trip to the camp. Since the professor planned to remain here, William and Elise were free to return to meet her parents at her sister's home. The professor would keep Richard under tight guard for at a couple of weeks. That would give the newly-weds plenty of time to return to the manor. William hoped that by seeing Elise get married this evening, the man would give up his need for revenge. If not, then William would have a heart to heart with him, to make sure he knew the consequences of posting further reward posters slandering Elise, or harassing her in any way.

The dig site was a beehive of activity, but the plan to put the meteorite into the wagon to take back to London changed after the cave-in. The stone was drug to a spot near the entrance of the cavern to await a final resting place once a science building was erected.

Since the professor had announced the building of a school for scientific study, more workers had started arriving from other villages and surrounding countryside.

People were eager to work for a decent wage, which had most of them in a jovial mood. More guards were hired, for with the good also came the bad, the ones who were too lazy to work and chose to steal from those who did. William had seen his share of that kind of evil while he served in the army.

"Even though there's been no further sign of the pagans, everyone must remain on alert." William spoke with the professor, as they did another inspection of the camp's perimeter and made notes of any weaknesses in the patrols.

As a warrior, he recognized the familiar feeling of unrest stirring within him that came before a battle. He couldn't shake it no matter how many additional guards were added to patrol the perimeter and grounds. Until a permanent stonewall was built to protect the property, there were too many boulders, hedges, and trees for an enemy to hide behind and wait for the right opportunity to attack. If someone was determined to sneak into the camp, they would find a way.

The professor approached William after he gave the new guards their assignments and sent them out on patrol. "I know you must return Elise to her family, but afterward, if you decide you'd like a new start, you and Elise are always welcome here. We can have a house built for you, so she can continue her scientific studies, and you could start a training camp, for we'll always be in need of well-trained guards."

"Thank you, professor. I'll talk it over with Elise. After we've met with her parents, we'll make the decision about what to do next." William felt the flutter of excitement within his gut knowing this might be the opportunity he had been waiting for. Elise would love to continue her studies, for she had a creative mind that pursued knowledge, like a thirsty man craved water.

He would have to wait to tell her about this new possibility, for he was instructed, by both Elise and Caroline, to stay away, as her time was consumed with preparations for the wedding ceremony this evening. He saddled Shadow and rode him around the property to make sure the new guards were following his instruction. Staying busy helped, but time moved too slowly for his purposes. His thoughts always returned to Elise and the details surrounding their trip back to the manor. It would be too late to start their journey after the wedding celebration, making it necessary to leave first thing in the morning. Elise agreed to pack only necessities for the trip, because they had to travel by horseback. One of the villagers had backed the water-hauling wagon into the professor's carriage leaving it in need of serious repair, before it would be safe for travel.

William rubbed at the ache of worry growing in his temple. Elise would stubbornly ignore the pain of her injuries, so as not to hinder their travel. He'd need to watch her for signs of weariness and find safe lodging to rest along the way.

He searched his mind for such places he must have passed along the way, but he'd been intent on finding Elise, and had slept on the ground most nights. With the exception of one inn, which he wouldn't mind stopping to declare to young Jeremy, Elise was indeed wed. The joy of seeing his surprise was short-lived, when angry shouts erupted from the worksite, ahead.

With a hand on the hilt of his short sword, he nudged Shadow into a run. When he arrived, it was merely a squabble between two brothers over who had used a missing shovel last. William spotted it behind a wheelbarrow and pointed it out, returning the peace. But their conflict reminded him of other conflicts he and Elice could face. Besides the pagans, who still roamed free, there was the Black Guard, and any number of evil people willing to attack a couple traveling alone.

With peace restored, William rode to Mr. Alford's farm, where he purchased one of his horses. William picked a pretty bay mare, which he deemed sound and well mannered. He had wanted to surprise his new bride with a carriage or a cart to travel in to make the journey easier on her until she healed, but there was none available. Since the bay was also broke to the harness, William hoped to buy a conveyance along the way to accommodate his new bride, though he suspected she would protest her need for one.

He arrived at camp and gave Desmond charge over the mare, who agreed with William, that she'd been a good purchase.

Their conversation was interrupted by a warning blast of a ram's horn, which could only mean trouble. He pulled his sword, and sent Shadow racing to the meteorite site to see what had caused the alarm. The professor was there when he reached the commotion.

"We caught them trying to get inside the cavern." With a bloody staff in his hand, and breathing hard, one of the recently hired guards, stood over a pagan, who lay on the ground unconscious.

The ram's horn blew again followed by the screams of more tattooed pagans rushing toward the mound, waving raised swords, clubs, and stones.

Men on patrol, and those at the building site abandoned their work. Armed with shovels, hammers and axes, they, too rushed into the fray.

William took charge, issuing orders and sending men with swords to guard the cavern as others fought against, at least a dozen, crazed pagans determined to gain access. He had little time to wonder what was so urgent that would cause the pagans to attack in daylight with so many men in camp. If they had waited until dark the camp would have had half as many workers.

~

*E*lise heard the alarm and stopped her sewing. Caroline had given her one of her dresses to make a wedding gown, but it needed to be altered, for Caroline was taller and fuller bodied than Elise. At least, it wasn't the other way around.

Putting the dress aside, Elise stood and hobbled out of the tent opening without her crutch. The camp was eerily empty.

"Got you!" Boney arms grabbed Elise from behind penning her arms to her side.

She screamed, twisted, and squirmed, against her captor's hold, to no avail. Her injuries burned with pain. Her ankles were captured and hastily tied together by another man wearing a long robe. She continued to scream, but a pagan with a tattooed face appeared in her vision and threw a liquid onto her face. The substance burned her eyes and took her breath. Voices grew faint.

"You didn't kill her?" Richard's voice rose in anger.

"Nay, just something we use on sacrifices to silence their screams."

~

*J*arred awake by pounding hooves on a dirt road, Elise realized she was tied to the back of a galloping horse, like a sack of potatoes. The pain in her head and the punishing ride made her sick to her stomach, until she feared she would retch, but the rag tied across her mouth made her fight the urge. Her eyes, nose, and throat burned from whatever substance that pagan had thrown into her face. She couldn't rub her face, for her hands were strapped to her side.

Desperate to be free, she struggled against her bindings to no avail. Every ache and pain demanded attention. Panic threatened to steal what breath she had.

She had to calm down. Think.

The last thing she remembered, after she was captured, was seeing the horrific tattooed pagan whose face looked like a skull. He'd painted black around his eyes and huge yellow teeth had been inked around his mouth.

Please, God save me. Thankfully, God could hear the cries of her heart, for she couldn't speak.

The sound of night birds and the cool mist of fog chilled her skin. She was so tired.

The next time she awoke, it was morning. Her eyes burned, but she squinted through the tears, seeing nothing but grass. No longer tied to a horse, she lay on the ground, but still bound tightly, unable to move. She drew a deep breath, thankful that her gag had been removed.

"Good, you're awake."

She was jerked to a sitting position.

"Richard!" She tugged against her restraints. "What have you done?"

He grinned and held a flask with water to her lips, which she gladly drank to ease her enormous thirst.

"I have captured my bride. Once my grandfather sees that I've taken you as my wife he'll gladly restore me into his good graces." He smiled as if it made perfect sense to kidnap and proclaim marriage to someone, he once declared he hated.

"Let me loose immediately! I can't feel my hands or feet." Her plea caused him to frown. Then he slapped her across the face.

"I told you once to never give me orders. You would think someone as smart as you would remember such a simple command." He glared at her, but he loosened the ropes that tied her hands and legs together. The prickly feeling of needles-and-pins began, as the circulation was restored. "See, I'm not without mercy." Richard's mouth contorted into something akin to a smile, but there was no kindness reflected in his eyes.

"Thank you." She said, through gritted teeth, dropping her

gaze, lest he see her hatred for him. Her injured shoulder and arm throbbed from the abuse. Somewhere along the way she'd lost her shoe. Her injured ankle was swollen twice its normal size, causing the bandage to cut into her skin, until she worked the knot loose. Removing the cloth released the pressure, but did nothing to relieve the pain.

Until she could stand on her own and runaway, she couldn't physically oppose him. Challenging Richard in his delusional state of mind would do nothing to aid her in persuading him to set her free. It would be best to play along and hope to gain favor until she could escape, find help, or William came for her. She drew comfort knowing her brave knight wouldn't quit until he found her.

Pray for your enemies.

"I'm hungry. Do you have any food?" Elise kept her tone civil, though outrage flooded her thoughts with revenge.

"Food?" He seemed puzzled at the question. "I didn't have time to gather supplies for our trip, but there's a farm nearby where I might find some." He frowned. "I shall have to leave you here while I'm gone." He jerked her to her feet and dragged her to a large willow tree, where he pushed her down, then dropped down beside her.

"Please, don't tie me up." Fear-filled desperation fueled her plea. "I'll promise to wait here until you return."

He paused, giving her hope he might heed her request.

"I was injured in a rockslide. See how swollen my ankle is?" She pointed to her injury. "I'm unable to walk without help."

"I don't trust you." His gaze narrowed. "If you get loose from your bonds and are not here when I return, I shall find you again, and you'll suffer the punishment of disobeying your husband."

"We are not married, Richard." She knew that was the wrong thing to say as his eyes grew wild with insanity.

"You are my wife!" His voice rose to a high-pitch wail. "That pagan priest chanted a spell over you that will bind you to me forever. He even spilled the blood of a sacrifice to seal the union." He pulled the ropes tightly around her waist and bound her to the tree tying the knot beyond her reach.

"Is this how you show you care?" She tried to keep her tone soft and pleading. Hope rose within her, as his expression of anger turned into confusion.

"I'll show you I can be a good husband…as long as you obey me." He tested the knot was tight, then mounted a horse waiting out of her sight, and rode off.

"Oh, that man!" Her frustration could no longer be silenced. Rather than curse her enemy, as her flesh demanded, she quoted scripture to counter the evil he'd left behind. "No weapon formed against me will prosper." The anger released her as she submitted to the Word of God spoken aloud. "My God and savior, Lord Jesus, is my protection against any demonic spell that heathen cast," defying Richard's declaration with one of her own. She sung scriptures of God's redemption and protection, as she pulled against the ropes that bound her.

Once freed, she could hide until dark, then make her way back to the camp.

Her body ached from her head to her toes, weakening any intentions to flee. Perhaps William would find her first.

Richard might be daft, but he tied a good knot. No matter how hard she tried, she only succeeded in making her bruised body ache and rubbing her wrists raw in her efforts to get free. Sweat ran down into the wounds making them burn.

She glanced at the sky to try to determine the time. The thick tree canopy didn't help, but by the shadows it could be midmorning. How long had she'd been unconscious and how far had they come?

The sun was high in the sky, when she heard several horses on the road coming her way. Dare she scream? Could it be William already?

The tree she was tied to was hidden off the road, but if she stretched, she could see through the branches. A feeling that something wasn't right filled her with dread. Could it be bandits or worse?

Her injuries, and being securely bound to a tree, gave her no option to run or fight. The doubt kept her quiet.

Three rough-looking men rode down the road. The sun reflected off their chainmail, but she could tell they weren't the king's men. The king's emblem was always emblazed on every item a soldier wore or used, and branded on every horse. These men and their horses had none of those markings.

Most likely bandits or... She gasped. Could they be the assassins, called the Black Guard whom William had warned her?

Had Richard confronted them? Dread pooled in her gut. If so, it was unlikely he'd survived the encounter.

The thought of being tied to a tree for hours or days caused her to squirm and tug against her restraints until the pain became unbearable. Her wrists were bleeding, but she had to get free. "Please, Lord help me."

"Be quiet." Richard slipped up behind her, making her squeal in surprise. He untied her and jerked her to her feet. "Those men are hunting me." He half-carried and half-dragged her to a sorrel horse, which she recognized it as one of the professor's carriage horses. Richard must have stolen it when he kidnaped her.

He mounted and kept a hold of the rope still tied to the wrist of her uninjured arm. "Give me your hand so I can pull you up."

She had no wish to remain behind with the Black Guard and pagans running about. She allowed him to swing her up behind him. She saw flames through the trees. A building was on fire. The thick smoke drifted toward them and the road.

"Stay quiet. We may yet get away, if we're quick about it." He started the horse in a walk, but as soon as they cleared the trees, and had a barrier of smoke to hide them, he kicked the animal into a gallop.

Elise had to hold on tightly to keep from being flung off. Every scripture of protection she could think of was whispered into her captor's back. The gallop lasted over an hour, causing the horse to stumble in its exhaustion.

"Richard, you know horses. They can only be ridden hard for so long. We don't want to risk the horse falling and injuring it or us. Please, stop. We all need some rest."

He grumbled something incoherent but slowed the animal to a walk until he spotted a stream and stopped. He reached behind, grabbed her arm, and swung her off before he dismounted. He led the horse to the stream, but tied it to a tree away from the water. Richard pulled her into the stream where they both satisfied their thirst. She quickly washed her face and the blood from her wrists. When Richard had his fill, he pulled her up onto the bank and led the horse down to drink. He kept a tight grip on the rope attached to her wrist, so she couldn't slip away while his attention was on the animal.

"I recognized those three when I reached the farm." He twisted the rope around his hand, as if agitated.

"How do you know them?" Elise dared to push him for more information. "A wife should know such things." She added hoping to keep him from another angry tirade.

He led the horse to a stand of tall grass and led it graze. A consideration she hadn't expected of him. At least, the animal was allowed to eat. "I owe a very powerful man, named Frank Haverton, a large sum of money from a gambling debt, which my grandfather refused to pay when he disowned me." He glanced at the slow-moving water, as if in deep thought. "A thug named, Thrasher is one of Haverton's hired enforcers, and the worse of the lot. He boasts he always gets the person he's after, probably because he gets a portion of what his boss collects." Richard's gaze reflected his fear. "I've heard what he does to those he catches." He cleared his voice and stood straight. "Thrasher, and the other two, have been hunting for me for months, but I'm too clever for them." He chuckled then frowned. "They must have found someone who told them where I'd gone. I hid until they left the farm, and I smelled the smoke. When I went to the house to find food, the house was on fire. I looked in the window and saw the farmer and his family lying dead on the floor." He glanced at Elise when she gasped. "I couldn't get inside to look for food because of the fire, but I found one wrinkled potato Thrasher must have dropped on his way out."

"Where is it? I'm hungry enough to eat it raw, but we could roast over a fire and share it."

"I ate it." He looked at her as if that were his right.

Her hunger and his selfish act had words of condemnation ready to attack him verbally even if she couldn't retaliate with force. The void in his gaze stopped her. No telling what he'd do to her if further provoked. One day he would reap what he sowed. She took a deep breath and released it with a prayer for strength. "Those must have been the men I saw ride past while you were gone." She rubbed her wrists. "I thought they were the Black Guard."

"Black Guard?" Richard frowned.

"William came to warn me about some assassins, called the Black Guard. He said they had been commissioned to go into all the land and kill all with noble blood. I feared those men might be them."

"Kill all of noble blood?" His eyes widened with alarm. "My grandfather is still in London last I heard. I must warn him. He must live long enough to reinstate my title before he dies, or all is lost." Richard rubbed his face. His expression turned into a wild gaze of confusion, which had him picking at the short stubble of his shorn beard.

"Richard, we can make it to London in time to warn him, if

we use wisdom. We must allow the horse to rest, and we need to find food and shelter for the night." She touched him to gain his attention. He jerked away and gazed at her as if he didn't recognize her. Slowly, as she calmly repeated what she'd said, he came back to the present.

"Aye." He smiled. "I shall like having a smart wife. We'll do as you suggest...this time." He led the horse away from the patch of grass and mounted, then reached down and slung her up behind him. Besides her rope-burned wrists, her arm and shoulder throbbed with pain from such ill treatment, but she kept her suffering to herself lest he become volatile and more dangerous. She feared he would consider her complaint as criticism against him. By his incoherent murmuring, which often turned to rants about her and his grandfather, he was hanging on to reality by a thread.

"There's an inn ahead where we can spend the night and get some food." He patted his coat. "I took a generous portion of the professor's money that he had given one of his men to pay the workers, so we have more than enough to use for whatever we need."

"What did you do to the man from whom you stole it?" The thought of him killing someone to escape made her ill.

He ignored her question and jerked her arm against his waist. "You will not scream, cry out, or try to escape. Our lives depend on getting to London. Those men hunting me will go to any lengths, even bribery, to capture me for their boss. They might have offered a hefty reward to any they met along the way, who will capture me and keep me in bondage until they return."

"I will do what is necessary to make it safely to London." But if he tried to touch her as a husband touches his wife, he would find her screams the least of his troubles.

They arrived in a small village and found the inn he remembered. Since they were both dressed in plain clothing, more suited to a commoner than gentry, they could blend in, as long as Richard didn't make a fuss about anything.

He helped her off the horse then dismounted and removed the rope tied to her wrist. He grasped her sore arm in a firm grip making her whimper from the pain. With a scowl and a warning shake, he helped her hobble inside. Her ankle had lost none of its swelling during the trip.

The air was tainted with the stench of spoiled meat and sour ale. As hungry as she was, she couldn't afford to eat tainted meat and risk becoming ill.

"Innkeeper, I need to stable my horse for the night with a full measure of grain. I also need your best room for my wife and myself." Richard's formal stance, haughty, and demanding tone, rang more of a privilege upbringing than that of a commoner. She recognized the superior attitude that seemed to spring forth from Richard whenever he addressed any of lesser standing than himself...which meant everyone.

"He's been beside himself, since the robbery." Without calling him her husband, she put a hand on Richard's arm, exposing the dark bruises and rope burns on her wrists, which the innkeeper eyed with suspicion. "We are very grateful to find such a fine place to spend the night. It's been a long and difficult journey, since bandits stole our cart and belongings. They bound us, and left us to die. We barely escaped with our lives." Elise tried not to grimace over the lie, but she had to intervene or Richard's demanding attitude would have them both thrown out without food or drink before the night was over. She felt him gather steam to protest and rushed on. "He was so brave and clever at saving our lives." Richard relaxed beneath her touch, as he accepted the praise. "He managed to save our meager funds by hiding his purse from our captors. We have money to pay for our room and shelter for the horse. All we want is to return home safely."

Richard took her cue and fingered out the coins needed to pay the innkeeper the price listed on the wall.

"Sorry, ye folks 'ave 'ad such a 'ard time of it. It's usually peaceful around 'ere." Sympathy and the coins softened his features. "I'll give ye me best room and bring ye some food once you're settled, —say in 'alf an 'our?" He reached for a key and led the way up the stairs. "I'll take good care of yur 'orse, too."

"Some food would be most appreciated, but," She hesitated as she hobbled up the stairs behind him with no help from Richard. "I've a delicate stomach of late, and he's been ailing since the robbery." She turned to the innkeeper, once they reached the landing. "All we need for now is bread and cheese, if you have them. Seems that's all I can tolerate in my condition." She couldn't face a plate of whatever she'd smelled earlier. She knew it sounded as if she were with child, but it gave her a good reason to order bread and cheese, a far safer choice.

"Aye. Me wife had the same problem." Once the door was opened, he handed Richard the key then turned and left.

"You did well. I knew you would make me the perfect wife." Richard went to the window and peered out. "We should be safe here for the night." He turned toward her with a curious expression on his face, and scanned her from head to foot.

"Lest you get any ideas, I should warn you, I sleep light." She pointed to the bed. "You can have the bed, and I'll sleep on the floor." Before he could protest, a knock came at the door.

"Who is it?" Richard asked.

"Sorry to disturb ye," the innkeeper said, "but I noticed the marks on yur wrists. I have an ointment, me wife makes, that will 'elp 'em heal."

Richard opened the door.

"Oh, how very kind." Elise limped forward and claimed the jar. She opened it and smelled the camphor and started smearing it over her injured wrists. To avoid more questions, she'd wait until the innkeeper left to put the ointment on her swollen ankle, too.

"I'll bring yur food, if ye be ready." By the way he eyed them, she wondered if he heard her warning to Richard.

"Oh, yes, please." She hurried to make up a story before he voiced the question reflected in his expression. "He gets cranky when he misses his meals. I warned him about his snoring. He'd better be quiet or he'll be sleeping on that bed alone." She watched the innkeeper smile with understanding. She hated to refer to Richard, as *he* all of the time, but if she used his name, the innkeeper might remember, if asked. Elise put a hand to her stomach to aid in her deception.

"Me wife has given me a few lectures about me snoring, too." He backed away. "I'll be right back with the food."

The cheese was hard, but after the mold was cut off the edges, it tasted fine. The bread was also not fresh but edible. At least, the meager food filled the void, but to hear Richard, it was one step below pig slop.

"If you complain loudly enough, maybe we'll be kicked out before we can rest." Elise was tired of his constant whining over what he'd lost. Of equal annoyance, was his panicked tirades to reach London before something happened to his inheritance. No worry for his grandfather, only about how the old man's death would affect Richard.

They finished the food in silence, which allowed the weariness of a long exhausting day descend on Elise, making it hard to keep her eyes open, but she needed to speak up.

"We need to rest, since we have a long journey ahead of us, if we're to make it to London before the week is out." She was relieved he didn't make a fuss about her taking charge. He settled on the bed, which looked far more comfortable than the cold floor, but she wouldn't risk being that close to him. "Maybe the innkeeper has another horse he could sell us. It would be more comfortable for me and we could travel much faster if your horse didn't have to carry my extra weight."

"I think I'd better sleep in front of the door, so you don't get any ideas about taking the horse and leaving me behind." He got up and pulled the covers off the bed and made himself a pallet in front of the door.

"Suit yourself. I'll gladly take the bed." She took a table knife from their meal and kept it hidden at her side. She had no wish to challenge him while her injuries hindered her movements, but she also would do what was necessary to protect herself. "I shall remind you that I'm a light sleeper. Keep your distance if you want further cooperation from me, or suffer the consequences."

He ignored her threat and stretched out on the blanket in front of the door. She settled on the bed and planned to remain awake until he was fast asleep, then she'd sneak past him and ride the horse back toward the dig site. Hopefully, she'd meet William along the way.

Exhaustion and pain had taken its toll on her body. She should be wed to William, not the prisoner of a madman. Tears blurred her vision. *Lord, please protect William and bring him to me.* She barely lay her head down when sleep overtook her.

A noise awakened her. Dawn lit the window with a rosy glow. She listened.

Boots on the stairs. At least two men, maybe more.

Her breath quickened with the possible danger.

She slipped out of bed and straightened her clothes, having slept fully dressed.

"Richard. Wake up." She whispered and shook him until he suddenly sat up looking wild-eyed and confused. "Be quiet and listen."

"You say you don't have any other guests but the two in this room?" The man's voice was none she'd ever heard, but Richard's eyes widened in obvious recognition.

"It's been a slow night." The innkeeper's voice held fear.

"Who are they?" The man asked then the sound of a slap.

"I don't' know their names, but they be commoners by their dress." The innkeeper backed away by the sound of boots scraping on the wood floor.

Richard pulled his shoes on and stood. "That's Thrasher." He whispered and backed away from the door.

Elise limped to the window and looked out. Barefoot, she wouldn't get far on the stony ground below.

The inn's tall roof had an overhang too far up to reach, but a shorter roof extended below their window. They could use a blanket and bed sheet tied together to lower themselves down and escape that way. She'd have to manage with her injuries. They couldn't take the chance that the men would break into their room and recognize Richard.

"They were robbed and have nothin' more to steal. No one you'd be interested in disturbing." There was a scuffle and a thump, then silence.

If she and Richard hurried, they could make it to the barn and saddle the horse before the men gained entry to their room.

She whispered her plan to Richard and he nodded. The bed sheet and blanket tied together held as Richard went down first and she proceeded after him. Her weaker arm caused her to slip, but he surprised her by catching her before she hit the ground. He carried her to the barn and set her down. While he was busy saddling their horse, she recognized the three saddled horses as belonging to the three men hunting Richard. She dismissed the thought of stealing one for herself knowing those type of men had probably trained their horses not to allow strangers to ride them. With one hand she managed to loosen the girths until the saddles were free and would fall off once the animal ran away. She pulled off the bridles and turned the horses loose. They took off in all directions. Richard mounted then pulled her up behind him. The sound of an upstairs door splintering was followed by angry shouts.

Elise held on tight as Richard kicked the horse into a gallop. They were gone before the men made it outside. But the assassins would follow as soon as they found their horses and their gear.

Richard pressed the horse into a run as far as was safe, and eased the gelding back to a walk to rest it.

Elise fought against the urge to delay their journey, to give William time to reach them, but they couldn't risk being caught by the murders chasing Richard.

"I know a way we can shorten our journey by days." Richard had been mumbling for an hour, and she feared the excitement had rattled his mind, so this show of clarity surprised her. "We need to gain passage on a boat."

"How far is it to the nearest port?" Elise knew every mile took her farther from William, but once in London she would find someone who could free her from Richard's bondage, assuming she and Richard were still safe and the king's soldiers had stopped the Black Guard before they arrive.

"Within the hour, I think." He rubbed his forehead. "When I traveled through here, my head hurt from too much drink, but I remember the smell of salt water and the sounds of fishing boats."

It was two hours before she heard the squawk of seabirds. She didn't recognize this place, but she'd never traveled this part of England. Soon, they arrived at a small port, where two battered fishing boats were moored. It was a small fishing village, the kind of place where the villagers would notice every stranger who appeared. Their battered appearance would certainly draw attention. They were met with open stares and curiosity on the weathered faces they passed.

A pub was the only business she'd noticed when they rode near the dock. Richard ignored the business and continued on toward the water. She feared he was going to ride the weary horse across the rickety wood dock up to the first boat, but he stopped at the edge of the wooden planks. He handed her off and dismounted.

"Go water the horse while I secure passage to London." His haughty manner was back. "I've already warned you what will happen, if you try to run away." His gaze narrowed. "I loathe to repeat myself. Do you understand?"

"I understand." Her tone was harsh, but she managed to silence the rant that rose within her when she gazed around and saw there was no place to hide. Without further comment, she grabbed the reins and led the horse to the nearest water trough and let him drink, wishing she could do the same. The pub might have a cuppa, for her throat was parched. A strong cup of tea would also help her headache.

If she could get Richard to agree to go inside, they could, at least, find food and drink.

"We leave within the hour." He grabbed her injured arm, which made her cry out.

She jerked away. He frowned and started to reach for her again, but she backed away.

"I'll scream if you touch me again. If enough people come to see the reason, you'll miss the boat and might never reach London in time." She hoped she had enough strength to carry through her hoarse threat. With three murderers not far behind them, she had no desire to be kept here sorting things out with whoever represented authority in this place. It would be safer for everyone, if she and Richard left on the boat as planned. She would meet William in London, or find a way to reach Sarah's and her family from there.

He glared at her, as if he'd like to do her harm, but a villager walked up to them.

"That be a fine horse. Be it for sale?" The villager's smile faded when Richard turned his glare to the man. "Ye can't take it with ye on the boat, and there ain't no stables to leave it if ye plan to return."

"Aye. The animal is for sale. How much can you pay?" Richard flashed a smile, but it didn't reach his eyes. They haggled over the price and finally settled at a cost far less than the well-bred gelding was worth, but both were satisfied they'd made a good deal.

Elise hated that the gelding would be lost to the professor and Caroline, but as the man said, there was no place to secure the animal until she could send word to the professor of its location. She did manage to get the man's name so she could send word to them once she was safe. They could reacquire the horse later. The cost would be considered a small fee for taking care of the animal.

She followed Richard into the pub, which also turned out to be a store. There were a surprising number of miscellaneous items, including hardware and a variety of foods. She watched as Richard took in the business with the eye of someone accustomed to getting the best, which was sorely missing among the items for sale here. Still, the limited choice of food was far better than starving the whole trip to London.

A man wandered into the pub right after them.

"Captain Herm, going to gone long this trip?" The pub owner, greeted the man as an old friend.

She overheard him tell the proprietor that the trip to London would take at least a couple of days, depending on how hard his passengers worked and how much fish they netted during the trip, for they would fish until their cargo hold was filled.

Richard stepped into his path, with a raised voice. "Captain, I need a word with you." The captain frowned but paused to hear what he had to say. "I paid you good coin to be taken to London. I should be treated as a passenger not a slave of your demands."

"This is nay a pleasure cruise, but a fishing boat. We need a hearty catch to make the trip to London worthwhile." The captain raised his hand to interrupt Richard's angry complaints. "As I tried to explain before, as part of the cost of the trip, I also expect you to do your share of the work alongside the crew." He glanced at Elise. "And since we lost our cook on the last voyage, I expect your woman to prepare the food for the whole crew." He turned his attention back to Richard. "Do you agree with my terms, or do I leave you behind?"

Anger pinched Richard's brow. He mumbled a curse. "Since I must get to London, I shall agree to your terms."

"I supply food for me crew, but ye need supplies enough to carry ye and yur woman for several days." The captain's eyes narrowed and he gave a sweeping gesture to the goods around them. "I suggest you pick out what ye want and not tarry, for we sail within the hour with or without ye." He handed a list to the man behind the counter and stepped away to have words with a man at the bar.

She stayed close to Richard and pointed him to more practical items than ale and tobacco, which he wanted. "We need things to eat on the trip." She glared at him. "I shouldn't have to remind you what it feels like to be hungry."

Anger pinched his lips, and he clinched his fists at his side.

She wasn't about to back down. "I will not go on this trip and starve, because you refuse to buy the items we need, like these blankets, soap, and towels. And I need a pair of shoes."

He grabbed her arm and whispered into her ear. "I will acquiesce to your demands this time, but you will regret it when once we are aboard, with none to save you from my punishment."

"You dare threaten me? Then I shall scream out the truth of how you kidnapped me, and be done with you." Elise glared at Richard and pulled out of his grasp. "'Tis not me those killers seek, but you." He stepped back at her stern reprimand, and doubt replaced the anger in his eyes.

"I will go to London willingly, only because I choose to do so. But if you think you can bully me further, I shall warn you that I'm more than capable of doing you harm. Since I will be doing the cooking onboard, it would do you well to remember that."

With no further resistance from Richard, Elise found a pair of sturdy shoes that fit, though she feared they would be ruined on a fishing boat. She would put them away until she arrived in London. After seeing the poor condition of the boat and its captain, she also included in their purchases, a large barrel to be filled with fresh water to be taken to the boat to use for cooking and drinking. She picked out dried oats and barley for a hot meal and dried fruit, a smoked ham, and fresh vegetables to make a soup. The captain had assured Richard that he had pots a plenty to feed his crew, but Elise added an iron pot to use solely for their food. When Richard complained about the amount she spent, she explained that a fresh pot would be the safest way to assure they ate well. When she nodded toward the captain, it was obvious he lacked even a modicum of cleanliness, by his filthy hands and clothes, both of which reeked of sweat, ale, and fish guts. Richard stopped his complaining and nodded his agreement.

With their purchases made, she quenched her thirst with two cups of strong tea, while Richard talked with the pub owner, as he downed a pint of ale. A crew member came to find them with a warning that the captain wanted them and their supplies aboard or risk being left behind. Richard and Elise returned to the dock and had their packages put onboard once they were assured nothing was missing, then they too went aboard. The boat sailed soon after.

CHAPTER 22

Back at the camp

The battle had barely begun when one of the pagans raised his hands, gave a shrill whistle, and waved his staff. The pagans, who were still standing, stopped fighting, turned, and fled. William signaled the men closest to him to give chase. Riding Shadow, William was able to reach the tree line as the pagans scattered in all directions. He paused to wait for his men to catch up, when the acrid stench of burning canvas filled the air.

"Fire!" The sound of alarm drew William's attention. A column of heavy smoke was coming from the camp. He and the six men with him, abandoned their pursuit and race toward the camp. When he arrived, he dismounted and tied Shadow away from the smoke before he entered camp. He saw Michael and Avery's tent in flames. A bucket brigade was formed to pass water from the barrels on the wagon onto the blaze. More water was poured on the tents nearest, to keep them from also catching fire.

William searched the crowd but didn't see Elise. Frantic, he asked everyone, but no one remembered seeing her.

"Elise?" William stopped at the entrance of her tent where her crutch lay abandoned.

Caroline arrived with two women from the village. "Oh, my goodness. What's happened here?" She and the women put down the laundry they carried. "Where's Elise?"

"She's not here. Didn't she go with you?" William stalked inside the tent, but she was not there. He saw her shoe set aside by a footstool. She must have been resting her bruised ankle. She was missing a shoe and her crutch, so she couldn't have gone far. Hope flickered within him.

"She remained here to work on a dress to wear for the wedding." Caroline followed him inside and picked up the dress that lay abandoned on the cot. "Elise was trying to get the alterations finished. She wanted to surprise you by having something nice to wear." She hugged the dress and tears pooled in her eyes. "I should have stayed and helped her, but when Alice and Murine arrived to do the laundry, she insisted I go with them. I had planned to return immediately, but it took longer than expected. We hastened back here when we saw the smoke."

"Help!" Desmond's cry released a fresh flood of fear in William. He hurried to the small grove of trees behind the tents. Others, who also heard the call, followed close behind.

"I went to check on the prisoner." Desmond knelt beside his friend. "Clarence's been stabbed." Fury filled his tone.

Brother Peter hurried forward and knelt beside the wounded man. "He's still alive.

Someone brought him a bucket of water and the monk wiped Clarence's face with a damp cloth.

"He stole the money." Clarence's words were hurried and hoarse. He moaned and tried to sit.

"Who attacked you?" The professor knelt beside him to better hear.

William stepped back to give them space and searched the ground for signs of what happened.

"Help me carry him to a tent." Brother Peter led the way as Desmond and another man carried Clarence to the camp.

"Take him to our tent." Caroline's gaze met the professor's and he nodded his approval She followed the men but the professor and William stayed behind to go over the scene to search for clues.

"Clarence said he saw the man who was supposed to be guarding the prisoner, run by him toward the battle and went to investigate." The professor wiped soot off his face with the sleeve of his tunic. "When he arrived at the place where the prisoner was supposed to be tied, Richard was free and had saddled one of the carriage horses. When Clarence tried to stop him, he pulled a knife and stabbed him. He remembers being searched before he passed out. The money I had given him to pay the worker's wages is also missing."

"But what about Elise?" William needed more information, but Clarence was in no shape to give it to him.

William noticed a blood trail, which led to a dead chicken nearby.

"Look at this, Professor." William waved him forward and pointed to a couple of dead roosters.

"The way they were killed suggests a sacrifice had been made, but why?" The professor frowned and confusion furrowed his brow. "The meteorite was not taken, nor anything from the cavern." His eyes widened with understanding. "Because Elise was the prize." His expression turned to disgust. "Unfortunately, I've greatly underestimated Richard's physical and mental state. He's had plenty of unsupervised time to plan the attack, his escape, and her kidnapping."

William feared he was right, but was it an act of revenge or something else? The pagans' appearance at the dig site had to be connected to Richard's escape. The new man guarding Richard appeared and swore he'd been called away by someone claiming to the professor, though the man he heard had stayed in the shadows. He ordered him to join the battle, so he did.

William sent him away to help with the wounded.

"But how did Richard contact the pagans? He's been under constant guard and tied up since he arrived." William remembered there had been a boy that often hung around the area around the wagon and where Richard was held captive. He'd seen Richard speak to the child, on occasion, and had warned the boy to stay out of reach of the prisoner.

William's hands clenched at his side. He'd made a mistake that might cost Elise her life. "Find that boy...what was his name?" He searched his memory. "Dewey! Bring him here and we might get some answers."

"I know the boy. Clarence felt sorry for the child, since he was always hungry, and didn't appear to have family nearby. He made sure the lad had food to eat and tried to get him to tell him where he belonged, though he wasn't forthcoming with that information, perhaps because he'd come with the pagans and been abandoned." Having left Clarence with Caroline and Brother Peter, Desmond had returned to the scene of the attack. "I think I know where he might be." He hurried away.

Out of breath, a guard rushed into camp. "The pagans...came back," He took a deep breath before he could continue, "and took their dead and wounded, while we fought the fire." His face was flushed from his run from the mound site.

"Did they hurt anyone?" The professor handed the man a cup of water, which he drank in one gulp.

"They just grabbed their people and fled. The guards watchin' the entrance to the cavern were lookin' toward the fire. By the time they noticed what was happenin', there was no point in chasin' after them and risk bein' caught in an ambush." The messenger accepted another cup of water and sipped it slower, as he regained his strength.

"They did right." The professor glanced at the smoldering

remains of the Michael and Avery's tent, then patted the guard on the shoulder. "To be safe, we need to double the guards around the cavern and the camp, in case they decide to return. Though, I suspect they'll be busy burying their dead and tending to their wounded."

"Aye." The guard returned to the dig site to relay the order.

"Found him. He was hiding in the trees." Desmond returned several minutes later with Dewey in tow.

"Let me go." The flaxen-haired child of nine or ten twisted and slapped at Desmond's hold on his arm. "I ain't done nothin'." The guilt and fear on his face suggested otherwise.

The professor took the child to the campfire and gave him some water and a piece of cheese and bread. The professor's method of interrogating a witness was a far kinder way than how William, as a king's knight, had been taught.

William paced to edge of the firelight and back to keep from interfering, while the professor stayed calm to gain the child's confidence.

The boy broke into tears with his denial, until the professor promised not to punish him if he told the truth. Between bites of food, he finally told his story.

Caroline came out of the tent where she had tended to Clarence's wound, leaving Brother Peter to keep watch over him. She paused as Desmond approach the tent.

"The professor promised the boy he could see Clarence so he could tell him he was sorry for what had happened." Desmond lowered his voice as he sent the distraught boy inside.

"Good idea." Caroline left Desmond to follow the child, and she went to the campfire. She glanced from her husband to William. "Was the boy helpful in identifying the attacker?" Taking the kettle of water from the fire, she made a cup of tea, then took a seat next to her husband.

"According to the boy, Richard vowed not to hurt Elise. He only wanted to protect her from danger by taking her to

London. He promised the boy a big reward if he would contact the pagan leader. He did, and told the scary man, the rich prisoner at camp would give him a great sum of money for his help." The professor shook his head in disbelief. "Our prisoner escaped without paying either of them what they were promised."

"The pagan's feeble battle was nothing more than a distraction to allow Richard to escape with Elise." William's voice rose in anger and disgust that he hadn't protected her as he vowed. He had to find her.

"When questioned further, the boy admitted to cutting off Richard's ropes and giving him the knife, but he hadn't expected him to attack Clarence, who had been befriended the boy." The professor stood as William went to Elise's tent and returned with his travel kit.

"From what Elise told me of the man's troubles, Richard plans are to take her to London for the sole purpose of tricking his grandfather into restoring his title and inheritance." William paused when the professor put a hand on his arm.

"Wait. You'll need help. I'll ask for volunteers to go with you. Two of our trained guards should be plenty." He turned and sent Desmond to the camp where the guards took their meals and rested.

"I'll gather the supplies you'll have need of for a few days. You can get more along the way if needed." Caroline appeared relieved to do something to help. She hurried away to complete her task.

Evening was fast approaching, but William insisted on leaving, once his two volunteers gathered at the camp. He knew the road and could track the stolen horse by a blacksmith's nick in one of its shoes, until it became too dark to see.

"We will keep you all are in our prayers." The professor put an arm around his wife as the men rode off.

By the time the sun went down, the men and their mounts

were tired and needed rest, but it was all William could do not to insist they continue.

At first light, he woke the two volunteers, Ed and Jimmy. He had trained both men as guards and he knew they could be trusted to help as needed. They wasted no time and were again on the trail of the quarry. Their cold breakfast was cheese and bread, but none complained. William found a woman's shoe on the road. A match to the one he saw in her tent. He stopped and picked it up.

"This belongs to Lady Elise." He showed the men and smiled. "We're still following the right tracks." He mounted and kept the pace steady, not to tire the men and mounts with him, but he was impatient to find Elise.

The tracks led to a rundown inn, not a place Lord Richard would seek a bed or a meal unless desperate. Hope arose within him that Elise might have sought aid here in escaping her kidnapper.

William checked out the barn first and found tracks of the nicked shoe of the horse they were following. There were signs three other horses had been tied in the barn by their droppings. Only the professor's horse had been stalled overnight. "Jimmy, stay with the horses while Ed and I inquire inside."

"Aye." Jimmy took charge of the horses and led them to the water trough.

The inn's door was wide open, but no one appeared when they entered.

"Innkeeper?" William called out, but there no answer, only an eerie silence about the place. The stench of burned food led William to the source. Some kind of meat had been neglected for some time on an old woodstove.

"Sir William." Ed's voice held urgency and drew William upstairs, where the guard had gone to explore.

A dead man lay sprawled across the hall.

"Looks like you found our missing innkeeper." William noticed the man wore a stained apron.

"By the saints. Why murder the man?" Ed mumbled his disgust, as William scanned the scene.

"I doubt Richard would risk killing the man who provided him shelter. We're looking at a possible robbery gone bad, or… perhaps others are hunting our kidnapper." The door to a room nearest the dead man had been busted open, by the evidence of the splintered wood frame.

Once inside, William glance around to find the room empty. The strong scent of camphor lingered in the room, which could have been left by Elise after doctoring her injuries. He picked up a small empty jar containing the remnants of the ointment, from the floor.

A make-shift rope, made from the bedsheet and blanket, had been tied to the bedpost to anchor it and hung out of the window, as if the previous occupants had used it to make a hasty escape.

"At least there's no sign of a scuffle or blood in the room." He stared down at the path below. No blood or scuff marks were there either.

William pulled the blanket and bedsheet inside and separated them to free the sheet and covered the dead body.

"I fear someone else is tracking Lord Richard and they are willing to kill any who get in their way." William led the way downstairs.

A patron of the pub wandered in.

"'ay what's you doin' 'ere pokin' about?" The old man shuffled up to the bar and glanced around. "Where's Arnie?"

"I'm Sir William Degraf. We haven't spoken to the owner. What's he look like?"

"He's shorter than me and much rounder. 'is hair is gray, what's he got left." The man shifted his stance and suddenly looked suspicious. "He's not one to leave the door open when he's not 'ere."

"Were you here last night?" William stepped closer. When the man nodded, hope sprung up in him. "Did you see a man with a scar on his face in the company of an injured woman?"

"Aye." He edged toward the door, but Ed blocked his way. "Said they be injured when they escaped thieves who robbed them and left 'em for dead." His voice lowered with fear. "Ye ain't them thieves huntin' 'em down, are ye?"

"I'm chasing a kidnapper and the trail led here. We're trying to free his hostage." William stepped back to gain his trust. "It's urgent that we find them before he does something bad to her." Urgency made William raise his voice and the man paled. "Did you see them leave?"

"Nay. Drink makes me sleepy. That's why Arnie makes me sit over there." He pointed to a table in the corner. "I do kind of remember three mean-lookin' blokes who showed up just around dawn. They be loud and orderin' Arnie about. But my 'ead hurt for being woke up so early, so I left to find someplace quieter." He frowned. "Did those blokes 'urt Arnie?"

"We found a dead man that fits your description upstairs." The information meant they weren't far behind, and Richard's horse was carrying two, which would require rest more often. If he hurried, William might yet catch up to them. He prayed with every breath that he reached them before the *mean-looking blokes*. "Can you see that the dead man's kin are notified?" When the man nodded, William motioned to Ed. "We need to go."

They hurried out to the barn to claim their mounts. Had the Black Guard tracked down Richard from the posters he'd left at the pubs? Or had the pagan leader taken offence at not being paid for a battle, which had resulted in the death and injuries of his followers? All he knew for sure was there were three murders who cared not for the innocent that got in their way while tracking Richard. Elise was not safe as long as she remained her kidnapper's captive.

He pushed the men and horses as fast as he dared, following the professor's gelding, with a right front shoe marked with a nick from the blacksmith's iron.

Half-a-day went by when the tracks led them to a fishing village.

The professor's stolen horse stood tied to the railing outside a pub, but no sight of the three that were following them.

It could be a trap. He drew his short sword from the scabbard.

"You both stay here and keep alert. Untie the professor's horse and be ready to leave in a hurry if necessary." William dropped Shadow's reins on the ground, which would keep him there until William returned. The horse snorted and his ears flicked from one direction to another, alert to his surroundings. "I'll check if Richard and Elise are there."

William went inside the pub. It took a minute for his eyes to adjust to the dim interior. Two men were present. One man had his hand on a mug of ale and the other stood behind the bar and greeted William with a smile.

"What can I do for ye?" The man was tall and lean with clear eyes of one who didn't imbibe. Hopefully, he had information that would help him find Elise.

"I'm looking for a man traveling with a woman who rode in on that bay tied to your rail. The man stole that horse and kidnapped the woman." William barely got the words out before the man with the mug stood to his feet knocking over the half-finished drink.

"That be my horse. I paid good coin for 'em." His hands were fisted at his sides. "It's mine, legal."

"The thief sold you a horse that didn't belong to him. The animal has a brand of the true owner that proves the truth of the matter." William held his hand up to stop the man from arguing. "However, I am willing not to press charges...and though, by law, I'm not required to give you anything, I'll give you a fair wage for caring for the mount, in behalf of its true owner." He quoted a sum equal to a stableman's charge.

"But…" The man huffed and grumbled in protest.

"Denny, that's more than ye paid the thief, so ye'd best be glad this man doesn't haul yur sorry hide to the constables and they hang ye for stealing it." The pub owner smiled and slapped the man on the back. "Accept the man's coin so ye can pay yur tab and take some home to yur missus afore she kicks ye out."

"Fine, give it to me ." He glanced at the pub owner when he cleared his throat. "Less the amount I owe 'im." He pointed to his creditor.

The transaction was completed and the man hurried out before William could question him further.

"Have you've seen the horse thief and the woman with him?" William grew impatient, knowing they weren't far behind, since the two were without a horse. "The woman is about this high." He measured below his chin. "And she has green eyes and brown hair. She's been injured and has a limp." The thought of her unable to protect herself made William's heart pound with fear of what else could happen to her at the hands of her kidnapper or those who sought him. "The man has a scar across his cheek and a haughty way about him. He's about same height as the woman, but has lighter hair."

"Aye. They were 'ere. They sailed on Hermann Osman's fishing boat this morn. They be bound for London, but it'll take 'em at least two days to get there, for I 'ear the fishin' ain't that great. Ole Herm will want to fill 'is hold with a good catch afore he docks in London." He rubbed his chin and frowned. "Ye ought to know some real mean-lookin' blokes also came by here lookin' for the same man. I told 'em what I told ye to get 'em to leave." He paused. "They raced out of town toward London like the demons of hell were chasin' 'em." The man rubbed his chin in thought. "If it takes more than a couple of days for Herm to get his catch, and those blokes don't kill their mounts, they might even make it to London afore the boat docks."

"Thank you for the information." William glanced at the shelves lining the walls. "I need a few supplies, then I'll be on my way, too." He picked out the items he needed and paid before returning to his men.

"Except for one man hurryin' out and givin' us the stink eye, we didn't see nothin' else to cause us to wonder if ye needed help." Ed grinned and straightened in the saddle.

William added his purchases to the bag on his saddle, as he told the men what he'd learned. "The pub owner said Richard and Lady Elise boarded a fishing boat this morning, which sailed for London. We'll need to ride hard to make it to London before the men who are following them."

"I'd truly like to go, but me family needs me back to 'elp with the farm." Ed said. He frowned. "I've ne'r been to London, but me duty is at home."

"Once ye get to London, ye won't need our help. All ye need is a few of your fellow knights to capture the man and rescue the woman." Jimmy took hold of the bay. "We'll take the professor's horse back to 'im."

"Ye on that big horse can travel much faster without us." Ed nodded to the stallion.

William handed them a hand full of coins each. "Here's enough for supplies to get you home." He shook each man's hand. "Thank you."

He mounted the stallion, replaced his short sword in the scabbard, and settled into the saddle. Shadow pranced in place, ready for a run.

With a salute to the men, William took the road that would lead him to London.

It was a relief to travel at his own pace, for the stallion's stride and stamina were far greater than the other men's horses, which were used more for farm work than long journeys or hunting down fugitives. Still, he owed the men a debt for their willingness to help him, and the professor would be glad for the return of his horse.

Good thoughts exhausted; worry stole his peace. The three assassins would be more than William could deal with alone, unless he could catch them unaware. He spent a good portion of the next miles praying for God's help and wisdom.

Had the Black Guard succeeded in killing the king and everyone on their lists? Was Elise's family safe? What would he find when he arrived in London? War or peace?

CHAPTER 23

*E*lise stood on the deck of the boat and frowned as the boat drew closer to London. It was not a city she would have picked to find sanctuary, but it was better than being stuck on this boat another minute.

There were times during the last three days when she wasn't sure she would ever see land again, due in part to Richard angering every member of the crew. He nearly caused the boat to capsize and sink when he dropped the sails in a storm. He'd almost been thrown overboard for more than one incident, and only through God's grace were those men's hands stayed as they held him against the railing ready to shove him over.

She had to ask God for forgiveness for thinking how much better it would be for them all if Richard paid for his misdeeds at the hands of those men. Then the Word of God rose within her, and she prayed for his salvation before he died. It was the best she could do.

Fortunately, Elise had gained favor with Captain Herm and his crew because of her ability to mend broken rigging and improve some iron fittings. They even appreciated her cooking, which she wished was more extensive than the few things she'd learned to cook at the dig site.

Barely a day out to sea when the captain had found a sailor drunk and passed out in the captain's cabin. At the risk of being thrown overboard, when questioned, he told all. Apparently, when Richard wasn't scrubbing decks or cleaning fish guts off the hooks, he'd had found a drinking partner in the young sailor. According to the young man, a keg of ale had been smuggled aboard by Richard's bribery. Elise assumed that was the reason Richard hadn't pestered her during the trip.

The angry captain had thrown the half-full keg overboard, in spite of the crew's plea to drink it dry first.

Captain Herm had the repentant crewman on deck to work through his hangover. He also had Richard tied up and put in the hold with the fish. Richard's threats and demands, to be set free, could still be heard from bow to stern as the boat neared the dock.

Elise leaned against the railing and searched for William among the men waiting to assist the docking of the boat, though she knew it was nearly impossible for him to have reached London before them.

If she had perfected her flying wing, he might have made it. She smiled at the thought. One day she would resume her work on it.

"Lady Elise, I thank you for your help." Captain Herm stepped up beside her. "Your skills as a cook and blacksmith were a welcome surprise to me and me crew." He glanced toward the hold of the ship when Richard suddenly stopped shouting. "And the main reason I didn't have yur man chucked overboard for the trouble he's been."

"I'm glad I was able to help, but Richard's not my man, but my kidnapper. I couldn't tell you, for fear of what he'd do if I spoke the truth. Once aboard, all I wanted was to get to London."

"I knowed somethin' weren't right the way you kept your distance. Who is he?" The captain frowned.

"He is a madman, who kidnapped me and threatened my life if I didn't come to London with him." She glanced up at the captain. "Thank you for keeping me safe during the voyage. I wasn't sure we'd survive that storm last night." It had been a harrowing experience. She couldn't wait to set foot on solid ground.

"Ye want me to turn him over to the king's men, or slit his throat and drop him overboard?" The captain grinned, as if the latter suggestion most appealed to him.

"Neither of us want his blood on our hands." Elise tried to ignore the thought of being truly free from Richard. But for as long as he had breath, Richard still had the opportunity to repent and accept Christ as his Savior. She had spoken to him about turning his life around during the trip, though he always made light of it. "Having him arrested would only delay your departure, and I know you and your crew are eager to return home." She rubbed her arm, which still ached when she moved it a certain way, but no longer required the sling. Her ankle was stiff, but she was finally able to wear the shoes she'd bought.

Where should she go? Richard had spent the little funds that remained from buying the supplies, to pay for the keg and to bribe someone to get it on board. Who of her parent's friends would still be in residence and not fled London for fear of war?

She had no money to buy a horse or rent a carriage. It would take days or longer to reach her parents at Sarah's house by foot, even if she could walk that far. With all of the unrest, it wasn't safe to travel alone.

The school may not offer her sanctuary, because there were still those who might accuse her of being a witch, just to see her suffer. She doubted the king's palace would admit her or believe her story, for she looked and smelled more like a beggar than nobility. What if the Black Guard were still lurking about?

She watched as the boat docked and prayed for direction. Now that she was here, her first decision was simple, get to shore. "If you could keep Richard confined until you have unloaded your catch and are ready to sail, it would give me the head start I need to get away."

"It shall be done." The gangplank was lowered to the dock, and the captain motioned toward it. "Leave now before the deck hands see which way ye go. Less chance he can bribe them with promises he can't fulfill." The captain yelled at the crew to get their catch ready to unload. He walked away, using his body to hide her from their sight as she departed.

Elise reached the dock and kept her head down, hoping no one would recognize her in her stained and badly wrinkled linen shift, which reeked of fish. Her sunburned face and bruised body would keep most folks from giving her a second glance.

Two blocks from the dock, she heard a commotion on the street. She stepped back into the shadow of a building, as six of the king's soldiers rode by. The knight's armor glistened in the sunlight. They were heavily armed, as if readied for battle.

If there was going to be a war, she urgently needed to find a place of safety until William could find her or she could gain passage to Sarah's manor. She prayed they were all safe.

She should have never gone on the expedition. As soon as the thought came, she knew she didn't mean it. It had been a grand adventure, until Richard showed up.

The feeling of being watched made her hurry to hide behind the corner of a brick building and wait. She peeked around the edge to the street but saw no one lurking about who appeared interested in her whereabouts.

After another squad of knights, also dressed in armor passed through the streets, stern-faced people rushed about pushing their way into shops past others coming out with armloads of supplies. The whole city seemed afraid of being swept into war at any moment. The street vendors closed up and disappeared. Within the hour, while Elise was wandering about without a true destination, the streets had thinned of pedestrians until it was easy to notice anyone suspicious.

She was exhausted. Everything hurt. She needed to find someplace safe to rest. Maybe her one of her sister's friends would take her in. As hard as she thought, she couldn't remember a single address. She hadn't paid that much attention to locations because they'd always had a driver. She sunk against the wall of a boarded-up bakery. Tears gathered in her eyes and hopelessness threatened to swallow her faith. "Please, Lord lead me to safety."

"Gotcha!" Richard's hand closed over her mouth to keep her from screaming. She was lifted off the ground and carried to a waiting cart. She had a glimpse of the questionable conveyance, with its scraped-together construction attached to an underfed horse with a graying muzzle.

"'Ay, mister, I don't want no part of no kidnappin'." The driver backed away from Richard.

"It's my disobedient wife and none of your business." As Elise struggled against his hold, Richard manhandled her into the back of the cart and kept his hand over her mouth. "Take us to Blackstone Manor. It's my grandfather's estate, and he'll pay you handsomely, my good man."

The driver eyed him with suspicion. "Ye don't look like no royal's grandson." He pointed to Elise. "Let her tell me. She has honest eyes."

Elise ceased her struggle once she knew where they were going. She was sure the duke would be reasonable and not believe Richard's lies. He dropped his hand from her mouth, but gave her a warning look. "It's true. He is Duke Blackstone's grandson."

The driver nodded and turned around to guide the horse to the manor.

Richard held her arms down and her body tight against his. "I told you I'd find you if you tried to escape." His breath was foul and hot against her neck. "I promised one of the crew a gold sovereign if he saw you leave the boat without me. He followed you then sent a friend to free me and bring me to you."

The trip to the duke's estate took only a few minutes. She'd been heading in that direction all along. Was it by accident or by the divine hand of God?

"Pull around to the servant's gate." Richard directed the driver to a set of large ornate iron gates with a stone guard house at the entrance. When they stopped, a guard stepped out of the one-room building and approached the driver.

"State your business or get along." The guard put a hand on his sword.

"I don't know you." Richard got out of the cart and pulled Elise out with him. "I'm Lord Richard Blackstone, Duke Blackstone's grandson. I demand you let me in to see my grandfather." It might have been more believable if Richard and Elise didn't smell like they'd been living on a fishing boat for the last three days. Surely, they looked more like beggars than royalty.

"Right. And me dear old mum's the king's sister." The guard drew his sword and stood in front of Richard. "Be gone with ye."

"What's the problem?" Another guard joined the first and glanced at Richard. His mouth opened in surprise. "Lord Richard. 'Tis good to see you're alive. Your grandfather has had men searching for you since you disappeared."

"Humphrey, tell this imbecile to let me and my bride inside immediately." Richard was his haughty self again.

"Of course, your lordship, but we have our orders. We must first get approval from Duke Blackstone before admitting you." He turned to the other man. "Inform the duke of his grandson's presence and that he's brought a...a bride." The man nodded and hurried away.

"'Ay gov'nor, pay me what's ye owes me, so I can leave afore the old man comes and sets the guards on me." The driver stepped down from the cart and held out his hand.

"Humphrey, pay the man. I'm short of funds at the moment." When the guard hesitated, Richard straightened and frowned at him. The man searched his pockets until he found the amount and sent the driver on his way.

"Standing about is for servants, admit me at once." Richard pulled Elise toward the closed gates.

The sound of approaching horses had Elise peering passed Richard to search the road.

The three men, who had been hunting Richard, rode up in a thunder of hoofs. The murderers stopped, pulled their swords, and dismounted.

Humphrey pulled his sword and shouted for more guards before he stepped up to challenge the armed men.

"We've come for Lord Richard…and his bride." The tallest of the three raked his gaze over Elise from head to toe, then he made eye contact with Humphrey.

"You need not die for this spoiled, pompous nave or his wench." A second man stepped forward. He had a large scar on his cheek, which disappeared into the neck of his chain-mail. "Come with us, Richard, Mr. Haverton would like a word with you." The man gave her a wicked grin. "And bring the woman."

Elise glanced from the duke's guard, to the men intent on taking Richard. All had raised their swords.

Richard jerked her behind him.

"You can't have her, Thrasher! She's mine." His eyes were wide and his voice shrill. "Run, Elise."

There was no place to run. The enemy barred the road and the closed gate stood between her and a safe retreat.

Elise search for a weapon, for she had been taught by the best.

Nothing. Not even a dead branch in which to deflect their swords.

The tall man raised his sword and swung it at Humphrey, disarming him in two moves. Thrasher and the other man met the estate guards, as they rushed toward them from their other posts. Once Humphrey was on the ground and bleeding, the tall man stalked toward Richard.

Elise made a grab for Humphrey's fallen sword. She was knocked to the ground as the battle grew in intensity. Two guards were felled by the hired thugs before she could stand and raise the captured sword.

"Haverton promised me a big reward for you" Thrasher stalked toward the unarmed Richard. "And your lady friend will be my bonus."

Elise ran to Richard's side, but he pushed her away and stepped in front of her.

Richard grabbed the man's sword and tried to jerk it from his hand. The man stumbled forward and plunged it into him, but Richard clung to the sword with both hands refusing to release the blade.

"Elise!" William rode up, dismounted while pulling his sword free of the scabbard, and rushed into the fray. Shadow reared and struck the nearest thug with its hooves, knocking him to the ground.

Surrounded by four guards, Duke Blackstone hurried toward the gate armed with a short sword. "Leave my grandson alone."

William and the manor guards disarmed Thrasher. After the battle, Thrasher was the only one of the three hired thugs who had survived. Two guards held him down as he yelled obscenities, cursing his boss and Richard, until one of the guards punched him in the jaw.

William hurried over to Elise, who was bending over the wounded Richard. A guard removed the sword, causing the blood to pool on the ground from his midsection. She turned him on his side to aid his breathing.

"Richard, you've been mortally wounded." Elise's hold on his hand was as firm as her words. "Please, receive Jesus as Savior before it's too late."

"Yes." Richard grimaced in pain then glanced up at her. "Tell me how."

He repeated the sinner's prayer after her, in a clipped hushed tone. A clarity and peace settled over his face. His smile grew into joy, which lit his eyes.

"Grandfather." Richard reached for the duke, who knelt beside him and took his hand. "I'm sorry. I wish…" Richard's voice cracked, and he grew pale. He coughed and his breath grew ragged.

"It is I who should ask your forgiveness, my boy." His grandfather's eyes filled with tears. "I should have been a better example of how to be a good man."

Richard squeezed the old man's hand. He opened his mouth, but no words came out. He released his last breath, and his body went limp.

Silence was broken only by Elise's sob, for Richard's wasted life.

"Thank you, young woman," the duke said, "for leading my grandson to the Lord. He has found the peace he's sought ever since his parents' death when he was but a child of six." The duke patted Elise's hand, which still held Richard's. "You can let him go now."

"Aaugh!" Thrasher used Richard's death as the distraction he needed. He jerked free from his captors, picked up a fallen sword, and lunged toward the duke.

"Death to you, Duke Blackstone. It's all your fault for not paying his debt!"

William stepped into his path and deflected the blade with a well-place kick with his pine peg, causing the killer to stumble back. William raised his sword, but the man's determination to strike the duke made him leap forward to try again. His momentum threw him into William's raised sword, which pierced deep beneath his mail.

The duke's guards grabbed the would-be assassin, pulled him back, and threw him to the ground. He died with a curse on his lips.

"You saved my life, young man." The duke glanced up at William. "Who are you?"

"He is Sir William Degraf, a former knight of King John." Elise smiled. "And the man I'm going to marry."

"Indeed." The duke reached up and William helped the old man stand. "It's not safe to linger out here. There is much unrest in the city." He glanced down at the body then to Elise. "I would be honored if you and your young man would come to my home and stay until my grandson is laid to rest. I have many questions."

To Elise, the old man seemed to have aged a decade while he'd watched his only grandson pass away. She put a hand on his arm to steady him as he bent over the guard, Humphrey, who was badly injured. He was being tended to by another guard. "Call for my personal physician, Colby," the duke said, "and see that Humphrey and the others who were injured are made comfortable until he arrives. Have my grandson taken to the solarium and call for the undertaker." He turned to Elise and took her hand. "I want to wait until my people attend to Richard, then I will escort you and your knight to my home, where you can freshen up."

Within a half-hour the dead bodies of the gambler's hired thugs were hauled off to be buried without honor in an unsanctified graveyard. Richard was taken to the solarium, then whisked away quietly by a mortician to be made ready for a funeral in three days. The injured guards were ministered to first, by the duke's personal physician, at Elise's insistence. He then saw to Elise's injuries.

By evening, William and Elise had bathed and dressed in new clothing, which had been brought to them at the manor by shop owners at the request of the duke.

That night's meal was kept simple. There were bowls of fruit, a platter each of cold roasted lamb, baked chicken, and three types of cheeses. Elise ate her fill and noticed William did so too, though Duke Blackstone ate nothing. He was a proper host talking about having met her father and mother on several occasions, and he gave insight on the progress of the building of the new workshop to replace the one destroyed at the School of Scientifica. "I sent a messenger to Barrington Manor to tell your family where you and your young man are and to assure them that you are safe and well under my protection."

"Thank you." Elise was able to take her first breath free from the fear she'd been under for so long. She sent a silent prayer of gratitude heavenward.

After the meal, Duke Blackstone, escorted them to his private study. After Elise and William declined his offer of sherry, he received a glass from his manservant who hovered nearby. Elise sat in a high-backed leather chair nearest the fireplace to soak up the warmth from the fire. William sat on the other side, with the duke at his desk nearest the window.

"I banished Richard with the hope that he'd finally learn by dealing with the consequences of his own doing, but all he's ever known is how to spend what he hadn't earned." He frowned. "I am truly sorry that his actions have caused you so much pain, Lady Elise." After another sip of his sherry, he cleared his voice. "Now, I would like to know more of how he found you and how you arrived here at my gate." He raised his hand before Elise could speak. "Don't try and spare my feelings. I've known the boy his whole life, so I'd prefer the complete truth."

Elise skipped the part about her first unpleasant encounters with Richard and his part in the destruction of the blacksmith's building, for the old man had heard it all from witnesses. She explained her reason for being at the meteorite site and what poor condition Richard was in when he appeared in the camp. She left out any mention of finding the cavern and skipped to the part where she was kidnapped and hurried on to the voyage that brought them to London. "As bad as the things he's done in the past, he did try to protect me from those men. His last act was one of bravery and honor. I believe it was worth it all to know that he accepted Christ as Savior before his death." Elise couldn't stem the tears that joy brought to her. The duke handed her a fine linen handkerchief to dab them away. "I'm still puzzled how he came to find me at the meteorite camp."

"I know the answer." William's gaze met hers "He had you followed once you arrived with your parents in London. People seeking a hefty reward left messages of your sightings at the Crooked Duck Tavern, as his poster instructed. Once Richard had solid information that you'd been spotted in England, he hired a man to follow you, who sent messengers to Richard at the tavern to tell him where you were headed"

"But where did he get the funds?" Duke Blackstone leaned forward as if not to miss anything. "I refused to give him any funds after he…" He waved his hand to dismiss the past.

"An unscrupulous man named, Frank Haverton loaned him a large sum to be added to his large gambling debt in anticipation of doubling his interest on the loan."

The duke nodded and leaned back to rest his head against the high back chair. "Go on."

William continued. "After Elise joined the professor's expedition, several people came forth to claim a reward for having spotted you. It took weeks of lying and cheating his way to that last village, where the man he hired waited for him, expecting the hefty fee he'd earned. Once he found out Richard was penniless and he wouldn't be paid, the man beat Richard badly and left him for dead."

"Oh, no." Elise couldn't hold back more tears of regret.

William reached over and patted her hand. "That's why he appeared in such bad shape when he arrived in the camp. But he came up with a plan after he heard the men talking about the pagans and, with the help a young boy whom he also promised money, he made a deal with the Druid leader to help him escape and capture you." William drew a breath and frowned. "He was very convincing when he wanted something and managed to leave many disappointed and angry folks when the riches he promised didn't come to pass."

The duke interrupted to ask for more details. Many of his questions were able to be answered between Elise and William, but not all of them, so he waved him on to continue with their story.

"After Richard's appearance at the camp the professor made sure that he was fed, cleaned up, and secured until the time he was sure he wasn't a danger to Elise or himself." The rest of William's story painted a more desperate picture of Richard's escape including nearly killing the guard who was watching over him, stealing money set aside for the worker's wages, and the professor's horse, which he assured Elise of its return. "Once I arrived in London, I felt that he would want to go home, to the duke's estate. I thank God that I arrived when I did." By the time William was finished with his story, the duke was visibly tired, as were they all. It had been a long eventful day. The old man pulled a thick silk cord that hung down against the wall behind his desk, and a servant arrived to show them to their rooms.

Elise parted company with William on the stairs, but not before she promised to speak with him tomorrow.

She slept late because of her exhaustion and the comfort of a real feather bed. By the time she dressed and went down to the dining room, the sun was bright and high in the sky.

William and the duke were nowhere in sight, but a servant assured her they had eaten hours earlier and had gone out together.

After a light meal of fruit and toast, Elise went outside hoping to find William. She realized how much she'd missed the servility of having servants tend to certain needs, like not having to prepare meals or wash her own clothes. She certainly appreciated those blessing far more because of her wilderness expedition. After she and William were married, she would once again be in charge of such chores, but with an occasional visit to enjoy the comforts of Brighton Castle or Barrington Manor, she wouldn't complain. She loved William and couldn't wait to become his bride no matter the sacrifice.

By noon, she still had not located either William or the duke. The servants seemed elusive and Elise became worried. Where could they be?

The doctor arrived to check on the guards' condition, but when she questioned him, he seemed not to be surprised at the duke's absence and told her not to worry as he hurried off to attend his other patients in London. She stood on the front steps and watched him leave. Before she turned to go back inside, a fancy carriage arrived and the duke stepped out then William, who was dressed as fine as any royal. Even his pine peg had been replaced with a highly polished and new nick-free one, giving him more the appearance of a wealthy pirate than a humble innkeeper's son.

He grinned when he spotted her on the stairs and hurried up to Elise, gathering her into his arms. "I have some rather shocking news to tell you."

The duke climbed the steps and joined them. "Now, William you promised to wait until I could give her the good news."

"Yes, sir, I did and I have kept that promise...so far." He kept his arm around Elise and waited to follow the duke inside.

"Hurry up, Greggory." The duke turned back to the carriage and frowned.

A stern-looking, well-dressed gentleman got out of the carriage carrying a small briefcase and followed them into the duke's study. He sat the case on the desk and poured himself a sherry as if he were accustomed of doing so many times before.

"Shall we get down to business?" He stood next to the duke, who sat at his desk.

"Greggory, give us a moment to get seated." The duke turned to watch Elise take a seat and William pulled a chair up next to her and took her hand.

"Splendid." The duke tented his fingers. "Lady Elise, this fine gentleman standing next to me is my solicitor and wise council." He turned to the man. "Now you may explain the reason you are here."

"I have come to update Duke Archibald Blackstone's will and to witness his signature on these legal documents declaring his adoption of Sir William Degraf, who will from this day forward be known as Lord William Blackstone. At the duke's death, Lord William will inherit the title and henceforth be called Duke William Blackstone. As the sole beneficiary of the estate, Lord William will be caretaker of it all."

Elise sat speechless. William smiled and nudged her.

"You will be marrying a nobleman after all." His grin pierced Elise's heart. She couldn't believe that he would forsake his name to gain a title for her.

"I did not fall in love with a title, but a man...a good man from a good family." She stood. Her hands were shaking with the magnitude of what she heard. She couldn't breathe. "I'm sorry I..." She couldn't finish without raging at the men who thought this was a good idea. She fled the manor for the cool shade of a large oak at the edge of the garden. A bench was there and she sat before she fell, having no more strength within her. Deep sobs racked her body and tears streamed from her eyes.

"Why are you so upset?" William's question was with sincere concern. He reached to touch her but she leaned away. "Talk to me, Elise."

"What were you thinking?" She turned to face him and accepted the linen handkerchief he pressed within her fingers. "What will your parents say when they find out you've forsaken their heritage for a title?" The grief of the question spurred more tears.

"I'm not forsaking anything. I shall retain my surname as a middle name and pass it on to our sons and daughters when the time comes." He gently turned Elise's face to him. "I know a title is not important to you and I didn't do it for that reason. In fact, I was downright rude to the duke when he first suggested it." William released her and leaned back against the tree and gazed at the magnificent manor with its manicured property. "The duke explained it to me. He has no other heir to pass on his title or fortune. He is earnest in his plea for me to accept this responsibility so that his life's work does not fall into the wrong hands and be used for evil."

Elise listened as William spoke of the good, he could do with the legacy of title, lands and power.

"I understand your reasons for accepting this offer, which are good and noble, but William you have no idea what you're facing. As a commoner, no matter your title, you will not be accepted as part of the Ton. The Ton is a tight group of wealthy, powerful people, who believe their ancestry makes them above all who do not hail from such nobility. Your acceptance will not happen in our lifetime, and may not in our children's. You will face fierce opposition at every avenue from both commoner and nobles no matter how righteous your intent or the good you want to do." She touched his arm. "Are you willing to take on such a heavy responsibility knowing you and our family will be ridiculed and disparaged?"

"I realize perhaps more than you, of being in the middle and not fitting in completely. I was raised by commoners who were also privileged to have close friends of your parents who were noble." He put an arm around her. "I am willing to take on this challenge if you are willing to do so as my wife. I won't do it without you." He tugged her close. "Let's pray and ask God's will, for if He is in this, He will guide and protect us along the way."

CHAPTER 24

"Stop fidgeting, Elise. We've only two days before the wedding." Lady Evangeline circled her daughter and tugged at the fabric in places, as she pointed them out to the seamstress, who remained quiet, nodded, and dutifully made the necessary adjustment to the gown.

It had been decided for Elise, her parents, and youngest sister to remain at her older sister, Sarah's home to prepare for Elise's wedding, since Brighten was days away from the cathedral in London where the wedding was to take place. William remained in London in residence with Duke Blackstone.

The next hour was excruciatingly slow for Elise, who wanted to run to her forge and complete the finishing touches of her own creation for her groom-to-be.

"You're free for now, Elise but don't be late, for we have guests coming for the midday meal." Her mother gave her a kiss and waved her off. She turned back to the dress alterations as Elise hurried out before she was caught by Sarah and recruited for more decorating or decision making. Her sister and mother were more than capable of making whatever decisions were necessary for this formal wedding. Elise would have been satisfied with the informal ceremony at the dig site.

Two weeks ago, the professor and Caroline had stopped by to see Elise. They wanted to drop off a bar of the special metal they'd processed from the large meteorite. They promised to return in time for the wedding, but didn't stay the night and journeyed on to London to begin the process of packing all of their belongings for their permanent move back to the dig site.

Elise was eager to start her experiments using their notes about the smelting temperature and the tinsel strength of the metal. It was the same lightweight element of the candlestick she'd bought in Spain and the cross they'd found in the cavern.

She'd used the metal to design a new leg for William that was both lighter and more functional than the old pine one. This one was fashioned into an elongated "S" that curved up at the end away from his body. The new curved design would flex and produce a spring action more like the muscles and tendons in his other leg. The flat, curved design would keep him from sinking into soft ground, because there was no pointed end, like the peg, to get stuck.

With an hour or so more polishing, it would be ready in time for their wedding. It would take time for him to adjust to the spring-motion, so she'd decided to give it to him as a wedding gift. He could get used to it in private, away from curious onlookers.

The warm feeling of satisfaction filled her being as she ran a hand down the smooth surface of the special metal.

The news of the elimination of the Black Guard rebellion and the overthrow of its leaders, which happened alongside the stopping of an invasion from French rebels, gave the wedding guests an additional reason to celebrate.

Even John and his wife, Julianna, were coming from Brighton to be at the wedding. They were bringing William's mother, Helen, and his youngest sister, Libby. His father stayed home to care for William's young brother, Timothy. Also missing would be his sisters, Martha, a newlywed and Silvia, who had a newborn.

Elise finished her project and went to her room. A messenger must have arrived from London in her absence, for she found two letters from William waiting for her on her side table. She washed her hands and face, changed into a clean shift, then curled up on a comfortable settee next to the window, which allowed plenty of light to read the letters.

She reread the first letter twice. After not seeing William for a month, she learned that he would arrive in the morning.

"The duke sends his regrets that his physician insists he's is not well enough to travel at this time, but he is looking forward to seeing us when we return from our honeymoon. I shouldn't tell you the surprise, but I can't keep his gift to myself. He has commissioned a beautiful home, which is being built now at the meteorite site so we can travel there whenever you need inspiration for your next project.

I must sign off and will write again tonight before I go to sleep. It helps me dream of you.

With all of my love, William"

The next letter was a bit battered as if it had been crumpled in the bottom of the letter bag.

"My Darling,

As much as I've wanted to be married and have you in my arms every night, I would not have been able to devote my focus on learning all about the estate and the duke's many holdings knowing you were waiting for me in our private quarters.

The duke is a determined teacher. He wants me to know all about his holdings so that I can carry on with minimum effort. He was especially pleased to know I speak several languages.

During this intense learning process, I've developed an enormous respect for him. His intelligence, and his ability to obtain wealth without cheating anyone to do so, has been formidable.

He recently insisted I refer to him as Grandfather Archibald. Since I've never known any of my grandfathers, this has also been agreeable to me.

To my relief, I feel as if I've also been accepted by his large staff of servants and guards during my stay.

He has treated me as an equal, making sure everyone we encountered know I am his heir. So far, there have been minimal negative comments, at least to my face.

I think the thing that has stunned me the most is the duke's wealth. Elise, I didn't know there was such in all of England. The knowledge has given me moments of fear that I might do something stupid and lose it all with one bad decision.

I pray constantly, as I'm continually learning something new.

To tease your sense of adventure, the duke owns many businesses in several countries, which will require us to visit in person, periodically.

There is so much more to tell you, but I shall see you soon. I can't wait to take you as my bride."

With all my love, your William

P.S. Did you invite Jeremy? I want to be sure he sees us getting married so he won't wait for you and miss his own true love.

CHAPTER 25

Three years later

Dear Mother,

"Thank you, for your many letters. I miss you terribly.

I know it's been a while since my last letter. William and I have been very busy, but know you are all in our prayers daily.

I'm excited to hear that John and Julianna are expecting again. Little Lois will be excited have a baby sister or brother. I'm glad they live near, so you can spoil the babies. I wish we lived closer, but like Sarah, with busy husbands, that is not possible.

I have to praise my brilliant and handsome husband, who has managed to make friends even among the Ton. They seem impressed with me, since the duke told them I went with William to visit three factories in three different countries the first year we were married. They insist that their wives would never agree to go to such faraway places like Africa to visit the duke's diamond mines, or India to visit the ceramic factory, or Persia to visit the factory that makes hand-woven carpets of such high quality there is a formidable waiting list.

Many ask about his leg wherever we go. Unfortunately, the metal to produce it is in short supply, but the design is sound. He's been offered a lot of money for it, but William said it's the love that went into its creation that makes it valuable. My heart is full of gratitude to God Who made it all possible.

The travel was enjoyable, but I was glad to return home to Blackstone manor once I found out I was with child.

I'm glad you were here for the baby's birth, as you were with Sarah's two sons. It's hard to believe little Archie is walking everywhere. Was I walking and getting into things so young? I always smile when I think of the joy it gave the duke that we named him Archibald Degraf Blackstone.

Grandfather Archie, as he insists, we call him after little Archie was born, actually delights in seeing little Archie every day. He tells everyone, the sounds of a child's laughter makes the house a home.

Unfortunately, he's not doing well after London's particularly cold and dreary winter. Please keep him in your prayers.

We commissioned a statue for the garden in his likeness to surprise him for his seventy-eighth birthday, which was last week. Even his solicitor, Greggory, approved. He has accepted the unofficial title of uncle to little Archie and has turned out to be a most valued and wise friend to us.

Mother, I know we planned to come to Brighton after Easter, but I find I'm with child again and traveling is not advised by our physician. William hopes it is a girl this time.

Perhaps Hanna would like to come and stay with us. My physician is young though talented and might be a good teacher to aid in her thirst to know more of healing.

Of all of your children, she is the most gifted healer. At fifteen, she might even find a suitor among the young men that visit here often.

Oh, my, I'm sounding more and more like one of those old matchmakers that used to pester me to find a good man and wed.

I hear little Archie. He's up from his nap, so I must cut this short.

How did you find time to do all you did while we were growing up?

Give Father and Hanna my love,

JAN DAVIS WARREN

Your devoted daughter, Elise
Lady Elise Blackstone, of Blackstone Manor

Did you enjoy this book? We hope so!
Would you take a quick minute to leave a review where you purchased the book?
It doesn't have to be long. Just a sentence or two telling what you liked about the story!

Receive a FREE ebook and get updates when new Wild Heart books release: https://www.wildheartbooks.org/newsletter

Book 1: The Secret Life of Lady Evangeline

Book 2: The Sword and the Secrets

Book 3: The Stone and the Secrets

ABOUT THE AUTHOR

Jan Davis Warren is a mother, grandmother, and a young-at-heart great-grandmother. Her wonderful husband passed away the same year she won the ACFW Genesis Award for Romantic Suspense. That win and many others are encouraging reminders that God wants her to continue writing even in the tough times.

Learn more at www.janwarrenbooks.com.

ACKNOWLEDGMENTS

I confess, unlike books 1 and 2, which stories flew onto the page, book 3, *The Stone and the Secrets* was like plowing hard ground, digging out one word at a time. I would like to blame my difficulty on the world pandemic, record breaking Oklahoma weather, and the myriads of decisions, which have required me to pray fervently, adapt and refocus daily to deal with every problem that arose, to try to keep life as "normal" as possible. It has all certainly taken a toll on my creativity.

I keep reminding myself that every adversity has the potential for me to dig deeper into my faith and ultimately to grow stronger in the process. It's not been easy, but by standing on the promises in the Word of God and with a determination to deal with one thing at a time, it's been possible to navigate through each uncertainty with a supernatural peace and assurance of a final outcome which will ultimately bring God the glory.

History is a good reminder that the world has seen it all before. I could easily have been overwhelmed by the research I found on the medieval time period. The dark ages had many similar challenges as has been common throughout history before and after, with political upheavals, wars, famine and plagues. In 1347-1350 AD, the Black Plague swept through the known world as a merciless harbinger of death, killing rich and poor, titled and commoner alike. In some countries, like Spain, over sixty percent of their population perished. Thankfully modern scientists are working hard to eliminate sickness and disease, but history dictates that for as long as people populate this planet, there will always be similar challenges to face until the final chapter when Jesus returns.

The Good News is there is help and hope for all who will believe: **Jesus**.

Christ the Lord is the only source of genuine lasting peace to quiet your soul in troubled times for He is the true Corner Stone on which we build our faith.

It is my heartfelt prayer that God's supernatural peace fill you to overflowing.

John 14:27-28: *Peace I leave with you, my peace I give unto you: not as the world giveth, give I unto you. Let not your heart be troubled, neither let it be afraid. Ye have heard how I said unto you, I go away, and come again unto you. If ye loved me, ye would rejoice, because I said, I go unto the Father: for my Father is greater than I.*

ABOUT THE STONE AND THE SECRETS

Writing *The Stone and the Secrets* was as much a joy as it was a challenge.

The hero and heroine of this book were first introduced in book 2, *The Sword and the Secrets*. Several readers loved Elise and William so much, they wanted to know more about them. *The Stone and the Secrets* is Elise and William's story.

Book 3, *The Stone and the Secrets* was also to complete the series, but as soon as it was finished, I knew there would have to be one more. I already have the title, plot, and the characters, but I'll share more about that another day.

As a writer, I love getting to know the characters. Before the story is finished, it's like I've known them their whole lives. It's fun, but challenging to allow the characters to evolve without pushing them to the end too soon. Spoiler alert. I absolutely LOVE a happily-ever-after ending. It gives me, as the author, a satisfying feeling of closure. You can laugh, but it's true.

The hero and heroine in *The Stone and the Secrets* are not the typical h/h you might imagine living in medieval times.

The beautiful and intelligent, Lady Elise Stanton has a long and impressive royal linage. Because of her heritage, protocol demands she marry someone with an equally impressive noble bloodline. The problem is, Elise has no interest in protocol, titles, or matchmaking, and refuses to be courted by empty-headed men who know nothing of using a forge, or mending a broken carriage axle. She's a scientist whose curiosity about the how things work has gotten her into trouble since she was old enough to take things apart. With her creative mind, she is always thinking of new things to invent. Her first attempt to fly almost got her killed, but for our hero, William Degraf's timely intervention.

He's saved Elise many times during their childhood—a challenge he gladly accepts for he loves her deeply. However, William's love for Elise is not to be. He must sacrifice his love so she can fulfill her destiny, which means marrying a man with title and wealth, neither of which he has. He is strong, handsome, and of noble character, but has not a noble bloodline.

Once Elise becomes of marriageable age, he realizes seeing her courted would be too painful, so he joins the king's army. By becoming a knight, he hopes to forget her.

As I got to know Sir William Degraf, a knight of the king's army, I can tell you, there's not a braver or more loyal man to be found in all of England.

In the title, *The Stone and the Secrets*, the *stone* was initially meant to represent the meteorites, which Elise is determined to locate. She feels they are the answer to finding a unique metal needed for a secret project.

To my unexpected delight, in the midst of writing this story, I realized the *"stone"* also represents the Lord, our Corner Stone, the Rock of Ages, the Stone that the builder rejected, and much more.

This is also an adventure story, so, of course, there's hidden treasure and several villains, each with a goal to kill, steal and destroy. Assassins, murderous pagans, and a madman intent on revenge, all who are determined to wreak havoc along the way.

Which begs to question. With so much coming against them…

Can William reach Elise in time to save her, this time from a fate worse than death?

And, with William being a lowborn commoner, and Elise of noble blood, how can they possibly have their happily-ever-after?

I'm so excited. I can't wait to tell you. They…

Oh, no, I've used up all my allotted words. Sorry, I guess you'll have to read *The Stone and the Secrets* to find out.

May God bless and keep you, and give you peace.

Jan Davis Warren

If you love historical romance, check out the other Wild Heart books!

Revealing the Truth by Lorri Dudley

His suspect holds a secret, but can he uncover the truth before she steals his heart?

When Katherine Jenkins is rescued from the side of the road, half-frozen and left for dead, her only option is to stay silent about her identity or risk being shipped back to her ruthless guardian, who will kill to get his hands on her inheritance and the famous Jenkins Lipizzaner horses. But even under the pretense of amnesia, she cannot shake the memory of her sister and Katherine's need to reach her before their guardian, or his marauding bandits, finish her off. Will she be safe in the earl's manor, or will the assailant climbing through her window be the death of her?

British spy, Stephen Hartington's assignment to uncover an underground horse-thieving ring brings him home to his family's manor, and the last thing he expected was to be struck with a candlestick upon climbing through the guest chamber window. The manor's feisty and intriguing new house guest throws Stephen's best-laid plans into turmoil and raises questions about the timing of her appearance, the convenience of her memory loss, and her impeccable riding skills. Could he be housing the horse thief he'd been ordered to capture—or worse, falling in love with her?

∼

The Petticoat Spy by Elva Cobb Martin

A Southern belle turned spy and a dashing blockade runner fight a hopeless battle against the British.

When Anna Grace Laurens's parents are murdered by the British and her Charles Town plantation burned, she seizes her only option for escape—a desperate leap into the Cooper River. She'll do anything to survive…and get revenge.

John Cooper Vargas is used to danger as he sails his sloop upriver through war-torn colonies, but seeing a woman plunge into the river amidst Tory gunfire is something he wouldn't have thought possible. Until now.

Rescuing her draws him into a web of intrigue, but he can't let her fight the British on her own. As the American Revolution closes in around them, it may take a miracle for them—and their love—to survive.

~

Avenue of Betrayal by Sandra Merville Hart

Betrayed by her brother and the man she loves...whom can she trust when tragedy strikes?

Soldiers are pouring into Washington City every day and have begun drilling in preparation for a battle with the Confederacy. Annie Swanson worries for her brother, whom she's just discovered is a Confederate officer in his new home state of North Carolina. Even as Annie battles feelings of betrayal toward the big brother she's always adored, her wealthy banker father swears her and her sister to secrecy about their brother's actions. How could he forsake their mother's abolitionist teachings?

Sergeant-Major John Finn camps within a mile of the Swansons' mansion where his West Point pal once lived. Sweet Annie captured his heart at Will's wedding last year and he looks forward to reestablishing their relationship—until he's asked to spy on her father.

To prove her father's loyalty to the Union, John agrees to spy on the Swanson family, though Annie must never know. Then the war strikes a blow that threatens to destroy them all—including the love that's grown between them against all odds.